SciAngels

SciAngels

Crazy, Mad Adventure

S.R. Shuja

First Edition

Cover page: Manzur Murad

Printed in the United States of America

Publisher: Mind Talkers Publishing

ISBN #:978-0-9878187-1-3

Visit www.mindtalkers.com

To all the kids – growing and grown.

Contents

Chapter 1

Vienna

The decision to take part in the prestigious Vienna Open Chess tournament was a simple one for Farina. Firstly, she was hoping to get her third and final norm for Grandmaster title. Secondly, she was looking forward to have an opportunity to play against *Aretha*.

She'd already impressed the chess world by achieving the first two norms for grandmaster title at a very tender age of fourteen. If she succeeded in getting her third norm in this tournament – at fifteen – she'd become the third youngest female grandmaster in the history of chess just after Koneru Humpy of India and Judith Polgar of Hungary.

In contrast, Aretha – a mysterious persona - had awed the chess world since she first appeared about two years ago. She'd easily beaten the world champion several times in friendly matches. Even the amazing chess playing machines couldn't put up any resistance against her. Many experts had said that her FIDE (world chess federation) rating would be in the north of 3500. The human world champion only had around 2800.

However, Aretha never played a single tournament in person. She played only via Internet and always rejected requests for pictures or interviews. Nobody knew where she lived or how she looked. As per regulation to be eligible for FIDE rating or title one must play the tournaments in person. That's why Aretha had no FIDE rating or the grandmaster title. Rumor went that one affluent person who had adapted her arranged her games with various organizations, often making large donations. This year, in addition to other prizes the champion was also promised to have the opportunity to play three games against the great Aretha, over the internet, of course.

It was late spring. School was open. Chess prodigy or not, Farina had always been very serious about school. Normally she'd never skip classes to participate in a tournament. But Uncle Shahed, husband of Aunt Abida – her only aunt from mother's side, convinced her by pointing out that very few females had earned the men's grandmaster title. It would definitely be a great achievement for a young girl and missing a few days of school was well worth the gain. He even took a few days off from his own work to accompany Farina to Vienna. For somebody who barely understood the game he showed immense passion watching each and every one of her games sitting nervously in the audience. He and his wife had been raising Farina since she was only a baby. The love and care that they bestowed her with would make any child jealous. Zaki, their nine-year old son – their only child – often showed all the symptoms of a jealous sibling.

In Vienna, winning most of her games Farina was breezing through the tournament. Four wins and one draw had easily put her at the top after five rounds. Even the most experienced grandmasters looked helpless when faced with her extreme aggression on the chess board. Her fan based grew dramatically. The students from all over Vienna flocked to watch her play. The city seemed to be taken by her charm.

Amid all this, there was this mysterious looking man who got her attention. She'd noticed him several times since the tournament commenced. He was tall, slim, tough looking with short, mostly-gray hair and a deeply tanned complexion. A thoughtful, anxious look hanged over his face pretty much all the time. He wore a dark set of sunglasses hiding his eyes completely. Nevertheless, behind his almost expressionless face there was an almost invisible smile that could be passed on as friendly. She caught him talking to Shahed once. However, later when she inquired Shahed couldn't remember anything. This was not surprising. At fifty his memory showed every sign of an ensuing collapse. Aunt Abida often ridiculed him – "O' forgetful! Have you forgotten me yet?"

Shahed would burst into laughter. He was a kind and gentle natured man. Farina had absolutely no memory of her biological father but had no issues in accepting this affectionate, big hearted man as a father figure.

After two more rounds Farina increased her lead over rest of the pack by a whopping one and a half point. All she needed to do was to draw the last two games. That would not only give her the championship but the final norm of the grandmaster as well.

Unfortunately, right before the next game she received a call from Abida. Bad news – just what she feared. Her mother was suffering from acute Pneumonia, once again.

Almost ten years ago a suspicious car accident had put Rajia - her mother - into a state of coma. Later she went into a vegetative state. She was unable to move any limbs of her body and could neither talk nor respond to any stimuli.

The only sign of life was her breathing.

She was staying in a specialized nursing home under the observation of trained nurses. Due to lying down around the clock she caught pneumonia very often. Farina knew that pneumonia was one of the major diseases that killed patients in coma. She wasted no time and took the first available flight home. Her mother was the most important thing in her life. Becoming a grandmaster could wait.

To her amazement, on her flight back home she noticed the tall man with the sunglasses was flying with her as well. He was sitting all the way back, near the washrooms. Even though her mind was filled with anxiety for her mother she couldn't resist her curiosity and took a few extra trips to the washroom just to check the man out a little closely. This – she knew – was somewhat risky but there was something about the man that didn't seem scary at all. He didn't try to hide himself or anything – even smiled once – at least that's how it looked to her. Still suspicious but without clues Farina decided to leave it that way for now.

Chapter 2

SciAngels

Once back home, Farina spent most part of the next few days by her mother's side. Fortunately Rajia was recovering from her pneumonia albeit slowly. It was a great relief for Farina. Though her mother was barely alive – at least that's how it seemed – Farina simply wasn't ready to lose her. Sitting by her mother's side, a portrait of a tireless and devoted daughter, she often wept silently wondering if she'd ever be able to talk to her mother again. The doctors made no reservation in stating that for Rajia to come back to normalcy nothing less than a miracle was necessary. It wasn't totally impossible – they had emphasized – but very unlikely.

Farina had no delusion. She tried to make the best out of the current situation. She spent hours sitting by her mother's side, holding her warm but motionless hand, speaking her hearts out. Did Rajia hear her? She wondered. How many times did she look for a signal - something as little as a twitching of the lips or a tiny movement of a finger? Nothing. Farina had learned to get used to the hopelessness of the situation.

A few days later, when visiting her mother she saw the tall man from Vienna once again. It was a mere glimpse but she knew it was the same man. He was scurrying out and seemingly didn't notice Farina. Shahed was with her but couldn't recollect seeing the man, as usual. Curious and somewhat confused Farina couldn't fully let it go out of her mind. She tried to dismiss it as simple coincidence, unsuccessfully.

A week or so had passed. Things were as usual until one afternoon when on her return from school she found – to her utter amazement – the tall man from Vienna was sitting in their living room, talking to Shahed! At her sight the man stood up and gently extended his hand.

"I am Roger Kogut." He'd a deep voice, something that gave his lanky appearance an unusual gravity.

Farina knew she didn't need introduction. He wouldn't be there if he didn't already know everything about her.

It wasn't long when the man broke the mystery. He was the convener of a scientific group called 'Science 24'. An enthusiastic and committed chess follower he was very impressed with Farina's achievement so far. His words ran so high with praise that even Farina blushed.

"...we need more talented young people like you to contribute in every area of our society, be it sports or science." He went on. "It's the minds like you that promise to build a better future for our old world."

Shahed was nodding generously, obviously overwhelmed in pride. "I am sure when she grows up she is going to do something stunning." He added with raw confidence.

"I've no doubt about it." Roger said. "I know a jewel

when I see one."

"Yes, she is one glorious pearl."

Farina wasn't sure exactly where this conversation was heading to. It was quite clear this strange man didn't come here to deliver a few words of praise. He definitely had something else in his mind. Could it have anything to do with 'Science 24' – Farina wondered.

"There is a reason for me to come here." Finally Roger decided to cut short the eulogy and get to the point.

This last remark did magic to tickle Shahed to his true senses. Alert and cautious he spoke choosing his words carefully. "She is only fifteen. We want her to complete her education first before getting involved into any other activities – beside chess – of course."

Roger chuckled. "Don't be afraid, Mr. Shahed. I didn't come with any absurd proposal. This summer, World Youth Science Tournament is going to take place in Vancouver. I am planning to sponsor a team there. I was wondering if Farina would accept the team lead position, of course with your blessings. Her school will be closed for summer. This could become a memorable experience."

"World Youth Science Tournament!" Shahed and Farina chorused. Who didn't know that it was the most prestigious youth tournament for cognitive activities in the world!

"Yes, that's right." Roger gently confirmed.

There were a few moments of silence as Farina and Shahed exchanged glances. Farina was clearly interested. Shahed was openly excited. He saw it as yet another opportunity for Farina to show her brilliance.

"Who else are in the team?" Farina asked.

Roger handed over a printed paper to her. "Six other kids. You'll find the names and addresses here. They are all from this neighborhood and attend Greens Village Elementary School. I handpicked them. They are smart, brave and bright. I also came up with a name for the team. *SciAngels*! What do you say? Sounds interesting? Everything depends on you. Without you there's no team."

It was an easy decision for Farina to make, especially when Shahed himself could barely confine his excitement – something that surely meant unconditional approval. Soon she found out Roger hadn't even contacted any of the kids on his list. He expected Farina to recruit them. This, she thought, was a smart idea. These kids lived nearby, in the adjacent subdivisions. She practically saw them grow up. Their parents knew Farina very well too. She was in a much better position to convince them than Roger was. At this point Shahed graciously offered a den in the ground floor as the temporary office for SciAngels. He'd special reason to be happy. Not just Farina but Zaki had made the team as well.

In the next two weeks Farina met the parents of the six kids - from Roger's list. Thanks to all the community work that she never passed on when an opportunity came, from free tutoring to cleaning up the playground. Everybody in the neighborhood knew her and adored her. Her offers were greeted with enthusiasm and complete trust. The World Youth Science Tournament had already built up enviable reputation. Nobody saw any issues. However, they asked to meet Roger, which was arranged. Roger's respectful demeanor and large expensive limousine helped evaporating whatever hesitation they had. The *SciAngels* was born.

The event was only eight weeks away. Farina didn't believe that was sufficient time to prepare for such a competitive event. She wasn't planning on only participation. Her eyes were set high – on one of the top three places. She hated losing. Her success in chess directed so much attention toward her that the last thing she wanted was to lose in anything and disappoint her fans.

However, soon she discovered that her team members weren't exactly willing participants when it came to preparing for the competition. They were, without much exception, a group of restless kids, in their preteens and teens. Brilliant students they were but still reluctant to study. The *Neighborhood Watch* – a kiddy version that Roger had introduced to educate the kids about their surroundings and to make them aware of the dangers that lurked around them – was a hit with them but not the brainstorm sessions where they worked on various scientific and analytical problems. Farina realized she'd her hands full with something that she didn't bargain for. Leading such a young and aimless team was not going to be easy. In fact it was going to be extremely painful.

Chapter 3

The Training

It was a Saturday morning. The meeting was supposed to start at 11. However, none of these recurring meetings ever started on time. There was no reason to think today would be any exception. Farina was on time as always, but there were no sign of the other kids, as always. No amount of scolding worked. How could anybody prepare for a big event with this bunch of irresponsible kids? Farina fumed.

Abida smiled at her dismay over this. She advocated for the kids. "Don't be so mad. They are just little kids. Don't expect them to have same sense of time as yours!"

Before Farina could come up with a bitter reply, Zaki burst in through the front door followed by heavily sweaty Musa. Both of them were nine years old, boasted to be best friends. Zaki was weary and calculative while Musa was recklessly brave - 'do first think later' type. He was an impulsive climber and attempted to climb just about anything that was climbable.

In the next few minutes the rest of the bunch showed up – slowly and steadily. Ivana was ten, careful and picky, unforgiving as a critic. Preeti was nine, a good speaker, often bossy, champion in sarcasm. Stanley was twelve. Bigger than his age, he was keen on showing off his strength. He loved lifting - chairs, tables, big rocks – whatever he could handle. The last member of the team was Oliver, twelve as well. Quiet in nature he always looked for willing participants to practice the Judo locks his dad taught him.

Their clubhouse - *The Laboratory* - was a 16 feet by 12 feet room. It had a large bay window with Venetian curtains. There was a round table at the center of the room surrounded by seven tools. On one of the walls hanged a large blackboard, which was an important part of any meeting.

Once everybody took their seats Farina glanced across the room. What she saw was nothing pleasant. The red faced, sweaty and out of breath kids – all six of them – were clearly more interested in going back in the sun than to sit inside and study math and science. They tried their best to show sufficient interest but the fakeness of it all was so apparent that Farina could only let go a deep sigh. This was all a big mistake.

Unfortunately, it was too late to back off. She tried to look at it in a different perspective. Winning was not everything in life. Just participating in an event like this was quite rewarding. This lightened her up a tiny bit, enough to allow her to break a smile. The guilty looks that the six kids bore on their childish faces were kind of funny – she admitted. The smile worked its magic through the kids. Finally they sighed in relief and eased on their seats. Farina wasn't mad. Thanks God!

The first thing in the agenda was the *Neighborhood Watch*, the undisputed favorite. Farina had reservation about this program but she played along, using it as a strategy to get their attention.

It turned out that the neighborhood was particularly

busy the past week. A two-storied house near the Greens Village Elementary School had a few suspicious looking visitors. Their appearances and demeanor wasn't like regular people. Using a digital camera with powerful zoom lens Zaki and Musa, who worked as a pair, even managed to take a few snapshots. However, it was impossible to identify anybody clearly in those distant blurry images.

Farina asked them not to risk taking pictures in future, even from a distance. If those guys were criminals and had seen them taking pictures there could be ill consequences. She noted down the address of the house – 312 Oak tree road – and decided to pass it on to Roger, who could check it out later and if necessary would inform the cops.

Ivana and Preeti worked as a team. They were assigned to keep an eye on Sunrise Boulevard, the street they lived on, in adjacent houses. They took their job damn seriously and any unknown face raised their suspicion. Preeti, an avid talker, grabbed the first opportunity to open her mouth.

"We saw two men of Chinese origin walking around. None of them live in this area. If they did I'd have definitely known. I've photographic memory! Nobody can fool me. Both of them wore sunglasses and had expressionless faces. They didn't talk to anybody. Isn't that right, Ivana?"

Ivana agreed, not something that happened very often. "They looked kind of weird but not like bad guys."

"I saw one guy driving around," said Stanley, "at least half a dozen times in the last few days. White, tanned. Always wears sunglasses. Very mysterious looking."

"I've seen him too. Unshaven." Oliver added.

Farina didn't pay much attention. These kids reported such sightings in every meeting. Later every mysterious person turned out to be perfectly innocent visitors. She put up a patient smile, trying not to be discouraging. Roger introduced this program to build consciousness among the kids. He believed once they learnt to observe people around them it would become harder and harder to prey on them. The threateningly high number of convicted sexual predators that lived in every neighborhood in this city was more than enough to put everybody on the defensive side.

The next half of the meeting was dedicated to the preparation for the science tournament. The tournament was held over two days only. Teams came from every corner of the world but primarily from America and Canada. Last year there were more than three hundred teams. Each team had to participate in a preliminary test. Passing that test was the only way to advance to the final stage. This final stage consisted of two rounds of tests. Each round had three parts – mathematics, analytical problems and general scientific knowledge. Duration – three hours. Only the top ten teams from round one would advance to the second and final round. Another three-hour test would determine the champion.

While Farina had no worries about the preliminary test, she wasn't sure if they could make it to the final round. Even the thought of not making it to the top bothered her. People had certain expectation from her. An early elimination would be truly embarrassing. But these kids were way more interested in acting detectives than to let their brains get soiled with academic problems. Especially mathematical problems were an unfailing yawn generator. Farina came up with several ideas to get their attention. Chocolate and cookies worked the most. What great inventions! Even the most reluctant children gave up on chocolaty temptation. Of course, Farina strictly restricted the amount. The last thing she wanted was a group of overweight kids hooked on sugar products. Fortunately, once the kids got into the mood they performed well.

One thing that Farina really struggled to teach them was team work. Working together as a team was the quickest way to solve a problem – she tried to educate them. Unfortunately, the attention spun of these youngsters was so short that they lost their interest even before she could finish the sentence. How can you get anything done when nobody seem to listen to you?

Her overall experience was painful – the continuous cycle of raising voice, repeating the same sentences god knows how many times and begging for any response, anything at all. Nevertheless, as the days passed by she could see some clear improvements though not nearly good enough to be in the finals. She knew she'd have to play a major role during the tests but the time to problems ratio was pretty low and she alone won't be able to answer even half of all the problems. This meant the kids had to pick up the rest. Like it or not, they must practice. She wasn't letting the silly bunch to put her down. This was a question of honor to her.

Chapter 4

Detectives in Trouble

Months had flown by. Summer was almost knocking at the door. Roger sent a new set of problems every week, which Farina practiced with the team. The World Youth Science Tournament was just around the corner. The kids didn't seem to realize the weight of this prestigious tournament. They were more excited about going away from home without any parents hovering over them.

Another Saturday. The practice session went considerably well today. There were several arguments – mostly heated and noisy – but at the end they came up with the correct solutions. Things weren't as bleak as it looked just a few weeks ago, Farina admitted. Of course, they won't be able to scream at each other in the actual tournament. Any such behavior would definitely quicken their departure from the tournament – with a kick on the buttocks.

Aunt Abida prepared lunch for everybody. After the meal the kids headed for the playground across the road. Farina accompanied them. As the weather warmed up after the cool winter, not just the kids, even adults could barely stay indoors.

The playground was jam packed with kids and their parents. The festive mode matched the bright sunny day. Instantly, Musa was up on the monkey bar. Preeti and Ivana dashed for the swingers. Stanley and Oliver carried a soccer ball with them around the clock. They headed for the adjacent open fields to punish the poor ball.

Zaki carefully climbed up to a slide. He wasn't as deft in physical activities as some of the other boys. His favorites were the slides – risk free entertainment. Watching him in a playground was truly amusing. His immense carefulness bordered insanity.

Half an hour later Shahed walked out of his house and called out for Farina. "Roger has sent for you."

Roger sometimes stopped by to see how the team was progressing. Sometimes he just sent his limousine to pick Farina up. Shahed, however, never allowed her to go alone. He trusted Roger but was determined to carry on his own responsibilities and always accompanied her. Before they left, Abida was asked to keep an eye on the kids. While the neighborhood was mostly safe, there was no need to take any chances.

Roger lived only a few kilometers away in an estate surrounded by brick walls. He was definitely rich. According to him, he was blessed with a fortune left by his late parents. Some good investment kept him going.

When they arrived at Roger's place, Shahed was cordially taken to a large living room while Roger pulled away Farina to his reading room for some private discussions. Shahed was served with delicious snacks as always. He liked good food and helped himself without any reservations.

Back in the reading room Roger looked worried. Today, Orenda - his girlfriend and long time partner - was present as well. Descendant of the native Indians, Orenda had a calm personality. She spoke softly and displayed patience without exception. A reputed scientist, she was known for her extraordinary contributions in environment related studies and discoveries.

Very pleased to see Farina she embraced her affectionately. "How are you genius?"

Farina could not hide her excitement. "Great! How are you Orenda? I haven't seen you for a while."

Orenda was about to say something when Roger unmindfully cut her off. "Farina, isn't there any way to stop the detectives?"

Farina shrugged. "They all want to be Sherlock Holmes!"

Roger sighed. "These young Sherlocks are going to get into some serious trouble. They are taking snapshots, watching through telescopes, stalking strangers! I am starting to lose sleep over this."

Farina was surprised. She hadn't yet told Roger about the snapshots. "How did you know?"

"I got my ways. I knew you alone won't be able to handle them. So, I keep my eyes open."

"They have been talking about suspicious people in the neighborhood." Farina tried to offer some kind of explanation.

"I know who these suspicious people are." Roger struggled to keep his calmness. "They are my guys - the Sygods." He ran his fingers into his hair impatiently. "We got to stop this before it goes out of hand. No more neighborhood watch. We are dealing with real bad people here. Trust me."

Farina vaguely knew Roger had a team of agents, strong and powerful, shortly called Sygods. Roger never elaborated.

"May be this wasn't a good idea to begin with." Farina said. "Unfortunately, that's the only thing that interests them. It's going to be difficult to stop them. By the way, who are your guys? Wouldn't it be better if we knew them?"

"I preferred you didn't because they are supposed to be undercover. Now, check this screen out."

There was a large LCD screen sitting on a table before him. He'd been occasionally glancing at it as he spoke. He turned it at her direction.

Farina could not believe her own eyes. Zaki and Musa were hanging from the grips of a gorilla of a man who was about to walk inside a house – with them. It was unmistakably the front porch of 312 Oak Tree Road.

Farina shrieked in complete panic. "They were at the playground! How did they get there? What is that man going to do with them? How come nobody is helping them?"

"Don't worry," Roger calmly said. "They were taking pictures and ended up going too close to the house. The man came from behind. It is amazing how stubborn these kids can be!"

Farina couldn't share Roger's calmness. The gorilla man pushed the doors opened and was stepping inside the house. Her mind went blank, heart pounded like drums, throat became paper dry. Why wasn't Roger concerned? She thought, horrified.

What happened next eliminated all her doubts. A man in all whites appeared from nowhere. He leaped in the air and threw a flying kick, briskly but forcefully, on the side of the gorilla man, crushing him to the floor without much resistance. Released from his grips, Zaki and Musa ran as fast as they could. The noise attracted couple of other heavyset guys who rushed out of the house.

They had barely any time to analyze the situation. The mystery man leaped in the air again and in quick succession released two strong kicks, hitting both on the neck. The two men looked almost comical as they slowly fell on the ground. The man in white somersaulted several times like a deft gymnast and quickly disappeared behind a series of houses nearby.

Farina sighed in relief. "Thanks God! Who was he? What was he doing there?"

"I can't tell you, not yet." Roger said. "He is there to stop things like this from happening. Those kids have good observation; I'll give that. But no more of this."

Farina didn't reply. She could still hear her heart pounding. How many times did she warn those kids not to do stupid things like that? Thanks to Roger for having somebody there, somebody who fought that well!

Later they spent some time discussing the team's progress for the forthcoming tournament. Roger's limousine dropped them home just before dusk. Shahed knew nothing about the incident that happened earlier. Roger tactfully expressed his desire to keep things like that hidden from Shahed. He could panic and terminate the whole plan. It could practically be the end of SciAngels.

That night Farina pulled Zaki aside and scolded mercilessly. He however blamed it all on Musa.

Chapter 5

The Fist Fight

Farina attended Green Village high school. Ninth grade. Even though she was exceptionally good at her studies and her teachers continuously pressed her to move up, Shahed wouldn't allow her to jump classes. He'd always said, "Enjoy your youth. Once gone, it's never coming back."

Farina was barely challenged at school, education wise, but she liked her friends. Though to her dismay, her fame as a talented chess player sometimes discouraged others to get too close to her. Many hesitated, not knowing how to mingle with a celebrity. Her beauty, beside brain, frequently attracted boys. However, there was no concept of dating in the family. She'd to gracefully deny all requests for dates. Despite the fact that both Shahed and Abida were progressive Muslims, they adhered to certain social traditions that had some element of conservativeness. Shahed took special effort to come as often as possible to pick her up from school. Farina had no difficulty figuring out what he was really up to. She enjoyed this extra attention.

Next day, on her way to school she noticed police cars in front of 312 oak Tree Road. The high school was located near the Elementary school. She'd to walk past it on her way to and from school. Roger must have informed the police, she thought. Two young officers stood on the front porch — patiently. Nobody responded to the ringing bell. Empty driveway. The house looked vacated. She saw the officers giving up on the bell and cautiously walking around the premises.

Farina kept an eye on the place between her classes. She didn't trust those kids. Given a chance they could group up and poke their noses into police business. Her main concern was Musa. He'd practically no fear.

Farina's school was about a kilometer away from home. After school she walked back home, like many others, unless Shahed came to pick her up. Usually Rani – one of her class friends who lived in a nearby subdivision – walked with her. Today Rani left early. Her mother picked her up around noon. Farina had to stay late after her classes to help out some students with their math. This was something she did voluntarily, twice a week.

When she stepped out of the school most students had already left. She didn't like to walk all by herself but had little choice.

The afternoon sun was bright and pleasant. She walked slowly enjoying every bit of the warmth. Her mother was doing well. This was a great relief to her. Pulling out of the tournament was somewhat disappointing, especially the missed opportunity to play Aretha, but she accepted it as a fate. More often than not, she observed, the natural turn of events guided individuals to directions they had never thought of. Perhaps this would somehow modify her future for better.

Walking past densely located houses, mostly brick, some stone, she stayed on the sidewalk that meandered through the midscale neighborhood and was so close to the front porches that one might wonder if the green yards were quickly approaching extinction in this rapidly growing city with shrinking yards.

Farina, however, was not worried about that. Her mind was occupied by Aretha. Who was she? Would they ever play each other? What chance Farina had against the girl who made little work of many top rated chess computers? Not to mention the crashing defeat of the human world chess champion in two different meetings. Could Farina   possibly win a single game? Or even draw? What was   Aretha's main strength? Two answers came in her mind – no blunders, no mistakes. Only a very advanced computer could be that accurate, time and time. Could she possibly be a computer? Farina wondered. Nobody had ever seen her!

If Aretha was another brilliant chess machine then she was better than anything the world has ever seen. Computers mostly relied on immense number of calculations coupled with an algorithm to navigate the decision tree in a most efficient way. The faster the machine the better. More calculations in less time. Humans on the other hand use their ability to recognize patterns and compensate for their lack of processing efficiency with creativity. This most often work to their advantage. Not against Aretha though. She'd examined some of Aretha's games. She was extraordinarily creative. The surprising combinations that she created from seemingly dull positions were beyond brilliance. They were simply work of unfathomable beauty. This clearly wasn't a footmark of master chess computers. Aretha had to be a real person, a human. If she could just beat her once! Farina dared to dream.

Taken by her thoughts Farina didn't notice the man who emerged out of a bush and followed her from a distance. The neighborhood playground - bordering woods in one side - provided a short cut to her house. Most days when she walked with Rani, this was where their ways separated. Rani turned left, Farina to the right and across the playground. At this time of the day there was nobody around. As soon as the sun weakened and air cooled, children of all ages would pour in here. The party would go on until dusk.

As Farina walked across the playground she didn't even bother to look around. Safety wasn't something that even crossed her mind.

When the man suddenly sped up, stepped ahead of her and blocked her way she was stunned. He was tall, dark, ruggedly dressed in old faded jeans and sweaty tee shirt that gave away strong odor. He probably hadn't taken a shower for days, possibly homeless, a new trend in this ever spreading city. It was hard to miss their presence – mostly healthy, young men, standing with a hand written paper board,   asking for work for food and accepting any donations from the passing drivers or pedestrians.

Farina didn't know what to do. For moments she looked puzzled, confused. The man took full advantage of her momentary bedazzlement. He swiftly came close to Farina, grabbed her hand forcefully and before pulling her toward the woods hoarsely said, "Not a single word. Come with me."

Terrified, Farina tried to jerk her hand off but to no avail. The man squeezed her wrist so hard that for one moment she thought it was going to break. Groaning in excruciating pain she quickly looked around. The playground was deserted. She knew her only weapon was her voice. She screamed at the top of her voice while putting as much resistance as she possibly could against a man almost three times heavier than her. The man, now totally mad, dragged her with brutal force. Farina tried to clasp on anything she could find to stop his progress but her fragile attempt had no impact.

Completely helpless, Farina didn't know what to do. She screamed a few more times hoping Roger's men might be around and could hear her. Seconds passed by, nothing happened. The man was about to drag her into the woods when a large, muscular man appeared magically and stood blocking the way. He was no less than six feet six, black, cleanly shaven with knee long shorts and sleeveless tee-shirt.

"Am I late for the party?" he calmly said.

The offender looked baffled for a long moment. This wasn't something he was looking forward to.

"You wanna dance with me?" The second man growled teasingly.

The perpetrator released Farina and attacked the second man with his fists closed. This was a bad idea. Even though he was almost as big as the other man, he proved to be no match in the skill and strength department. What ensued in the next thirty seconds was particularly pleasing to Farina. The muscular man danced away from the hastily thrown blows before advancing ahead in lightening speed with a quick combination of a jab and hook, breaking the attacker's nose and possibly jaw. Blood gushed out through the broken nose. Next came a blazing upper cut, knocking the criminal down on the ground like a sack of dirt, senseless. "Don't be afraid." He calmly said. "Go home now. And do me a favor. No shortcuts."

Shaken but relieved Farina managed to say, "Thank you for saving me. Shouldn't we call the cops now?"

"Don't worry about that. I'll take care of it." There was a slight touch of ambiguity in his tone.

"Sir, do you work with Roger?" Farina collected

enough courage to ask.

He shrugged, clearly impatient. "Duh! Can you just go home, please? I've to take care of this dirt-bag, don't I?"

Farina muttered a quick 'yes of course, thanks' and hurried back to the sidewalk. The man had just saved her from a trouble of epic proportion. The last thing she wanted was to piss him off. As she paced back home she couldn't help wondering if she should have stayed back there until the cops arrived. Now that she'd left the scene how was he going to explain the situation? Was he really one of Roger's men? She decided to bring this incident to Shahed's knowledge.

Chapter 6

The Magician

The front door was closed but not locked. As Farina stepped inside the house she could hear Shahed talking in his study – a small room right next to the living room where he usually received his close friends. A full professor of economics, he taught classes in the University of Toronto. A courteous, polite and friendly man – he made friends quickly. He'd visitors practically every day. Farina knew most of his friends. Just by listening she could tell who was who. Today it was Jafar, senior police officer. An Egyptian Muslim who came to Canada twenty years ago. He was one of Shahed's frequent visitors.

Farina stood quietly outside the study, struggling to make up her mind. Should she tell them about the incident in the park? Her instinct said 'No'. If her savior was truly one of Roger's men then bringing it to Jafar's attention without talking to Roger first could be asking for trouble.

She heard Musa and Zaki running around on the second floor. This was Musa's second home. He slipped in whenever he found an opportunity. Both of his parents worked long hours. They considered this as a blessing. Abida didn't fully share the feeling. When Zaki joined forces with Musa, things could and did get a little stressful for everybody in this household. They were like two busy beavers, always in hunt for novelty.

The exhaust fan in the kitchen buzzed loudly. Abida must be cooking. Farina could smell the aroma of traditional Indian spices. She was tiptoeing past Shahed's study when something Jafar said got her attention. Right or wrong, her curiosity emerged victorious. She stood by the door silently, listening.

"One thing I just can't understand Shahed," Jafar was saying, "recently the crime rate has jumped both in USA and Canada. Especially drug and mob related crimes have doubled. Yes, you might say economic downturn may affect the crime rate but such large scale spike is unheard of."

"I heard large supplies of illegal weapons made their way to North America." Shahed said. "Maybe the mob bosses are trying to settle things up. Or maybe the terrorist groups are orchestrating this to destabilize our social stability. What do you think?"

Jafar lowered his voice. "Have you ever heard of *The Magician*?"

"No. Not really. Who is he?"

"Well, he is sort of a legend, obviously not as a magician. He is a secretive scientist and got that name for his fascinations with magical applications of science. We have very little information about him. Guy is filthy rich. We know that for sure. But we have no clue where he lives or who he works for. Many believe that he is hiding somewhere in South America. "

"What is his role in all this?"

"Well, I heard he is very whimsical and fosters deep resentment against the rich and powerful countries. Just a few days back General Derek Bowman – chief of Bureau of Crime Reduction, submitted a report to the president. Secret report but I found out - don't ask me how – that the report is pretty much all about the Magician. General has practically blamed him for the increase of crime rate and several other offenses. According to him both America and Canada received several large shipments of illegal weapons from an unidentified country in South America. I guess this is what you heard too. Anyway, most of these weapons ended up in the hands of the organized criminal groups and the arm dealers who are selling them to the small time thugs. Naturally that caused a surge in criminal activities. Now, these are strong, modern weaponry that even the police department doesn't have the ability to fight against - the report   mentioned. "

"What is his motive?" Shahed sounded doubtful.

"According to the General the Magician is plotting to influence change in the current American government. His first goal is to create anarchy. When people would start losing their confidence in current governance then he'd move in with his preferred politicians, who would ensure that his interests are served. A simple plan!" Jafar paused for a moment. "This is just an assumption. There's no evidence to support this theory. Anybody who knows General Derek won't be surprised. He is known for his wild speculations. May be he is trying to keep the president happy."

"I heard nasty things about him as well. Hell with him. Tell me more about the scientist. He sounds interesting."

At this point Farina heard Musa and Zaki running down the stairs. She quickly moved away. On her way up the stairs she passed the two. None of the busy bugs took much notice of her. Once in her room she locked the door and called Roger from her cell phone.

Roger was ahead of her. "I heard. Are you okay?"

"I am fine." Farina said. "He is one of your men, right? He beat the crap out of that thug. However, I don't think he reported the incident to the cops. I haven't heard any police siren."

Roger assured her. "Don't worry. I'll take care of it. The man who attacked you is a convicted felon with several cases of sexually abusing underage girls. I can't believe they let this guy loose!" He paused as if to shake off his annoyance. "Anyway, you be careful. Another thing, police didn't find anybody in 312 Oak Tree Road. Please make sure our Sharlocks don't show up there again."

"Strange! Who were those people?"

"Drug dealers. A few kilograms of heroin were recovered. High quality. That's close to a million dollars right there. Anyway, nothing to worry about. My boys are staying close. But please make sure nobody in your team tries to talk to them. That might destroy their camouflage."

Farina promised to stop the neighborhood watch program temporarily. Things needed to cool down a little bit before these overzealous kids ended up getting into another trouble.

She asked how many men Roger had in the area but got no specific answer. She decided not to press. Roger was always very secretive about his team. Instead she thought of inquiring about the scientist. "Can I ask a quick question?"

"What is it?" Roger sounded cautious.

"Who is the Magician?"

There was an uncharacteristically long silence at the other end. Finally when he did talk his voice was cold. "How did you hear about him?"

"One of Uncle Shahed's friends mentioned him. He is a police officer."

"He is a mysterious person." Roger said after another short silence. "Nobody really knows much about the man."

"Is he some kind of a criminal?" Farina had this

strange feeling that Roger wasn't saying everything.

"That's what my impression is." Roger quickly moved away from the topic. "Anyway - about the tournament - I've a great idea. Next week when the school closes for the summer how about you and the kids stay in my house for a few days. This would give us plenty of opportunity to test our readiness for the tournament. What do you say?"

"Sounds like a plan! Do you think our parents would allow that, especially Uncle Shahed? He is going to make a big fuss about it. You know him."

Roger laughed. "Leave that to me. I can handle him. Be alert."

Roger disconnected. Farina connected to the internet and tried to find some more information about the Magician. She got lot of hits but most information was clearly ambiguous. Opinions about him varied. He could be a drug lord, or an arms dealer or even a terrorist determined to shake down the world. Roger knew more but he won't share. Why not? She wondered. Could she approach Jafar? Bad idea. If Shahed heard about it he'd get alarmed. Not a good thing. She decided to leave it there for now.

Almost an hour passed since the assault. Looking out the window she saw no sign of police cars. Clearly Roger didn't want cops to interfere in his business.

Chapter 7

The Attack

The Unionville nursing home, located in Unionville - a small historic town near Markham - was a relatively small facility. However, in a town two hundred years old it fit in just fine. It was hardly noticeable apart from the rest of the restored houses and stores in the town. Nevertheless, it had high reputation in Greater Toronto Area, mainly due to professor Aleya Ibrahim. An Indian Muslim, she was in her golden age. Her reputation in Neurology was world known. She lived in this small town with her husband, away from the bustling city of Toronto. Close to her house she rented a two storied building and started this nursing home. Her long time acquaintance with Shahed was the only reason why Rajia was spared a bed in this place. In total there were fifty to sixty patients. Most of them were suffering from serious mental illnesses. Only Rajia was in coma. She was kept in a single room at the tail end of the second floor. Two doctors and ten nurses took care of the patients around the clock. An armed guard was always on duty at the entrance. Doctor Aleya was very particular about the safety of her patients.

The guard change usually took place around 10 am. Jonathan, the guard for the new shift had just sat at his desk with a cup of coffee when two monstrously big men, each one well over six feet tall and heavily built like bodybuilders, appeared before him almost magically. They both had short hair trimmed uniformly. Jonathan shrunk in front of their blazing eyes. He was only five feet ten and weighed about one hundred and sixty pounds. These guys could literally pick him up on their pinky and spin as long as they wanted before smashing him on the ground. Still, putting up a brave face he stood straight with one hand on his gun. "How can I help you?"

"Where's Ms. Rajia?" They growled in unison.

Jonathan now noticed that these two were identical twins. With the exception of a red pimple on one of their left cheek there were virtually no other differences that he could notice. Shaken within, Jonathan tried to keep his composure. It was clear that these two meant trouble. The man with the pimple became impatient and threw a forceful blow on the wooden reception desk, which crumbled without any objection. Jumping back two steps Jonathan quickly drew his gun. But before he'd any chance to use it the second giant snatched the gun from him like taking candy from a child and easily bent the barrel. He returned it to him, nicely. Next, ignoring him completely they burst through a pair of heavy doors and disappeared inside the nursing home.

Frozen in panic, Jonathan didn't fully understand why they let him live. It was close, very close. It took him a few long moments to get into his senses. He quickly pressed the silent alarm button that was installed under a hidden panel. This signal was directly connected to the local police station. Cops would be here in five minutes. But five minutes were a long time for something bad to happen. Still shaken, he fearfully followed the giants into a specious corridor and froze instantly.

The two brothers were holding a female nurse high in

the air. "Where's Rajia?" They shouted in chorus.

The middle-aged nurse, desperately trying to breathe, pointed at the stairs. She was immediately dropped on the floor as the brothers rushed upstairs. Jonathan had no clue why they were asking for Rajia. She was in such vegetative state that she couldn't even move her fingers, forget about talking. In the next few minutes the things that happened could easily be the most memorable event in his entire young life.

Two lightly built, average height young men silently came through the doors. From their movement and absolute serious posture one could easily make out that they meant business. Jonathan couldn't catch a clear glimpse of them as they sort of flew toward the stairs and climbed up briskly. Both of them wore loose white dress and flat sole black karate shoes. They looked to be of Chinese ethnicity. Not thinking clearly Jonathan followed them. After all he was the guard. He'd some responsibility.

The time it took him to climb up the stairs quite a bit had already happened. The shorter guys had attacked the giant brothers. Their legs and hands were moving faster than eye could register. With every movement they hit the brothers ruthlessly. The giants seemed to be totally taken aback by such unthinkable speed and skill. Their every attempt to hit back went in vain as the attackers effortlessly moved away and hit with even greater force. Their rhythmic body movements, quick change of position and the plethora of kicks and punches took away every bit of energy from the big brothers. They did the only thing that they could possibly do – run. They dashed down the stairs and rushed out of the building. The attackers followed them out as well. In a moment everything was quiet, normal, as if nothing had happened. Jonathan had dived on the floor to get away from harm's way. Now, in front of dozens of curious and fearful eyes of the doctors and nurses he slowly stood up. The police siren could be heard from a distance.

He cleared his throat. "Everything is fine" he said, struggling to make his voice as steady as possible under the circumstance. "Nothing to worry about. Cops will be here in no time."

Coming back to his post he collapsed into his chair. He still couldn't believe what had just happened here in last few minutes. If the broken parts of the security desk hadn't been there he probably would have just waved it away as daydream.

Roger was the first one to show up in Unionville Nursing Home. On his way there he also picked up Farina. Shahed was in the middle of a class when he was informed about the incident. He dismissed his class and drove to home to pick up his wife and son and joined Roger and Farina in less than an hour.

There were two cops guarding the facility. Farina was still in a shock. She simply couldn't understand why would anybody in the world try to hurt her mother? The two saviors were Roger's men, she was told. Luckily they were close by.

Sitting right by her mother's side Farina tightly held her hands. Obviously Rajia had no awareness of what had happened. Trying hard to stop her tears from rolling down Farina whispered, "Don't worry mom, we won't let anything happen to you. You just get better. I miss you so much."

Roger affectionately touched her shoulder. "We'll have to move Rajia to another place."

"Who were they, Roger?"

"Don't know, but there's reason to believe that they

didn't really want to harm Rajia. They just wanted to stir things up. According to my guys they ran without putting up much of a fight."

"I don't really understand this. Why mom? She was just a young scientist before the accident! "

Roger thoughtfully nodded. "Right. It's puzzling."

Later that day Rajia was moved to another nursing home. Only the closest relatives were informed about it. Nobody was to visit her for the next few days.

Chapter 8

A Glimpse into The Past

That night, back in his room, Farina tried to concentrate on her studies. The final exam was closing on but she couldn't put her mind to study. A few things were eating her up. She didn't believe for a moment that Roger's men were in the area accidentally. Either they were following the two attackers or they were keeping an eye on the nursing home. Why? Is there anything that Roger knew about her mother that Shahed and Abida didn't? But how was that possible? They didn't even know Roger until just few months ago. Of course, he'd become a good friend of the family in a very short time. Shahed had quietly inquired about him and found nothing negative. He trusted Roger like his own brother. And yet there was obviously something that Roger knew and wasn't sharing with them. What was it?

Knock on the door. Two quick ones followed by a single strong one. It was Shahed.

"Yes, Uncle Shahed?"

"Can I come in?"

"Yes. Sure."

Shahed came inside and sat on her bed. "What a day! Huh?"

"The last thing I ever expected." Farina said, thoughtfully.

Shahed noticed it. "What else bugging you?"

"How much do you and Aunt Abida know about my mother?"

Shahed scratched his head. "Exactly what we told you before. When we first came to Canada as immigrants – twelve years ago – your mother was teaching in some American university. She barely had any contact with her family back home for years. And you know why."

"She'd an affair and her family didn't approve it. I know."

"I guess she could never forgive her family for that. Anyway, couple of years later when she suddenly quit her job and came to live with us here in Canada, we were very surprised. But we didn't ask her anything. Your aunt was so happy, especially seeing you! You were a five-year-old angel. We didn't want to do anything that might drive her away. Obviously we were more worried about you than her. Things were going very well.

"However, that happiness didn't last too long. Your mother had just taken up a new job in Toronto. One night, while driving back she got into an accident. The fire brigade had to cut the car to get her out — it was that bad. She'd a severe trauma in the head and was already in a coma. She never recovered. That's all I know. " Shahed felt guilty. He wished he knew more. Farina had every right to know her mother better.

Farina heard all this before, numerous times, with different wording. It didn't give her any answer. She'd always wanted to know about her father. She never had the courage to ask, Shahed and Abida never offered any details. It was a taboo subject among them. Today she was determined to seek an answer.

"I know nothing about my father. Not even his name.

No pictures, no letters. Why? Who was he?"

Shahed sighed heavily. "I told you everything I know. Your mother never told us anything about your father. One time when Abida pressed her hard she acknowledged that she broke up with her boyfriend who she never married. Is he your father? We never got a clear answer. She kept it a total secret from all of us."

"So nobody knows who my biological father is?"

"I am afraid so. Rajia was very secretive about it. A mother out of wedlock wasn't exactly something to be proud of. Not in our culture."

"Didn't her ex-boyfriend try to find her?"

"Not to my knowledge. But I only know what Rajia told me. Anyway, why this sudden interest?"

"I am just trying to make sense of this attack." Farina gloomily said. "Why would anybody want to hurt her? Was there anything else in her past that she was hiding from you and Aunt Abida?" She ran her fingers into her hair thoughtfully, not really expecting answers.

"Did she ever mention about Roger?" She suddenly asked.

"Roger?" Shahed was surprised. "How would she know him? We just met Roger couple of months ago. He has been living in Toronto for last twenty years, I checked. Rajia lived somewhere in Connecticut. I am not sure I understand your line of thoughts."

Farina shook her head in frustration. "I am just exploring all possibilities. Never mind."

Shahed patted on her shoulder. "Don't get drawn into this. Everything is fine. Study for your test. Remember, the world is watching you, genius."

Farina chuckled. "Yeah! Some genius!"

Shahed smiled, kissed her on the forehead and left.

Farina knew she needed to study for her test but she could barely concentrate. What was she missing? What she didn't know?

Chapter 9

The Mansion

Roger's ranch style house was located at the northern end of Markham. Though Farina had been there numerous times she never really had a chance to check the place out. Her visits were solely business. None of the other kids had ever set foot in that premise. However, that was about to change.

Farina didn't think for once that the parents would actually permit them to stay in Roger's ranch — overnight — all by themselves. Apparently she didn't know Roger very well. He visited every kid's house starting with hers, had a frank conversation with the parents and didn't leave until they agreed to his proposition. What he wanted was simple. The World Youth Science Tournament was due to start in couple of weeks. Before that he wanted to have the opportunity to get them ready for the tournament. This, he argued, couldn't be done from a distance. Most parents had blind faith in Shahed. Hence when he agreed to it they had no reason to object.

Roger did have one condition. Parents weren't allowed to stay overnight with their kids. They could visit but only for short time. With the exception of Shahed none of the other parents showed much interest anyway. Nobody in their right mind could pass on such an opportunity to spend one whole week without the nuisances these kids created.

Shahed, as always, looked so worried that Farina joked, "We are only going three kilometers away, not to the North Pole! Chill out!"

Zaki echoed. "Yes dad, you need to chill out sometimes!"

"I bet you don't know he is going to Vancouver with you." Abida said smilingly.

"What?" Farina and Zaki screamed in disbelief. "Why?"

"To spy on you, what else?" Abida was enjoying it. "He already took three days off from work for the tournament. I feel sorry for you, kids."

Shahed was not embarrassed at all. "I can't just let them go like that," he calmly said. "Roger is a good man but I've a responsibility to make sure that the kids are safe. I can't do that sitting in Toronto."

It was meaningless to argue with him, Farina knew. He was coming, no matter what.

Roger brought the team to his ranch in the first week of July after schools closed for summer. The novelty of this whole thing – going away from home to stay in a mansion – had the team boiling in excitement. They even displayed unusual patience when Shahed tagged along on the first day and took hours to meticulously examine the house and the surroundings to ensure that the place was safe for the young kids.

The house had several armed guards working around the clock, a gray haired butler and two maid servants. Shahed made no apologies as he badgered them with his questioning and didn't stop until he'd a good knowledge of their family trees. He was a firm believer of strong family values. Roger graciously went along and instructed his

47

employees to cooperate.

Shahed left at nightfall. Roger and Orenda personally served dinner to the kids, spent a little time after dinner and then helped the kids into their beds before retiring in their own room. They wanted the kids to get good rest before the training started the next day. Farina – still worried about her mother – had difficulty sleeping. There were too many unanswered questions running down her mind.

Next day, the kids woke up at the break of dawn, all of them. The cumulative excitement must have had some kind of group effect on them. As their hosts slept they showed no mercy and instantly went into their usual restless, chaotic feat.

Farina - in a vacationing mode herself - decided to give them a break. This was the first time they lived under the same roof all together. This was exciting.

Musa took the liberty to navigate through the house to the back door, unbolted it and slipped out of the house to the backyard. The rest of the team swarmed out in a blink, including Farina. The rear of the house was partly surrounded by dense woods of matured pine, oak and birch trees bordering large stretch of green fields followed by rolling hills that extended hundreds of yards where a high wire fence clearly marked the boundary of this property. The nice balance of wilderness and the vast openness was quick to win over them, making it feel like a camping trip. Soon they found themselves playing a game of tag. It took little time for a calm morning to turn into a screaming tournament, so loud that even the dead might rise.

Roger and Orenda joined them little later. It wasn't clear whether they were early risers or a helpless couple who couldn't sleep in all the commotion that was in progress. Once the 'Good morning's were exchanged Roger gathered the team around him. He challenged them to solve a mathematical problem.

"Let's say there are four tigers in this wood." He pointed at the woods. "While passing through it four animals out of every hundred get eaten. Now my question is - if an animal has to go through this wood fifty times, what would be its chances of staying alive?"

This was not an easy problem for the elementary graders. However, Farina had no problem solving it. She could do this in her sleep.

As 4 out of every 100 animals went into the tiger's mouth, 96% actually came out alive after their first trip. This essentially meant that the probability for any of them to come out alive was 96% or .96. Similarly the probability to come out alive after two trips was .96 x .96. After fifty trips this number would become (.96) to the power 50.

"Zaki!" Farina called out, "what's .96 to the power 50?"

Zaki always wore an oversized hand watch with a calculator. He swiftly pressed a few buttons and almost abruptly came up with the answer. "12.9%."

"Thirty seconds", Roger sounded happy. "Not bad. But don't forget there'll be lot of good teams. If we want to win we got to do even better. In the next few days we are going to try out a truck load of problems. Are you guys ready for the challenge?"

Nobody answered. Obviously this was the last thing in their minds. Farina cleared her voice a few times, signaling the team to show some enthusiasm. That worked, just a little bit.

"Yes. Sure." The kids mumbled.

"That's all I get?" Roger was persistent.

Orenda chuckled. "You just ruined their day. Thank you!"

Roger managed to smile. "No worries. We'll make a great team. But first we need to eat breakfast. Hungry?"

"Y-e-y-y-y-y!" The response came quickly and loudly. They were starving.

Roger guided them to the dining room, at the table. The maids served French toasts, eggs, fresh orange juice and plenty of jam and jellies. The sight of the food did magic to them. The gloomy faces turned all bright and smiling. In seconds the breakfast table turned into a bazaar. Farina's all attempts to bring back some order went unheeded. Even Roger roared in vain to get their attention. He shrugged hopelessly. "Is this how they are all the time?"

"Pretty much." Farina grimly said.

Orenda was amused. "Kids will be kids! Let's eat."

Farina put up a forced smile. This was kind of embarrassing for her. She wished this restless bunch acted a little more sensibly in the presence of Roger. After all he was their sponsor!

Roger allowed the team more time to adjust before he gathered them in his study later that day to start the prep work. It took a little while to warm up the team but eventually they started to show true interest, to his relief.

The next few days they trained incrementally longer time and moved into more difficult problems. He made no attempt to hide his eagerness to top this tournament. He'd been planning for this for a while and had several sets of question papers ready. Besides brushing up their knowledge and skill in science and math Roger's other goal was to educate and train them in team work. They needed to understand how important it was for each and everyone in the team to contribute in solving problems instead of depending only on Farina. Despite the varying degrees of attention deficit – something that he simply learned to live with – Roger looked content with the overall progress. His confidence in the team continued to grow as the week progressed.

In the mean time, Shahed visited the kids every day. Eric – Roger's chief security guard – respectfully allowed him in the house and the maids guided him to the large living room. Butler Krishna Murthy personally served him specially made snacks and exotic tea. Clearly Roger wanted him happy but not nosy. Shahed didn't need too many clues to figure that out. He spent most of his time there talking to Orenda who was nice enough to keep him company for hours discussing current weather to world politics.

Chapter 10

Sygods

Since they came to Roger's mansion Farina and the team fostered high hopes of meeting Roger's mysterious team members, especially the Kung fu masters and the giant boxer. However, days passed by and Roger didn't mention anything about them. Eventually the killer curiosity became so stressful that they could no longer keep silent. Realizing how eager and excited the kids were to meet the Sygods, one day Roger gathered them in his specious study room. At the center of the room sat a projector facing a large white rectangle screen hanging on the wall just ahead. Roger had them all seated.

"I know all of you are dying to meet them." He smiled apologetically. It was impossible to miss the greedy looks and the visible tension among the kids. "Unfortunately," he explained, "they couldn't be here in person. But don't lose heart just yet. We have this." He pointed at the projector.

"For now you'll know them by pictures. They'll be responsible for your safety during the tournament. That's why it is very important for each and every one of you to remember their faces. One more thing – they do not work for me. They are volunteers working for an organization called – as you already know - S.Y.G.O.D.S., shortly Sygods, acronym for Strong and Young Globally Organized Demon

Stoppers."

There was a wave of appreciation in the audience.

"Do they kill bad people?" Stanley asked.

"Do they have guns?" Oliver.

"They don't need guns. They are master kung fu fighters." Zaki and Musa confidently echoed.

Roger raised his hands to calm them down before it turned into another chaotic session.

"They don't kill people. They just try to stop the bad guys and hand them over to police. That's all you need to know."

He stopped for a moment to add," Remember you cannot talk about them to anybody else. This is our secret. Deal?"

"D-E-A-L!" The gang was quick to agree.

"What do they actually do?" Farina tried to get little more details.

"They are basically crime fighters." Roger selected his words carefully. "Vigilantes, like Spider man, Batman. When they see a crime is being committed, depending on the situation, they either report to police or take action."

Farina decided not to press for more details at this time. Obviously Roger wanted to keep it to minimum. If this was a vigilante group, it could very well be illegal in the eyes of law.

Roger turned on the projector. Orenda joined them at this time. Her presence lightened up the room immediately. She was greeted cheerfully by the crowd. Farina was truly impressed with her. She was smart, loving and easy going. Farina wondered why the two of them - Orenda and Roger – didn't yet tie the knots? They obviously loved each other and both had immense respect for institutionalism. Someday when the time was right she'd ask

Orenda – she thought.

The first image on the screen was of two identical young men of Chinese origin wearing traditional Kung fu dresses. Both had sharp eyes carved on expressionless faces. The only noticeable difference was in their built - one heavyset, muscular while the other one was lighter, acrobatic.

"Hong brothers." Roger spoke. "The bigger one is Hong Lee. He has legendary strength. He can break rocks with his bare hands. The skinny one is Hong Shien, extremely agile body. He can jump seven feet up in the air."

"We saw Hong Shien!" Zaki and Musa cried out. "He beat up those bad guys like hell! He just kicked and kicked and kicked!" A ripple of excitement and admiration passed through the kids.

Once they calmed down Roger moved to the next slide - a big black man with a friendly face.

"Dylan Woodsman. Boxer." Roger introduced. "He can break a brick wall with one punch."

"Wasn't he the man who saved me the other day?" Farina inquired.

"Correct. He might have been a little rough on you but he is not known for his sensitivity."

The next image was of a Caucasian man in his early twenties. He was medium built, blonde and had a lazy harmless appearance. "Miller Shovchenko", Roger said, "brilliant with handguns and rifles. He was a talented Russian shooter."

Next was Rana Agarwala. Of Indian descent, he was average built and wore thick nerdy glasses.

"Cool and calm, black belt in Judo." Roger said. "Very calculative. A computer whiz."

The next image that followed was of a female of light

stature, wearing slightly loose, well-covered black outfit. A dark embroidered scarf covered her hair neatly. Her childlike face and a pair of bright curious black eyes clearly suggested that she was only at her late teens.

"Johra!" Roger declared. "Egyptian parents, Muslim, an expert gymnast who marvels in throwing knives. "

Farina was surprised. The last thing she expected to see was a pretty, young girl as a vigilante. "How old is she?"

"Nineteen. A wonderful discovery!" Roger could not hide his admiration. "She is the music of this team, the rhythm."

"She is so pretty!" Stanley exclaimed.

"Oh yes, very pretty!" The rest of the boys voiced their approval.

Orenda broke into laughter. "How cute! I'll let her know that."

"Is she dangerous?" Stanley looked nervous.

"No less than anybody else in the team." Roger smilingly added as he turned the projector off.

"Interestingly," he dramatically added, "As they battled against the criminals over the last few years, common people have come up with affectionate street names for them. Hong lee is the Deadly Dragon; Hong Shien is Ruthless Tiger; Dylan Woodsman is Black Hammer; Miller is Killer   Miller; Rana is Cool Finger and finally Johra is Lightning Beauty."

"How long have they been with Sygods?" Farina asked.

"Each one joined at a different time." Roger didn't elaborate on this. "I am sure they would love to share their stories with you when the time is right."

"When can we meet them?" Ivana eagerly asked.

"Soon. In Vancouver." Roger said. "They'll be staying

very close to us. I can't tell you too much on security reasons."

The – *security reasons* – part was taken with great enthusiasm, as if it was the sure sign of a very exciting trip. Watching their eyes brightened up Roger felt a little alarmed. One thing he didn't want in this trip was trouble.

"When are we going to Vancouver?" Several voices asked in unison.

"In three days." Roger said.

"And how are we going there?" Preeti sharply said - her usual tone. "Shouldn't we have planned about it already?"

"I have." Roger replied patiently. "I've a small jet but big enough for all of us. We'll be flying in it. Day after tomorrow I'll drop you all home and pick you up the following evening for the flight."

"Does my mom and dad know that?" Ivana asked.

"Yes, they do." Roger said. "I've already spoken to them."

With that the questions ceased. Everybody was clearly ecstatic. Keeping aside the science tournament, just going somewhere together out of parental guidance was quite appealing to them. They barely cared about the details.

Two days later Roger dropped the kids in their respective houses. They were advised to have a good night's sleep and pack up for the trip. Zaki was dog-tired and went to bed almost instantly. Farina was both excited and nervous. Despite her plethora of experience in playing nail biting chess games she still didn't feel fully ready for the science tournament. Perhaps the fact that she never participated anything of this nature might have had an intimidating effect on her.

She'd difficulty sleeping that night. So she got up in the middle of the night and finished packing for both her and Zaki. Before going back to bed for the second time she made a mental note to visit every member of the team next morning to ensure that they didn't forget to pack the most essentials like the tooth brush, their favorite toothpaste, a pair of sleepers etc. While the two girls – Ivana and Preeti - showed some maturity, the boys had none. Even though Roger would be there with her she was still apprehensive of managing these six restless kids in Vancouver. This was a great responsibility and there was no room for error. That was the last thing she had in her mind before falling asleep.

Chapter 11

Vancouver!

Farina didn't want to leave for Vancouver without visiting her mother at least once. But Roger advised her against it. Police didn't yet have any clue about Rajia's attackers and their motives. Neither did Roger. Since Rajia was moved from her previous location only Shahed and Roger visited her. Farina was spared the whereabouts of Rajia citing her safety. What she learned from Shahed that Roger went out of his way to help him on this. The trust that had built among the two in such a short time was unusual. Shahed persistently claimed that he knew a good person when he saw one. Roger, according to him, had a heart of gold. Farina didn't necessarily disagree with that but the amount of control that Roger was gaining over their family worried her. Especially she didn't like the fact that even she couldn't see her mother. She didn't totally buy the safety concern.

On the night of departure they all convened at Buttonville airport in Markham, a town northeast of Toronto. Roger and Orenda had arrived earlier. Roger had offered to pick the team up but the parents decided to see them off and drove them to the airport. Roger's ten-seat jet, a falcon 50 was parked nearby. It wasn't anything spectacular but was good enough to awe the small crowd that stood before it. Roger graciously gave them a tour inside the plane. For many of them it was the first time inside a private jet. While the young ones were more excited because they were about to fly in it, the adults showed plenty of admiration. Many desire such luxury, only few actually have the means.

It wasn't before another hour when the plane took off, little after nine. Shahed, as arranged, flew with the team. Fortunately, he was so satisfied with the comfort of the flight that he made a generous declaration. He'd not interrupt the fellow passengers in any way. All he was looking forward to was a good nap thousands of feet above the ground. Nobody believed him.

Roger himself was flying the plane. Orenda sat in the cockpit with him. After a flawless take off the plane rose above the clouds to settle down at the proper altitude. It was a clear star lit night. White cottony clouds hung way down below. Farina was mesmerized by the quite, dark yet so amazingly beautiful sight. Shahed, sitting by her, was already attempting to take his promised nap. The kids were quick to get out of their seat belts and were back into their usual silliness. In less than ten minutes they successfully messed up the neatly organized compartment. All that running and jumping Shahed could tolerate but the screaming contest broke his patience.

"Can you guys give it a rest? " He yelled. "You`ll make a mummy rise from its grave. "

The kids were quite for thirty seconds before a throw-everything-at-everybody contest started. After several yelling it subsided only to make room for another disturbing idea to pop up in their fertile minds.

Sensing trouble Orenda stepped inside the cabin with her trademark smile. "Hungry, anybody? I am going to be your hostess tonight. "

Most of the kids had no interest in food. Not Stanley

though. He'd eaten his supper before the flight but food wasn't something he could easily pass on, hungry or not. Orenda offered him a low calorie snack, promising a meal later. The rest slipped past her into the cockpit. Roger happily explained some of the basics of flying and answered several questions before sending them back to their seats to rest. Orenda served them some snacks and juice hoping to calm them down. That worked for a little while before they started arguing about some movie characters.

Shahed shrugged in frustration. "Can you guys get some sleep?"

Farina chuckled. "Just use earplugs. They aren't going to stop."

Shahed was seriously looking for something that he could use as earplugs when Orenda walked to him and occupied the seat facing him.

"I doubt if you are going to get any sleep at all. Coffee?"

"Why not?" Shahed tried to lighten up.

Orenda served him a large cup of coffee. For herself she took a cup of green tea. Farina wisely moved to another seat, providing them the opportunity to have an adult conversation.

As they drunk their beverages Orenda opened up a little bit.

"They are quite handful, aren't they? " She joked.

"That's a very moderate way of putting it." Shahed shook his head in frustration. "They can annoy people to death. You guys must be repenting for picking them. As you have already found out, they are exceptionally noisy."

"And very bright!" Orenda added, grinning. "We both love kids. Surprisingly we don't have any of our own!"

"Why not? If you don't mind me asking."

"Honestly, I don't know. I want it, he doesn't.

Perhaps he doesn't want to have children out of wedlock. We never really discussed."

"Why not tie the knots then?"

Orenda looked a little unmindful, just for a few seconds. "Good question. I once took a vow not to wed ever. I am even ready to break it for him. But he doesn't want that." She sipped into her tea unmindfully. "May be he is scared. He is involved into too many things. Risky things. Raising kids could become a responsibility that he is not ready to accept. Not now."

Shahed nodded. "I understand. Raising kids is not an easy job. These little angels can get to your nerve more often than you might think."

"I won't mind that." Orenda smiled. "Only if Roger wanted."

Vancouver – a coastal city and major seaport – is located in British Columbia, a province of Canada. It is bounded by the Strait of Georgia, the Fraser River and the Coast Mountains and was named after a British explorer Captain George Vancouver. Unlike most part of Canada it has an unusually warmer climate with average yearly rainfall about 48 inches. Winter is less severe with temperature rarely going below -10°C. It is about three thousand miles away from Toronto, a six-hour flight.

Half an hour later when Orenda returned to the cockpit Roger took a break. The jet was flying on autopilot yet he preferred to keep a close watch. Orenda was not a licensed pilot but she knew in and out of flying. He taught her over the years.

After hours of anarchy the kids were finally exhausted and retired into their seats. Farina advised them to take a nap but that went unheeded. Some of them played their pocket games while the rest continued chatting. When Roger stepped inside and sat on a chair the situation in the cabin instantly changed. He was quickly surrounded by the kids.

"I have a question." Zaki took the first opportunity to open his mouth.

"Shoot!" Roger was inviting.

"Why aren't the Sygods flying with us?"

"I said it was too risky for us." Preeti replied. "They are dangerous. We shouldn't be too close to them. We are just kids."

"She is right." Ivana said. "But these silly boys won't agree."

"What are they saying?" Roger asked, curiously.

"We think there's more than the eyes meet." Stanley roared.

"Yes, we think you have a plan." Oliver added.

Roger frowned. "Are you boys calling me a schemer?"

The boys looked at each other. This was moving into unfavorable territory.

Roger smiled. "Relax. I am just kidding! The truth is they went to Vancouver ahead of us. That way they'll have more time to detect and eliminate danger. There's no scheming going on here. Sorry to disappoint. Also, if you have noticed, there's no room here for them anyway."

"We were right, kind of." Preeti proudly declared.

"No way!" The boys objected.

"Yes, we were." The two girls held on.

As they got into another bickering Farina broke her silence. "What kind of danger are you expecting?"

"Honestly, none." Roger said. "However, after the attack on your mother I don't want to take any chances. There's nothing to be scared of. Everything is in control."

Shahed, who had been listening to Roger with an anxious look, sighed in relief. "Good to know. I am a teacher not an adventurist. I don't like trouble. But I must admit I am also dying to meet the Sygods. They seem to be a terrific bunch. How did you find them?"

"It wasn't easy." Roger briefly said. "Each one of them has a story to tell."

"Is it even legal?" Shahed asked. "This vigilante operations?"

Roger moved uneasily in his seat. He coughed to clear his throat. "Sometimes legality may not necessarily translate into justice. Police and judges work for the government to put the bad guys to jail. Their job is tough. We as citizens may have to give them a hand in their battle against the evil. That's what the Sygods do. They work as an extra hand, a shadowy hand."

"A shadowy hand!" Shahed repeated. "Interesting! Now I am wondering whether we should even meet them. We won't be in any kind of trouble, right Roger?"

Roger smiled. "Our records are clean. Now," he stood up," I've to go back to the cockpit. Enjoy the rest of the flight." He walked out of the cabin, clearly reluctant to continue on this line of discussion.

Shahed and Farina exchanged glances. Shahed wasn't sure whether he should be worried or relieved. The six kids went back to their seats and started another of their worthless arguments.

Shahed once again tried in vain to take a nap. Farina wasn't sleepy. She looked outside through the window. The dark sky with all its stars and mystery stood there like a ubiquitous background. She closed her eyes, trying to untangle some thoughts. There was something that didn't fully fit into place. She couldn't quite grasp it. Was Roger being completely honest? Was he saying everything he knew? Was it even a good idea to accept his invitation to this tournament? Too many things had happened centering Roger in a very short time. What was cooking?

The plane reached Vancouver around 10 PM. The local time was three hours behind Toronto. Roger landed the plane in Vancouver International Airport - nice and easy. His skill as a pilot was beyond any question. They were quickly led out of the airport by security personnel. A dark shining limousine was waiting for them in front of the terminal. As soon as they all climbed into the car the driver immediately pulled out. He was a tough looking man with a pair of huge sunglasses covering good portion of his upper face.

"The car is bullet proof." Roger said as a matter-of-factly. "The driver is one of the best. So, just relax and enjoy the short trip to the hotel."

"Bullet Pr-o-o-o-f!" The kids jumped off their seats. "Really? Is somebody going to shoot at us? Look out, there comes James Bond 007!" It was an instant hit.

Shahed couldn't hide his anxiousness. "Roger, now you are starting to freak me out. Why a bullet proof car? And the expedited service in the airport. Were you serious when you talked about danger? I don't want to take any risk."

Roger tried to ward off the fear with a big grin. "I am just a security freak. If there really was a risk do you think I'd bring these kids here?"

Shahed looked at Orenda, perhaps to get a second opinion. But Orenda was looking outside. Was she avoiding him? Shahed had no way to know.

The kids, especially the boys, continued in the 007 line and were pretending to have a gun battle inside the car. The screaming and shoveling was beyond acceptable limit,

Farina concluded. She felt as the team lead she needed to step in and discipline the team.

"Guys, stop it! Take your seats, please!" She scolded.

This was a bad idea. While the younger ones dared not to talk back to Farina Stanley and Oliver sometimes did.

"This is not your car!" Stanley promptly replied. "You can't boss around here."

There seemed to be a public consensus on this point, though nobody really voiced anything.

Farina was disappointed but she tried to hide it. She realized sometimes it was necessary to be more diplomatic with them. If she'd to keep this team together she needed their love and respect. She wondered if she'd gotten used to being a little bossy with them. It was her first time as a lead and perhaps she needed to find a right balance between friendship and leadership.

Roger must have felt her embarrassment. He lightly said, "It's okay to be silly sometimes. Relax. As long as they don't start jumping out of this car, I see no issues."

Farina shrugged. She just hoped this silly bunch would act sensibly during the tournament.

Chapter 12

The Mysterious Boy

The limousine stopped in front of the hotel Hiat-Regency. It was a twenty-nine storied building with a very stylish outlook. A group of elegantly dressed young male and female hotel employees were cordially welcoming the guests at the main entrance. As the limousine pulled into the Guest drop area two of them quickly stepped forward to greet them only to be cut short abruptly by a towering black man who appeared from behind and gently shoved them aside.

"We'll take it from here." He coldly announced.

Farina recognized the man. It was Dylan Woodsman, the boxer. Hong brothers were right behind him. From their calm, expressionless faces it was next to impossible to guess that they could be any more dangerous than a pair of harmless lambs. They stood near the rear end of the car, not directly looking at anybody. Dylan stood halfway down the length of the car but didn't attempt to open the car door. His eyes roamed around like a hawk.

Farina thought the driver would climb out and open the door for Roger. Not so. He didn't move from his seat.

Roger opened the door himself and stepped out. "Come on Shahed. Guys." He signaled them to climb out.

Once everybody was out of the car he gathered the kids around him.

"We are going to follow this big man here. His name is Dylan. You remember him, don't you?"

All six heads nodded. Who was going to forget the giant?

"Behave." Dylan growled. "No screaming, no running around. Follow me."

The group was led to the nearby elevator. Hong brothers lazily walked behind them, as if they had no business here. A white male was holding one of the elevator doors wide open. Miller Shovchenko.

"Killer Miller!" Stanley and Oliver excitedly whispered.

Miller showed no emotion in his calm, cold face. He touched his lips with his pointer asking the two to remain tight-lipped. Once everybody walked into the elevator Miller let the door slide close. Dylan and the Hong brothers stayed back. To ease the tense situation Roger smiled at everybody. Shahed didn't find any comfort in that. What was all this hush-hush about? Was it a bad idea to bring these kids here? How was he going to face their parents if anything bad happened to any of them?

The elevator stopped at the eighteenth floor. They stepped out into a wide corridor. An Indian man – Rana Agarwal – was waiting for them.

"You are the planner!" Ivana exclaimed. "I like to plan too!"

"Me too!" Preeti said. "Not the boys though. They are the trouble makers."

"Hey, watch it!" That was a roaring warning from Stanley.

Rana smiled at them but didn't say anything. He silently gestured them to follow him to their rooms.

Six rooms were booked for them. Three on each side

of the corridor, face to face. Farina, Preeti and Ivana decided to stay together. Musa and Zaki insisted to be in one room. Shahed didn't want them to be all by themselves. So he became their third roommate. Stanley and Oliver occupied the third room. Roger and Orenda took the fourth one. There were still two more rooms unoccupied. Everybody assumed they were reserved for the Sygods.

"Should the girls stay alone?" Shahed anxiously said.

Roger understood his concern and looked at Orenda.

"I guess I could stay with them." Orenda knew what was expected from her.

"Why? We are not babies." Preeti was clearly offended.

"We can definitely take care of ourselves." Ivana added.

"We'll be fine." Farina assured. She'd no desire to separate Roger and Orenda. Orenda wanted to be with Roger, she sensed it.

Before anybody else had a chance to say anything a young, slender and noticeably pretty woman in black trousers and full sleeve shirt stepped out of the elevator and boldly walked to them. She was averagely tall and had large soft eyes. It wasn't hard to figure out her Middle Eastern inheritance. She wore an embroidered black scarf on her head covering her hair.

"Johra!" The words vibrated through the crowd.

"Here I am," Johra spoke in perfect English, "at your service guys and girls. I was dying to see you all."

"Remember what I told you." Roger was all smiles.

"You exaggerate." Johra gave him an affectionate frown.

Farina readily knew she (Johra) was the daughter Roger never had.

Johra might have overheard part of the conversation they were having just moments ago. "Don't worry Mr. Shahed." She said confidently. "I am going to stay in the room right next to them."

Shahed gave in. "Looks like they will be in capable hands."

"You bet!" Johra warmly said. "I've heard so much about them, I feel like I already know them."

"You mean the girls?" Ivana wanted to clarify.

"Girls and the boys." Johra grinned. She was definitely aware of the rivalry between the genders.

The boys melted. Since she appeared their eyes were glued on her. She noticed. "Boys, you want to say something?" She asked, giggling.

Stanley and Oliver shyly shook heads. Zaki was the artistic kid in the group. He captured this opportunity to speak out. "You are so pretty Johra!"

Farina gave him a hard pinch. "What do you think you are doing?"

"Just complimenting."

Johra laughed. Musa had moved away from the crowd and was halfway up a nearby supporting pillar. Preeti saw him first. "There he goes again."

Johra rushed to the pillar. "What are you doing?"

"Don't worry about him." Farina said. "He is a human monkey."

"All boys are." Preeti added.

"Watch it!" Warned the boys.

Roger gave them an hour to freshen up. He'd made special arrangements for dinner in the large dining room located on the ground floor. Normally the hotel dining wouldn't be open this late but Roger had his ways with everything.

Shahed wasn't in favor of having a grandiose dinner at midnight. School going kids needed to go to bed early.

Roger read his mind. "A little indiscipline once in a while wouldn't ruin them." He confidently said.

Shahed shrugged. He was a disciplined man and believed it was an important part of growing up. Nevertheless, he decided to let it go this time. Why kill the excitement?

The lobby was pretty busy even at midnight. Contestants from all over the world arrived in random intervals. Roger had invited a few teams to join them for dinner. Served buffet style the food was abundant but Roger had asked his team to eat sensibly. Nobody needed a contestant with upset stomach. After a busy day Musa was very tired. He'd no interest in the food. Soon he put his head on the table and dozed off. Zaki ate little as usual. The girls were health freaks and tried just a little salad. However, Stanley and Oliver seemed to compensate for the lack of appetite for the rest of the team.

Farina ate very little. She could never eat that late in a day. Watching the two feasting got a little sickening after a little while. She took her eyes of them and looked around the dining room. She noticed – though not clearly visible – the Sygods were sticking around. Dylan was standing behind a pillar, while the Hong brothers were sitting on a bench pretending to be reading from the same newspaper. Rana stood quietly in one dark corner of the dining room, frequently checking around. She couldn't readily see Miller or Johra but assumed they were nearby as well. Such security was   unusual, by any comparison.

The tournament organizers had arranged ample policing inside and outside of the facility to ensure safety of the contestants. None of the other teams seemed to have security concern. The seed of doubt that had previously settled in her mind reemerged. Why was Roger acting so cautious?

She tried to shake the thought out of her mind. She was tired and needed a good night's sleep to clear up her mind. But she knew Roger would never allow her to go back to her room all alone. That wouldn't be safe! Realizing that she'd little choice but to wait until everybody finished, she relaxed into her chair and lazily browsed around. There were more than thirty people in the dining area, mostly young participants. They sat close to the center, occupying a handful of tables among several dozens that were spread out in the specious room.

The two persons who sat at a distance at the far corner immediately got her attention. One of them was an old man with long snow-white beard who wore a heavy exotic gown and a large head cover, almost like the turbines that the Sikhs wore. He'd a fancy looking walking stick resting against the table. He sat in such an angle that Farina could barely see any part of his face. His companion, a small person, was completely clad in a long black cloth that twisted around his shoulder and ended over his head in a veil, covering almost all of his face except the stronger looking jaws – the type teenage boys start to develop.

The old man and the boy ate slowly and silently. Farina was about to take her eyes off them when the boy raised his head and looked directly at her. He'd a pair of unusually sharp eyes on a handsome face. Farina felt nervous for a moment. A rush of strange feelings filled her mind momentarily. Did he know that she was observing them? He didn't look happy. Farina wanted to look away but she couldn't. She felt mesmerized. Why did the boy look so familiar? She wondered. Under the veil she saw a pair of thick eyebrows, a big forehead and a small pointed nose.

As their eyes held on each other for a long moment she finally snapped out of it and quickly looked away. Her heart throbbed. This had nothing to do with romance, she knew. It was more like staring at something strange, something that gave an impression of having the potential to turn into trouble.

Fortunately right at that time Roger inquired if everybody had finished eating. Stanley and Oliver weren't but they were cut short to their abysmal disappointment. He asked everybody to head back in their rooms. Farina quietly followed the rest. She felt an irresistible urge to look back, just to have a quick peek of that strange boy, but somehow managed not to.

That night she could hardly sleep and had several weird dreams.

Chapter 13

The Tournament

The tournament venue was an oversized, high ceiling hall room inside the hotel. Next morning all the teams gathered there. Farina took special effort to ensure that they arrived on time. This wasn't an easy task. Especially pulling Stanley off the bed was stressful.

As per tournament regulation every team was allowed to have one adult, for supervision only. Roger urged Shahed to be part of the team. Shahed didn't mind at all. In his youth he used to participate in competitive debates. He didn't really shine but who cared. He joined the team at the center while Roger stepped back and stood in the area designated for spectators. This area was cordoned out by ropes and had plenty of sitting arrangements. A few hundred people had come to watch this unique competition. Journalists and TV cameras were hoarded into one corner. A group of law officers were meticulously checking their identities. Beside the organizers they were the only other people who were allowed to go near the contestants.

Farina was feeling a little restless since morning. As the initial formalities of the tournament progressed she frequently looked around, not exactly knowing what she expected to see. Roger was there in the audience, she noticed, so were the Sygods. Not in plain view but they were around. She could sense them.

There were over two hundred round tables set in neat rows and columns at the center of the hall. Each table was surrounded by eight chairs, one for each member of the team including the adult supervisor. A huge electronic scoreboard hanged from the ceiling flanked to one of the sidewalls. The board was programmed to show score for the top twenty teams.

Farina browsed through other contestants - most were young, in their pre-teens or early teens. Everybody looked happy, excited. She now carefully examined the audiences, quickly, not willing to reveal her weariness to Roger. She detected a few plain cloth security guards among the spectators. Her sharp eyes had no trouble identifying the small bulges under their armpits – concealed guns.

Shahed knew something was bothering her. "What's wrong?" He whispered into her ears.

Farina shrugged. "Probably nothing. Too much security. And I am not just talking about Sygods."

"Could be part of regular security measures." Shahed said.

Farina shrugged again. Could be.

Farina and her team were assigned a table near the center. As she took her seat Farina couldn't help noticing the old man and the boy in black from last night were sitting at a table at the far end, away from her. They had five other kids sitting with them - three boys and two girls. Like the night before, the old man almost shadowed the boy. Farina had that strange unexplainable feelings again. She looked away. She didn't want to give any wrong idea.

It was another hour or so before the test started. All

participating teams were given three sets of question papers on math, analytical and general knowledge on scientific affairs. Exam time three hours. Most mathematical and analytical problems didn't have any specific solutions. Each could be solved in various ways. The judges would reward points based upon the brilliance and novelty of solutions. As the bell rang indicating the start of the test the big hall room went abruptly quiet. After a few moments slowly the quietness was replaced by frantic whispering, as the teams discussed the problems and worked on solutions.

Farina was happy with the teamwork. All those torturous practice sessions were definitely paying off. Instead of quibbling the silly bunch was actually discussing like civilized people. What an improvement! Farina could not help feeling a bit proud. Nobody could deny her role in this conversion.

The mathematical problems were a breeze. While Farina solved majority of them, she'd plenty of help from her companions. However, during the analytical phase things were about to get out of hand. Each problem presented them with several acceptable solutions. The difficulty aroused in rating the solutions. The idea was to take the highest ranked answers.

In several occasions arguments broke down, tempers lost, voices raised beyond permissible level. There were several between Zaki vs. Preeti, a few Ivana vs. Stanley, even one Musa vs. Oliver – that one had nothing to do with analysis. Musa claimed he could climb up one of the fifty feet columns located inside the hall, a claim Oliver laughed at, which obviously agitated Musa. Farina kept her cool and handled them calmly. One thing she'd learned in the process of tutoring these kids – she must not lose her composure.

That was the key to manage them.

Suddenly, a high pitch scream broke the silence of the hall room. It echoed briefly before the next series of screams rippled through. Startled, everybody was silent for a long moment, anxiously looking around to find the source of this chilling shriek. The guards quickly moved in, fully alert, their hands on their weapons. Soon the source of the commotion was identified. Strangely enough it was the mysterious veiled boy.   The elderly man, who sat beside him, held him closely and spoke gently into his ears. That worked. The boy calmed down slowly and within minutes went back to the test. The old man, very embarrassed, waved his hands apologetically.

"Autistic?" Shahed whispered.

"Probably." Farina looked thoughtful. "That voice didn't belong to a boy."

"What do you mean?" Shahed asked.

"She could be a girl." Farina said.

Shahed didn't agree or disagree. He refrained from making any comments. Farina needed to go back to the test.

Farina took another quick glance at the table where the old man and the boy sat. The old man was still holding the boy closely and speaking to him, occasionally patting him on the back. The boy looked absolutely focused, composed. The momentary relapse disappeared, as if it never happened. Farina couldn't help noticing the boy was the only one working on the problems. Rest of the kids just sat there patiently. Did that mean he didn't need any help? That was hard to believe.

The veiled boy finished way ahead of others, by tens of minutes. Farina and her team finished at number four. She was relieved. Only first ten teams would advance to the next level. If they couldn't clear the initial test, it would have been very embarrassing. However, finishing ahead didn't guarantee a birth in the final. The score wasn't due until 10 pm that night. They could only wait and hope for the best.

Roger had arranged a late lunch for them. Interestingly Orenda was absent. When Farina inquired about it Roger briefly mentioned that she'd returned to Toronto in a morning flight. Somebody had to be in the mansion to handle regular organizational activities. She found it a little unusual. Was he trying to protect Orenda from any possible danger? In a way she was the backbone of the Sygods with her inventions and gadgets. Roger's concern was understandable. Though, the question still remained – what kind of trouble was he fearing anyway?

Chapter 14

Danger on the Suspension Bridge

After lunch the kids showed keen interest in visiting the Capilano suspension bridge. Vancouver, a scenic city, has many attractions spread over the city. The Capilano suspension bridge is located in North Vancouver, just a short distance away from the hotel.

Roger agreed to take them to the bridge, to Shahed's dismay. He (Shahed) was truly concern about the safety of the kids but didn't want to jeopardize his popularity by objecting to something that they really wanted to do. If it was fine with Roger it must be safe, he reasoned. The Sygods were coming with them anyway. That definitely increased his confidence. He joined Farina and the team in Roger's limousine. The Sygods climbed into two separate cars and followed the limousine closely.

After the short trip through Stanley Park and over Lions Gate Bridge they reached the comparatively quiet location of the suspension bridge on Capilano road. The first thing that they noticed was the series of totem poles - monumental sculptures carved from trees, usually cedar, by the indigenous people – were erected with distinct artistic signature portraying popular legends, clan lineages or notable events.

They climbed out of the limousine and advanced toward the ticket booth led by Roger. Shahed stayed near the back making sure everybody followed. He was particularly concerned about Musa and to some extent Zaki. They were notorious for wandering away.

The driver of the limousine remained back in the car. This was necessary for quick gateway. Rana and Miller, who were driving the other cars stayed back, while rest of the Sygods followed Farina and the kids, keeping a fare distance, trying not to make the connection too obvious. The kids were instructed earlier not to recognize them in public. Roger did not want to compromise security, he'd made it clear.

The totem poles were an instant winner. Shahed lined up the kids at the foot of the totem poles and took a few snapshots. Roger purchased the tickets and called them to the entrance. He looked alert, watchful.

The suspension bridge – located in the serenity of the West coast rainforest, is Vancouver's oldest tourist attraction. Originally built in 1889, it stretches 450 feet across and 230 feet above Capilano River.

The sight of the spectacular suspension bridge hanging between two ridges with lush temperate rainforest surrounding it was simply mesmerizing. For some it perhaps a little scary as well. Zaki – owing to his acrophobia (fear of height) turned pale and flanked to Farina. Shahed didn't do any better, despite his desperate attempt to put up a brave face.

"This is really high!" He nervously laughed. "Looks like fun though."

Musa wasted no time. He was halfway down the

bridge in a blink.

"Come on guys," he called out, "come quick. We'll go to the Treetops Adventure. Zaki! What are you doing there?"

"Keep going," Zaki struggled to keep his voice steady. "I'll catch up with you in no time."

"Wait for us." Shahed shouted. "Don't go all by yourself."

Musa hesitated for a moment, finally decided to wait for the rest of the team. After all, going alone wasn't much fun.

Stanley and Oliver had little difficulty on the bridge. They seemed to adjust to the mild swing of the bridge easily as they walked on it. After going about halfway down Stanley stopped, put his hands around his mouth and tried a Tarzan call, which sounded nothing more than a distorted howl.

Preeti and Ivana were cautiously walking behind Roger, who moved slowly allowing the two girls to catch up with him.

"Stop it!" Preeti yelled out at Stanley. "You are going to start a rock slide or something."

"Yeah!" Ivana giggled. "It sounded like elephant hiccups!"

Stanley tried a second time, just to badger the girls.

Farina, holding Zaki close to her body, took a few small steps into the bridge. The minor swing was more than enough to freak Zaki up.

"I don't want to go any further." He declared. "I'll just stand here."

"You are only two feet from the ground!" Farina chuckled. "Just hang on to me. You'll be fine."

"Zaki, did you bring extra pants?" Ivana teased.

"My turn will come." Zaki warned.

"This is not too bad." Shahed muttered. "I am coming

with you, Zaki. Don't worry."

"You are more scared than I am." Zaki smiled faintly.

Minutes later, holding each other's hands, the three had managed only ten more steps. Farina labored to fight back the irresistible laughter that simmered inside her. Zaki was a sensitive boy. He wouldn't appreciate being laughed at, especially not by Farina.

"Are you guys okay?" Roger asked. He was approaching middle of the bridge, where Stanley and Oliver joined Musa. Ivana and Preeti fell a little behind but advanced steadily holding the hand rails.

Stopping for a break, Farina looked around and was completely taken by the sheer beauty of the place. The towering Douglas fir trees, the dense vegetation and the flora and fauna unique to this part of the world, the ribbon like river hundreds of feet below – cumulatively they created an amazing visual experience.

Zaki had his eyes practically closed. Any glimpse down could be devastating for him. Shahed stole occasional glimpses, but was still a nervous wreck.

"Take it easy guys; you are not going to fall." She tried to lighten things up with a chuckle.

"Don't laugh. This is not a joke." Zaki objected readily.

"Do you want me to give you a hand?" Roger asked.

"No, no, we are just fine." Shahed nervously said.

Roger moved forward with rest of the team. Looking back Farina noticed the Hong brothers, Dylan and Johra were still following them keeping a safe distance. There was a good crowd on the bridge, mostly giggling tourists who were determined to make it to the other side, screaming every time the bridge shook under their feet. It was a gorgeous day with no trouble on sight, Farina thought. She wondered if there was any need for the Sygods to follow them like zombies.

Just seconds later, Farina had just taken another step forward when something unexpected started to happen. First she heard a few running steps, quickly approaching the bridge from the other end, then she saw the two gigantic men emerging from the bushes and hopping onto the suspension bridge, forcing it into a frightening swing.

As they continued to rush forward another three men galloped into view and raced toward them, sending the bridge into another frantic vibration.

Roger had just enough time to envelop the kids with his two extended arms and dive on the floor, making sure they didn't get thrown out of the bridge. There was at least couple of dozen visitors on the bridge. This sudden commotion caught them all in surprise. Seconds later, the surprise turned into pure panic. Shouting and screaming they moved out of the way of the rushing giants, holding onto anything that looked strong enough.

Farina, holding Zaki tightly with one hand quickly grabbed the nearest railing, pressing hard on her legs to maintain balance. Shahed, caught unprepared, fell on his back but was able to quickly stabilize himself. As he wobbled into a standing position he realized what was happening.

Unsuspecting, Farina yelled at him, "Grab the side rail, Uncle!"

Shahed wasn't listening to her. He was looking at the two darting giants, who were quite obviously heading toward Farina!

"Watch out, Farina!" He screamed.

Baffled, Farina followed his direction of sight and immediately knew what was about to happen. She was under attack. She panicked.

"Uncle!" She screamed at the top of her voice sending echoes that rippled through the forest.

The Sygods made no mistake assessing the situation. Hong Lee and Hong Shien moved with lightening speed toward Farina. Right behind were Dylan and Johra.

Her heart pounding wildly, Farina tried to think. The Sygods weren't close enough to intercept the attackers before they reached her. All it needed a minor shoving, and she'd be thrown out of the bridge along with Zaki, all the way down to the rocky river bed more than two hundred feet below.

Shahed, in a desperate attempt to put up any kind of obstruction, quickly placed himself in front of Farina and Zaki, his fear suddenly gone. But with his slight built he looked literally transparent to the approaching human gorillas.

Farina, not knowing what else to do, knelt down on the bridge, embracing Zaki with her right hand so hard that he cried out in pain. With her left hand she unsuccessfully tried to pull Shahed down. One of the attackers shoved Shahed out of their way onto the bridge floor in one quick sweep of his hand. Their pursuers, just few steps away, came charging. One of them, a grim looking heavy set man, suddenly jumped like a leopard in the air. With a thunderous cry he attacked the two men ahead of him. His strong blows threw the two men off balance and forced them to hug the floor.

However, they quickly stood up only to face sharp kicks from the Hong brothers. But even that wasn't enough to stop them. Somehow they broke free of the defenders and rushed toward the exit. The Sygods and the three pursuers went right after them. Unfortunately, the chase ended abruptly as the attackers climbed into a waiting van that zoomed away. A second car picked up the three pursuers and rocketed in the same direction.

Sygods quickly returned. Roger had brought the kids safely back to the ground. "Where did they go?" He asked.

"They had cars waiting." Dylan quickly said. "Two different cars."

Roger looked thoughtful.

"We need to go back to the hotel." Shahed almost demanded, still trembling from the frightening experience. "Who were they? Why would they attack us?"

The questions were aimed at Roger.

"Don't know." Roger dryly said. "I doubt it was aimed at us. Must be gang related."

"They attacked me!" Farina couldn't stress any harder, surprised with Roger's remark.

"It looked like that, I admit." Roger soothingly said.

"We see them before." Spoke Hong Shien, in broken English.

"We see them in hospital." Added Hong Lee.

With this new information the atmosphere quickly turned grave. It was now evident that somebody was trying to harm Farina and her mother. They raced back to the cars and were on their way back to the hotel in seconds. While the kids had a blast discussing the chase and the fight sequence, Farina, Shahed, and Roger were quiet. Roger hid his face behind a Times magazine but he couldn't conceal his embarrassment and anxiety.

Around 10 PM that night scores for the first phase of the tournament was published. Roger personally went to check the result. Farina and the kids were instructed to stay in their rooms and not to make any contact with anybody without asking the Sygods, who were guarding the corridor.

He brought back good news. Farina and her team came second, beaten squarely by a team led by a girl named Aretha. Instantly Farina knew Aretha had to be the veiled girl who she took for a boy. She just knew.

Final phase of the competition was scheduled for the following day. Top ten teams would compete for the championship. The format of the test was to remain same though understandably the bars would be raised. It was an eventful day and everybody was tired. Roger had ordered room   service for supper and sent the kids to bed before midnight. Farina, shaken and drained after the frightening incident on the suspension bridge, decided to hit the sack early as well, hoping to put it all behind with a good night's sleep.

It wasn't before another long hour when she could finally rest her mind and fall asleep.

Chapter 15

The Kidnapping

Farina woke up amid a big chaos. Confused, she looked into the darkness for a few moments, trying to understand what was going on. She could hear the loud sirens of several fire trucks going nuts, almost burying a series of chilling screams.

Springing out of her bed she rushed to get Ivana and Preeti sleeping in the other bed across the room. The girls were already up.

"What's going on?" Terrified, they screamed at the top of their voices.

Farina didn't answer. The wailing sirens of the fire trucks got louder and louder. Was the hotel on fire? She tried to stay calm.

"Get up," she shouted at the young girls. "We got to get out of this room."

"Where are Uncle Shahed and Roger?" Ivana sharply asked.

Farina didn't know. She didn't try to answer. Holding the girls she rushed toward the door. She smelled no smoke. This was good news, she thought. May be fire didn't spread that far yet.

Suddenly, the deafening fire alarms in the hotel went berserk, startling the three to death. This wasn't right. Did anybody ever check those devices? Farina wondered.

Standing next to the door she was about to yank it open when the wide glass panels located on the outside wall shattered into pieces and a dark, sturdy figure jumped inside through the opening. The figure swiftly reached for Farina and hit her on the shoulder with a quick but delicate move of his hand. Darkness immediately swallowed her. Before the bewildered eyes of Ivana and Preeti the intruder effortlessly picked Farina up on his broad shoulder and slipped out through the broken window.

Seconds later Dylan kicked the door open and rushed in, followed by Johra.

"Where's Farina?" Dylan asked.

The two girls could only manage to point at the window. Johra turned on the lights, hurried to the window, and briskly examined outside. "Came down the roof, on a rope."

"The Magician got her." Dylan snorted.

"We'll get her back." Johra calmly said. "First, we need to get out. The fire may spread."

She grabbed the girls and burst out of the room. Dylan shadowed them as they ran toward the stairs at the end of the corridor where they stumbled upon rest of the group.

"Where is Farina?" Shahed asked anxiously.

"We must start right now." Johra spoke to Roger.

Roger remained silent but his pace increased almost to a running speed as they headed toward the stairs.

"Where is Farina?" Shahed impatiently demanded.

"She has been kidnapped." Dylan muttered, quickly walking past him.

Shahed couldn't believe his own ears. "What? Why? How? Oh, God!"

"Don't worry." Johra tried to comfort him. "She'll be

back unhurt. You have my word."

Shahed almost collapsed on the ground. His legs felt weak, lethargic. Why would anybody kidnap Farina? His whole body started to tremble in fear and anticipation of something very bad. Rana came from behind and held him strongly.

"Are you okay?" He asked.

Shahed nodded. He knew he'd to move on. The kids needed him. Still shaking, he followed the rest of the team down the stairs as the fire alarms continued to wail.

After rushing down eighteen floors along with hundreds of other hotel guests when they finally stepped out to the street the miraculous view that greeted them was not anything any of them had ever seen. The multistoried hotel was completely engulfed by deep red flames of fire with no smoke, no heat, no smell.

"Why it's not hot, dad?" Zaki asked.

Shahed was puzzled. They were standing only fifty feet away from the fire but felt no heat. He looked at Roger expecting an answer. Roger was on his cell phone, quickly giving instructions. Moments later he hung up.

"Magician's trick." He gravely said.

"Magician!" The kids exclaimed in unison.

"A magician kidnapped Farina? Why?" Shahed was shocked.

"He is not just any magician," Roger grimly explained, "He is known as The Magician. Not a real magician. It is his hobby. He is a rogue scientist called Dragon Valcovich."

"The Magician! I heard of him." Shahed looked bewildered. "Why in the whole world he'd have any interest in Farina?"

"We'll find out." Roger briefly said. "But he is well

known for his insanity."

"We are not afraid of him." Stanley roared with his usual vigor. "We'll bring back Farina from his evil web."

Oliver punched in the air. "Absolutely. We'll show him who got the guts."

"I am coming with you." Musa eagerly said.

"Why are you boys so thick?" Preeti quipped. "Do any of you have any idea who this magician is and where he took Farina?"

The boys looked at each other, blankly.

"We'll find out. We are the SciAngels." Stanley declared, confidently.

"Yeah! SciAngels! You can't even see your toe." Ivana muttered.

"Hey, I am not fat." Stanley objected. "Am I, Oliver?"

"Of course not. You are healthy." Oliver stood by his friend.

The girls flapped their hands in the air, dismissing the two.

"Do we know where he took her?" Shahed anxiously asked Roger.

"We'll find her." He said confidently.

"Why Farina? I just don't get it." Shahed threw his arms in the air in total frustration.

Roger cleared his voice. "He is known for his interest in intelligent kids. I believe he is building an army of smartest brains to become world's most powerful scientist."

Shahed shook his head in shear disbelief. "How come you never mentioned this to me before? I heard he was just a thug, sold weapons and drugs. I'd no clue about any of this!"

Roger shrugged helplessly. "I took all precautions!"

"Apparently it wasn't good enough." Shahed bitterly

said. "What happens now?"

"We'll bring her back. We already know her approximate location. Now it's just a matter of getting her out."

"You know where she is?" The kids growled.

Roger raised a hand to calm them down. "I can't tell you that – for her safety – of course. But we won't rest until she is back. In the mean time, Johra will take care of you."

A caravan of fire trucks had just stopped in front of the hotel. Baffled, the firefighters examined the strange reddish cool flames. Soon they found out water had almost no effect on it. Realizing that the flames were harmless they decided to keep a watchful eye on it as they explored their options.

Next arrived dozens of police cars with their sirens tearing through the air. Stunned, the officers tried to cordon off the building but not before some curious observers had time to walk up to the fire and try to touch it. Surprisingly, the flames danced around their hands without burning a single hair. The large crowd, awestruck, hummed in sheer joy of watching such amazing, unbelievable display. This must have motivated Stanley, Oliver and Musa because they suddenly took off, running through the police cordon, to the flames.

They had barely touched it when one of the patrolling police officers chased them away.

"These boys have no sense whatsoever." Preeti blasted.

"Tell me about it." Ivana sneered.

A dark limousine quietly cruised to the front of the hotel, stopped near the crowd. Roger's phone rang. He picked it up, mumbled something. "I got to go." He told Shahed and headed toward the waiting limousine.

Shahed followed him. "I must come with you." He insisted. "I am like a father to her. It's my duty."

"I understand." Roger softly said. "But you will only hinder our mission. The kids need you here. They are handful. Johra will need help. I am counting on you."

"What do you want us to do?"

"When the fire stops go back to the hotel, stay in your rooms and wait to hear from me. I'll call. Promise."

He quickly slipped inside the car. Shahed could not see him through the tinted windows. The car silently took off.

Shahed felt helpless. Roger was right. He'd be no help to them. Dejected, he walked back where Johra stood with the kids, all quiet, peaceful.

"They are kind to you." Shahed couldn't help pointing it out.

"They are good kids, in their own way." Johra managed a dry smile.

Shahed shook his head unmindfully. Johra saw the agony he was going though.

"You can trust Rogers." She calmly said. "He'd never let anything happen to Farina."

Shahed shrugged silently. His mind wasn't working anymore. The flames had started to fade away, slowly but steadily. The hotel authority requested people to go back to their rooms. They had done necessary inspection and found everything was functioning and the hotel was fully safe. Johra rounded the kids up and headed for the hotel lobby, closely followed by dispirited Shahed.

The Kidnapping

Chapter 16

Sygods to the Rescue

The two cars zoomed through the dark and empty Highway One at the early hours of the morning. Miller was driving the first car – a black Mercedes carrying Hong brothers and Dylan. He drove fast, as usual, well over the posted speed limit.

The black limousine that followed closely was Roger's. Rana was riding with him.

"Sir?" The driver spoke through the intercom.

"Yes, Roland?"

"We are moving too fast."

"Slow down. I'll call Miller."

Roland immediately slowed down, quickly falling behind.

Roger called the car ahead. "Careful, Miller." He urged. "We don't need highway patrol on our tail."

Miller did not talk. He'd a natural distaste for authority and did not like to be instructed. However, he responded well to reasoning. Not readily but eventually he slowed down to a safer speed, twenty – thirty kilometers above the posted speed limit. Roger often worried about him. He was a bomb waiting to blast.

Roger looked at Rana who was attentively monitoring a GPS device. "How far are they?"

"At least one hour." Rana replied. "I think Dragan is taking Farina somewhere deep in the Coast Mountains. Luckily, he hasn't suspected anything about the transmitter yet."

"The transmitter is in Farina's stomach. Unless he performs intensive tests he'd never find it."

"How long will it stay there?"

"2-3 days. It is supposed to stick to the stomach muscle loosely. If she uses the bathroom too often it might lose its grip quicker due to all the muscle contraction."

Rana looked thoughtful. "Even if we find him do you think we could catch him?"

Roger shrugged. "I hope so, unless something goes miserably wrong. I've done extensive homework on him. He doesn't believe in big team. He keeps the company of only a few but very trustworthy assistants. His power is science. If we can somehow go past his scientific illusions we can definitely catch him."

"Which, I reckon, not going to be easy." Rana added.

Roger's mind raced into the past, many bitter memories flashed through. Dragan had been a consistent source of sufferings and humiliation for him. Once he'd cornered the illusive man in a house in Florida but surprisingly he disappeared without a trace. So many years have passed after that but Roger still had no clues on how he did it. He looked through every inch of that house. There was no hidden   escape route. That was very embarrassing. A living human being couldn't just disappear. He'd to have a means to physically get away.

Anyway, shortly after that miraculous escape big changes happened in Roger's life. He retired from army and dedicated himself in building Sygods. His primary goal was to catch or stop extremely dangerous men like Dragan, who the conventional legal system couldn't touch.

Roger sighed. Apparently he was not very successful either. The mad scientist was still out, doing his sick things. He was always one step ahead of Roger. Sometimes Roger felt the man was playing with him. Dragan – he'd come to accept – was after all a man with a great sense of humor.

The phone rang. "How far are they?" Dylan inquired.

"Another hour, at least." Roger said.

"I guess we'll have to camp in the mountains tonight." Dylan said.

Roger looked at his watch. It was two in the morning. "We have a few more hours of darkness. We'll have to move forward."

"Yes." That was Hong Lee.

"Yes, Yes." Hong Shien echoed.

"I don't see very well at night." Dylan muttered in dismay. "Especially in the mountains."

That drew laughter from both Roger and Rana. Dylan had no problem with his sight. He was just scared of darkness. For a mountain of a man who was brave and strong this was a hilarious flaw.

Dylan disconnected.

"He is mad." Rana smilingly said.

"As always." Roger looked distracted. A series of wrinkles popped up on his forehead, a sign of concern.

"You worried?" Rana asked, casually.

Roger groaned. "I am. We might have taken too much risk."

"We are in full control, aren't we?"

"I hope so. But you can never be sure, not when you are dealing with multiple adversaries."

"Dragan is one. Who else?"

"Do you remember General Derek Bowman?" Roger said, distastefully. "He is also looking for Dragan."

"For what?"

"He made some kind of agreement with Dragan. Gave him tons of government money. I tried to stop that. Never believed in anything Dragan said. Soon I got moved to another project. Bowman is a capable man. That's when I retired from U.S. Army and moved to Canada. Anyway, Dragan took the money and disappeared."

"How?" Rana was genuinely surprised. "Bowman must have had something to bind him to his commitment, didn't he?"

Roger chuckled. "He wished. Dragan played him like a puppet."

Rana pondered for a moment. "Does the general spy on you?"

"He sure does. I got many proof of that."

"Does he know you are in Vancouver?"

"I'll be surprised if he didn't." He turned the intercom on. "Ronald, keep an eye on the road."

"We are clean, Sir." Roland spoke in a deep, professional voice.

"You are the best."

"Thank you, Sir."

Roger nodded in appreciation. He'd great confidence in Roland, an ex-army - special force. After losing a leg in an assignment in Iraq he was put to desk jobs. Roger knew him from before and trusted him. He offered Roland a job as his close assistant cum chauffeur. Roland accepted it. Since then he'd been with Roger.

Chapter 17

In the Rough Terrain

Farina woke up with a light headache. She found herself in a specious room, lying on a queen size bed. There was no visible light source inside the room but yet the room was illuminated in soft blue light. Still lying on her back, she tried to assess her situation. She remembered going to bed in the hotel room along with Preeti and Ivana. There was some kind of huge commotion in the middle of the night, she was about to step out of the room holding the two girls when something happened and she blacked out. She couldn't remember how and when she ended up in that strange room. Was it a dream? She pinched herself. It hurt.

She carefully climbed down the bed, walked to a wall and tapped on it. It felt like stone. She looked around for a door. To her surprise, the room had no doors or windows. How was that possible? There had to be an entry to the room. There was more to it then the eyes met – she knew immediately. One name bubbled up in her subconscious mind. The Magician! She didn't know why but it just stuck in her head. Nothing made sense to her. Why would anybody kidnap her? She neither had money to pay ransom nor was she important in any way aside from being a chess grandmaster.

Farina checked time on her watch. Half past three in

the morning. This meant she wasn't brought there too long ago. They went to bed around midnight. The fire alarms must have gone off between 12 to 1 AM. If the kidnappers drove after capturing her then she couldn't be more than couple of hundred kilometers away from Vancouver. Of course, she could also be in a house right next to the hotel. There was no way to know.

Scared and restless she paced around the room for a little while. She knew she'd to get hold of herself. Panicking wasn't going to help. She'd to stay calm and focused.

"Stay calm. Stay cool." She spoke softly to herself. "It's going to be okay."

This worked, slowly but surely. She knew there was not much she could do except waiting. The best way to use this time was to observe, explore and analyze. Whoever brought her here had something in mind. She was still alive and free to roam. So they didn't intend to kill her, at least not yet. At some point they would make their move, whatever it was. Just like chess she must now wait until her captors made a move. She'd to be strong. She'd to be brave.

"I can handle this." She whispered to herself. "I've to handle this until they come to rescue me."

She really wanted to believe that Roger and the Sygods were rushing to rescue her. Would they even know where she was? How? She sighed deeply. The possibility of a quick rescue looked bleak, she'd to admit.

Suddenly something got her attention – a buzzing sound, faint but clearly audible. She looked around expecting to see a bug, saw nothing. The buzz quickly traveled close to her, stopped.

"Farina?" Someone spoke right into her ears. Pleasant, human like voice.

"Who is it?" Farina was clearly startled.

"I am Flyball." The voice spoke again. "Horrible name but there's not much I can do about it. My Boss – the Magician - likes it. How distasteful! I am a machine, not a ball."

So, her hunch was right. It was the Magician who brought her here. Not that it was any more comforting. "Flyball!" Farina called out. "Where are you?"

"I am right behind your ear." The faint voice said. "You must have already figured out I am a tiny machine. Turn your head to your right and I'll blink like a cricket."

Farina did as asked and saw the bright blink very close to her head. "You are small! How is your intelligence?"

"Well, I've a small brain, naturally. Not much room. But don't just count me off yet. I can still hold you ten-fifteen moves in a game of chess."

"How do you know I play chess?" Farina was genuinely surprised.

"What are you talking about? Even the walls here know that. Literally. But no more talk. Sleep now. You need rest. Who knows what happens in the morning. The Princess is very unpredictable."

"Who is the Princess?"

"Boss's daughter. Who else? Such a tormentor! But don't be alarmed. I'll be with you. Big guy's order. If you need me just call. Oh! Try to keep your voice down. The Princess has millions of ears." Flyball lowered its voice further to a whispering level. "I can't tolerate the girl. Super evil. She treats machines like us worse than bedbugs."

Farina had no clue what the strange machine was talking about. "Why?"

"We are old technology. Now there are so many sophisticated intelligent machines. She thinks we are last century. If she can catch us we are mashed potato."

"How many of you are out there?"

"A few thousands. We are still kicking just because of the big guy. Not only had he made us, he actually believes in us. We are small but effective. Wise guy. Okay, too much talk. Sleep now. My order is to put you to sleep. I am good at lullaby songs. I can sing them in one hundred twenty languages. I'll sing the 'Rock a bye baby' for you."

"Save me the torture." Farina surrendered. "I'll go back to bed. Don't know if I'll be able to sleep."

She lied down on the bed. There was no use walking around anyway. Moments later she'd an itchy feeling behind her right ear. She raised her left hand to scratch the spot but stopped midway as she sunk in deep sleep.

"Sweet dreams!" Whispered Flyball.

The Sygods drove on an unpaved road for almost fifteen minutes before reaching at the foot of a big mountain. This was part of Coast Mountain. The region consisted of miles after miles of rugged, difficult and treacherous mountainous landscape with peaks as high as ten thousand feet.

After the limousine came to a total halt Rana stepped out of it. He was holding a GPS receiver in his hand. Hong brothers, Miller and Dylan climbed out of their car and joined him. They all bent over the well-lit screen of the receiver.

"What do we have here?" Dylan inquired.

"We are about few kilometers away from her." Rana said. "However, it's difficult to determine her exact location considering the nature of the landscape."

"How are we going to find her then?" Miller asked.

"As we close on, the signal would get stronger." Rana tried to sound optimistic.

"We have to move forward." Roger said.

"Why would Dragan take her in the mountains?" Dylan looked annoyed.

"Puzzles me." Miller shook his head.

Roger shrugged. "He might have built a kingdom in there. I won't be surprised."

The Hong brothers looked restless. "We go mountain." Hong Lee impatiently said.

"We waste time." Hong Shien added grimly.

"Hold your horses, boys." Dylan said. "We got to think before we do something, not after."
Furrowed brows, the brothers gave him a cold look. "You scared."

"No! I am not scared."

"You no like dark."

Dylan shrugged. It was useless arguing with the brothers. They never relaxed. Always on the edge. He, on the other hand, could handle a few humors even at the worst of the times.

"The faster we reach there the better." Miller said. "They won't be expecting us this quick."

Roger agreed. "That's right. But we have to be fully prepared. We don't know what to expect."

They quickly grabbed their small backpacks with essential kits and were on their way up the slope in a single file in less than five minutes. As always the Hong brothers were at the front, leading the party. They both were legendary climbers. Fable went they could climb up a vertical mountain in bare hands. Miller, carrying a rifle on his shoulder, stayed next to the brothers. He'd two other guns tucked under his garments. Dylan, Rana and Roger stayed at the end of the line in that order.

It was a clear but dark night with only the stars

blinking above their heads. They had to put on their night goggles with infrared capability. They walked as fast as they could under the circumstances. It would be dawn by five in the morning. They wanted to make as much ground as possible before the daylight broke.

The plan was to follow the signal from the GPS device and hope that it would take them close to Farina. If Dragan took her somewhere in these mountains then, presumably, he must have had some kind of establishment, whether it was a hidden kingdom or a few log cabins. Once they knew what they were up to then they would plan for a rescue mission. If necessary they would wait for the next nightfall to take any kind of actions. First thing was to find them.

After climbing up for about half an hour they walked through a patch of flat land and started to descent. A few hundred yards of climbing down was followed by another ascent.

The youths had no issue with the up and down maneuvers but Roger started to feel the pressure. At younger age he could run for hours on mountain trails. With age some of that toughness was gone. Watching the team navigating through the rugged terrain with such confidence gave him immense satisfaction. Building a strong and disciplined team was never easy. He'd to go through many hoops to get these talented youths teamed up.

"How are we doing?" He whispered to Rana.

"Can't say yet. I'll have a better idea once we cover a little more distance." Rana's eyes were fixed on the device.

The Hong brothers stopped abruptly, forcing rest of the team to huddle on each other. They signaled everybody to be quiet. Bent near the ground they cautiously examined the surroundings. It was clear they had either heard or seen something suspicious. Nobody dared question their senses.

The mountains were quiet with a gentle breeze blowing through the leaves. Nothing unusual. The brothers exchanged quick glances and shook their heads in agreement. When they moved again they looked much more careful. Silently and slowly the team followed them around a mammoth boulder to a flat patch of land covered with tall grass and sparsely populated trees.

Chapter 18

Sygods and The Shaolin Monks

Just past the plains the land took a sharp dive into a huge valley thousands of feet below. The valley – more than a mile wide in each direction - was surrounded by a series of tall peaks almost secluding it from the rest of the mountain range. At the center of this pack stood a summit, narrow and vertical, rising above the rest so high that its tip shrouded in mist. On this tip stood a enormous medieval castle, an extravagant blend of Byzantine style domes, gothic style pointed arches intermingled with Renaissance style symmetry,   offered a magical and commanding glimpse, boldly declaring its power and supremacy over the mountains, the valley and the forests that lay below.

Speechless and astounded the visitors stood with bulging eyes, gawking at the amazing structure that hung right before their eyes.

"Is that some kind of trick?" Miller gasped.

"You mean something like a mirage?" Rana said.

Dylan sighed in disbelief. "Holly crap! How did he do that?"

"He is not called the Magician for nothing." Roger calmly said.

The Hong brothers had little patience for the magical puzzle. They were far more motivated at stepping inside it and snatching Farina out. With a quick gesture of hand Hong Lee signaled the rest to follow.

Still overly cautious he and Hong Shien advanced in short, quick strides through the waist high blades of grass. The edge of the plain was only a few hundred feet away leading to a long and steep slope racing to the valley at least half a mile below.

The team stayed close, often meandering through densely grown patch of vegetation and large boulders, watchful, alert.

Suddenly a gust of air carried a thick fog that shrouded them completely. Blinded and tensed the team stood calmly and quietly, anticipating something strange to follow.

To their relief, the fog started to move down the plain shortly. As their vision cleared up, they found themselves standing before a group of fearsome Chinese warriors, just yards away! Wearing loose traditional dark black Karate outfits and unusually long snow white beards the warriors stood with expressionless faces and piercing eyes that could intimidate the bravest of the opposition.

"Take me God!" Dylan exclaimed. "Where did they come from? Is there any Buddhist monastery here? "

Hong Lee raised his hand, urging quietness.

"Shaolin monks?" Confused, he whispered to his brother.

"Shaolin monks!" Hong Shien whispered back.

Miller raised his rifle fearing aggression but Roger quickly walked to him and lowered the barrel.

"We don't want Dragan to get an advance warning." He said calmly. "A shot fired here can be heard from tens of kilometers away."

"They are definitely his men. He must already know

that we are coming." Miller said.

"May be. We don't know that yet. Let's give the brothers a chance." Roger said.

"Make sense to me." Rana supported.

Miller didn't argue. Primarily because the Hongs had just taken a few steps forward to face the worrier monks, thirteen of them, standing close to each other in a half circle. As the two parties carefully eyed each other Roger gestured the rest of the team to step back.

"Can the brothers beat them all?" Dylan was apprehensive. He knew how ferocious fighters the Shaolin monks could be.

"If not..." Miller shook his loaded rifle.

"I am not sure you'll have time to reload that thing." Dylan said.

The Hong brothers did something strange. They bowed gently.

"Respected Shaolin monks, no fighting. We go." Hong Lee gently said.

The monks studied them with dispassionate eyes. A short silence was followed by events that shuttered the serenity of the plains into pieces.

With chilling battle cries the elderly kung fu masters sprung up and attacked the two brothers. The Hongs quickly flipped in the air like expert gymnasts and moved away from the line of attack. The monks divided into two groups and surrounded the Hongs from two opposite directions.

Dylan, thinking the brothers were in trouble, was about to step in when Roger lightly patted on his shoulder.

"Not yet." He said.

"Are you sure?"

Roger shook his head. He'd seen the two defeating formidable opponents.

The rivals walked in circles a few times, measuring each other's strength. Then, in a blink, all hell broke down.

It looked as if the Hongs just exploded into these incredibly swift fighting machines. Their bodies twisted and flipped in the air like tornadoes; their fists, elbows, and the feet smashed everything that came into contact. The monks tried in vain to move out of the deadly counter attacks. Scattered and confused they soon became easy victims as the brothers picked them up individually and clearly overpowered them in quickness, technique and strength. After the initial disarray, some monks regrouped and attacked with similar tenacity that the brothers had just displayed.

Hong Lee, subjected to a deadly flying kick, spectacularly spun in the air, dodged the kick, twisted his body up and hammered the attacker with a swift round kick. The monk dropped on the ground like a sack of sand.

Just yards away, Hong Shien desperately looked for a way to stop two stubborn fighters. As he stepped back to recoup the two monks came rushing at him, throwing deadly blows at lightning speed. Hong Shien turned around, ran briskly toward a tree, took two long strides across the length of the trunk, gained enough momentum to leap backward, sprung over the head of the two rushing men, and fell heavily on their back with his full weight. Their backbones broken, the two assailants became motionless under his muscular body.

The battle stopped as abruptly as it had started, which felt like just seconds ago. Only a handful of the monks still stood on their feet.

"Dangerous Dragon! Ferocious Tiger!" One monk hissed in pure trepidation. "You are better than what we thought. Much better."

The Hong brothers, ready and alert, kept careful eyes on the enemy. They knew that the worst attack could come when the battle was almost won. But the monks had enough. As they quickly collected their injured members another heavy screen of fog appeared from nowhere — blinding the Sygods. Seconds later, when the fog cleared up, there was no sign of any warriors. They had just disappeared in thin air!

"What the hell!" Dylan couldn't believe his eyes. "Where did they go? They were just here two seconds ago."

"Some kind of magic, I guess." Miller bitterly said.

"Dangerous Dragon! Ferocious Tiger!" Rana muttered. "How did they know?"

"How else?" Miller quipped. "They are Dragan's men. He knows we are coming. I told you."

Nobody replied. They truly hoped Dragan didn't.

The Hong brothers wasted no time talking; they were already marching to the edge of the plains, ready to descent down to the valley. The rest continued behind them.

The descent was steep but negotiable. They again formed a single file and carefully walked down the rocky surface. Roger labored to move on the tough, slippery surface but he was determined to tag along with the team. Clearly, age was catching up with him. He stopped frequently to catch his breath. Rana must have sensed his fatigue. He stayed close to him.

"Do you think Dragan really know we are coming?" He asked, thoughtfully.

Roger shrugged. "With him nothing is impossible. You can plan as much as you want, but he can figure it all out in seconds. The devil has a genius mind, got to admit."

"Great!" Dylan said sarcastically. "Instead of creeping in now we'll have to be kicking in. There goes the surprise!"

"I got enough bullets." Miller defiantly said.

"Man, can't you think beyond the guns?" Dylan sighed.

"We can't just shoot our way in." Rana said. "Farina is with him. Don't forget."

"That's right." Miller said. "We'll shoot our way out then."

Dylan laughed. "My man got sense of humor!"

The Hongs weren't in a mode to loosen up. Descending silently through boulders and bushes they frequently checked around for possible booby traps, often stopping to examine fallen tree branches or small openings on the ground.

As they approached the valley dense pine forests greeted them with lush greenness. Just past the forest a sprawling field extended for kilometers, merging into a rushing body of water originated from a waterfall that stood hundreds of feet high. Standing at the foot of the forest they could hear the running water humming away into the cluster of mountains.

Chapter 19

The Fearsome Ninjas

Half an hour later, when they finally made it across the pine forest and reached the core of the valley, it seemed right to take a break and let the sweat dry up. Climbing down a mountain was not particularly an easy task.

Roger needed the rest. How fast time had passed, he wondered. Wasn't it just that day when he could carry a man on his shoulder without flinching! The dawn was still hours away but the starlit clear sky had diluted the usual darkness of the night. A steady cool breeze flew across - comforting, soothing.

Sitting under a tall pine tree, legs spread out, Dylan opened his water bottle. Rest of the team – except the Hongs –was resting on the ground nearby, relaxed. The Hongs, looking fresh and strong, stayed on their feet as they discussed something in their native tongue frequently pointing at the castle, which now seemed to be high up in the sky.

Frowning in annoyance and perhaps a little bit of jealousy, considering the brothers' unending endurance, Dylan had just taken one sip from his water bottle when something hard hit it throwing the plastic mess yards away. Glancing behind he caught the glimpse of a silhouette quickly   disappearing behind a tree. The trademark black outfit and the stealth, swift movement had clearly told Dylan what it was. He instantly plunged on the ground screaming at the top of his voice, "Ninja! Take cover!"

Everybody hugged the ground. A long few moments passed, nothing happened. Glancing around Roger saw no sign of Ninjas. Just the woods, the natural movements, and the rustling sounds as the air passed through the leaves.

"What did you see?" Roger whispered to Dylan.

"I don't know. Surely looked like a creepy Ninja." Dylan mumbled. "Something hit my water bottle."

Another few moments passed quietly. A strong breeze flew, the leaves shuffled. Looking keenly through the dense woods they saw no sign of suspicious movement.

"You sure you are not hallucinating?" Miller teased.

Dylan had crawled a few feet back and recovered his water bottle, a part of it anyway. It was cut half in the middle. He raised it inch above the ground.

"You want to end up like this, dude?" He said.

Having seen the decimated item all doubts disappeared. There was still no unusual movement, anywhere.

Impatient, Hong lee slithered through the bushes quietly. Hong Shien signaled everybody to move back and take better shelter. The team slowly and silently crawled backward looking for either large boulders or thick bushes.

Miller, his rifle in his hand, was looking for an excuse to go crazy. Rana took out his blowpipes. He'd excellent aim from a close distance. The poisonous tiny arrows could run havoc in the enemy line. Dylan was good at throwing rocks, a skill that he picked up keeping situations like this in mind. Blessed with his knuckles he'd a natural detest for weapons. He quickly filled both his pockets with rocks.

"I hate ninjas." He grunted. "I am a boxer. How can I

beat the heat out of them if I can't even get close to them?"

Roger was an expert freehand fighter and could easily tackle a few strong men. However, lately he didn't depend on his fighting skill as much and started to carry couple of guns. One had real bullets while the other had poisonous pins - Orenda's innovation. Once the pins hit somebody the person would become immobile for hours. He preferred not to use real bullets unless the situation absolutely demanded. Killing wasn't in his nature, no matter how heinous the enemy was. He picked up the gun with the pins.

They quietly waited, expecting the invisible enemy to strike. Long, painful moments ticked away, nothing happened. Everything seemed perfectly normal. No unusual sounds, no suspicious movements.

Hong Lee had disappeared more than a minute. The team had a protocol for communicating in this kind of situation. They used birdcalls to convey various messages. At night, owl calling once stood for dire situation. Repeated calls in quick succession meant safety. Two or three successive calls with longer intervals indicated warning - move with caution. Till now there was no signal from Hong Lee.

Hong Shien was clearly worried for his brother. It shouldn't have taken Hong Lee more than thirty seconds to identify danger, if there was one. He moved like a snake, observed like a vulture, and listened like a bat. He wouldn't miss even the faintest movement on the blade of a grass.

Roger started to get little worried as well. Hong Lee was taking uncharacteristically long time to send a message. He looked at Rana – meaningfully. The general rule was – at least one of the Hong brothers must stay with the team. In a free hand combat any one of them could hold a small army. This meant when doubtful about the safety of Hong Lee, the team-tracker, somebody else beside Hong Shien must go to check on him. Smaller and agile, Rana was the next best choice unless Johra was present.

Rana readily understood what was expected from him. He'd already started on the trail of Hong Lee when a single call of an owl broke the persistent silence of the woods. Just moments later, the woods suddenly came alive with numerous shouts followed by a scuffle.

Hong Shien wasted no time. He sprung up from the ground and dashed toward the source of the commotion. Rest of the team knew they had to act, even though they couldn't be sure whether Hong Lee was in trouble. Quickly up on their feet they rushed into the dark.

Less than twenty meters inside the woods they suddenly found them completely surrounded by dozens of Ninjas. Their sharp edged ninja stars whistled through the murky air, looking for human flesh. There was little time to think. They dived on the ground scrambling to find anything to use as a shield against the deadly stars.

Safe behind tree trunks Roger, Rana, Miller and Dylan could now see Hong Lee battling several masked men. His body leapt in the air frequently and his hands and feet moved with lightning speed, accompanied by the sure sound of broken bones and the agonizing scream of the fallen enemies.

Hong Shien somersaulted and rolled as he miraculously dodged the rain of ninja stars and broke through the attackers with powerful kicks to help his brother who was now getting heavily outnumbered by the Ninjas. Hong Shien issued a chilling war cry as he darted to help his brother. Momentarily the ferocity of the battle doubled. The springing bodies of the two brothers made mockery of the opposition, as they were beaten in every faculty of martial art – skill, speed and strength.

However, the enemy tried to overpower the brothers with numbers. No matter how many of them were beaten and thrown, more kept coming. Roger knew the Hongs couldn't possibly continue fighting for the rest of the night. He'd to intervene, though from past experiences he knew the brothers weren't going to be happy about it.

Keeping low to the ground the team crawled ahead fast. Miller fired his rifle a few times, rapidly. He believed in kill-the-thugs strategy, but out of respect to Roger limited himself in shooting only to immobile the enemy, when possible. With every shot he took came a painful scream, clearly suggesting he wasn't missing. Very rarely he did.

Attacked on two fronts the Ninjas changed their battle plan. They quickly divided into two large groups. One group continued to press hard on the brothers while the other group counter attacked the Sygods. Roger realized if they waited too long they wouldn't have a fighting chance against the pouring Ninjas. He signaled a full-blown attack.

Not yet fully convinced that a deadly means was needed Roger decided to continue to use his pin-gun and shot carefully targeting, making a point not to miss. He was only carrying three boxes of pins each containing fifty pins.

Rana joined the onslaught with his blowpipe. Hiding behind trees he skillfully blew a series of poisonous arrows, hitting several of the approaching foes.

Dylan, more eager to beat the Ninjas up, tried to close on them but retreated when the deadly stars rained on him. He swiftly moved out of their sight and returned the favor by hurling stones at them.

Miller happily continued his shooting spree, not as careful to spare the lives of his rivals any more. This, he believed, was a more dangerous situation and required a serious approach.

To their relief, they noticed the Ninjas had little answer for the combined attack of their rivals and had opted for a safer distance. The question was how long would they hold back? Roger didn't think it would be too long before they decided to overpower them with sheer numbers.

Another few minutes had passed, overall situation hadn't changed much. There seemed to be no lack of supply for the Ninjas. The fallen Ninjas were replaced by the fresh ones. Wounded and dead bodies piled up, air turned heavy in agony of the injured, even the Hongs was clearly tiring up. Roger knew they had to do something to stop this unending battle. If it continued for too long they would be exhausted to death. Unlike the Ninjas, they didn't have any backups.

Roger had a few tricks saved under his sleeves for extreme situations. Orenda had invented and manufactured some useful gazettes, each with specific functions. They came in different sizes – from marble size balls to tiny dust like particles – and were anything from deadly to annoyance. Roger tried to think which one would be the most effective under the current circumstances.

Chapter 20

The Bloodthirsty Wolves

Suddenly, a strong breeze blew; trees shook in unison; leaves murmured. A chilling wolf's call echoed in the valley, again and again. The Ninjas stopped, listened carefully. Something very strange happened next. Clearly panicked, they scurried back into the woods and simply vanished in the darkness. Perplexed, Sygods looked at each other.

"What's with the wolf?" Miller asked.

"Beats me." Dylan shrugged. "I hope it's not one of those werewolves. You know - the ones that can stand up on their hind legs and suck the blood of pretty girls."

Relieved that the Ninjas had fled, nobody mind in this untimely humor. Roger always enjoyed Dylan's sarcasm and was about to smile when the sanctity of the night was broken for a second time with a chorus of blood shuddering howls of a pack of wolves. Moments later they heard the pack charging toward them right through the woods, fast.

The quick turn of events must have stunned them because they stood there confused for a few long moments. What was exactly marching at them in such a menacing pace? The howls got stronger, the rushing footsteps sounded like a forthcoming storm with the potential of mayhem. There wasn't enough time to analyze the situation. Some kind of beasts were about to attack them.

"I guess this is when we run." Dylan tried to keep his composure.

Rana nodded strongly. "I second that."

The Hong brothers had been listening carefully to the howls. They gave their full approval to the idea, unusually quickly, and ran over the hedges and through the bushes like two possessed men. The brothers knew their limits. People they could handle but not wolves. The rest followed without any words, running as fast as they possibly could.

"Across the valley, to the creek." Roger shouted.

His plan was simple. The creek ran along the length of a rocky mountain that stretched for miles with sharp drops ranging anywhere from thirty-forty feet to hundreds of feet. If they could cross the creek and somehow climb up the rocks they would probably be safe from the fierce beasts. Hopefully the four legged animals wouldn't be able to negotiate vertical ascent with their hooves.

"Whose nightmare was this?" Rana said, sprinting.

"The evil Magician's, of course." Dylan yelled back. "If I could just get my hands on him…."

"This can't be true." Miller shouted. "Where would all these wolves come from?"

"Why don't you ask the wolves?" Dylan joked.

"I'll, with my guns." Miller sped up. He was carrying the rifle and was falling back.

"They are too many. We can't shoot them all." Roger reminded.

The creek was at least a kilometer away. Sprinting across the grassland, zigzagging through the wild bushes and spread out trees, they must have made it to the creek in record time as the terrifying howls behind them continued to grow louder and louder.

Gasping for air they looked back. What they saw was

simply mind boggling. The pack of wolves, hundreds of them, had just emerged out of the woods like a swarm of locusts and was approaching them with raging speed. Their sharp, shinny teeth glittered in the faint light of the predawn sky, their heavy footsteps shuttered the piece of the valley. There was little doubt about what the beasts were capable of doing.

"Take me God!" Dylan exclaimed. "What sin did I commit? Okay, okay, I'll go to the church, once a year. Now get these creeps of my back. Please!"

"Once a year!" Miller frowned. "That's the best you can do?"

"I was talking to God, not to you. He has mercy."

The creek was about sixty feet wide, not more than four –five feet deep at any point. They walked right through it as quickly as they could.

Hong brothers had reached the other side first. They quickly surveyed the near vertical rocky surfaces trying to find a part that they could climb up. The one they set their mind on was a vertical wall about thirty feet high from the ground – one of the lowest, made of pure, comparatively smoother rock. The brothers had little success trying to climb the wall in free hands, as there was almost nothing to cling on.

Dylan carried a rope for situations like this. He took it out from his backpack. The rope had an anchor attached to it. He threw the anchor over the vertical wall. After couple of tries the anchor stuck to something. When the rope endured a few good pulls Dylan knew it was strong enough to hold one person. He signaled the team to climb up one at a time.

Roger went first followed by Rana. The wolves had picked up speed and were now rushing in alarming velocity across the flat land. It looked unlikely that everybody would have time to climb up the rope. Hong Lee was the stronger one between the two brothers. He stood close to the surface with half folded knees and spread out palms. Hong Shien took a short run up, jumped on his brothers open palms, sprung high in the air and magnificently managed to grab the corner of the wall with the tips of his fingers. He then easily flipped over and stood on the flat rocky surface at the top of the wall.

Dylan was an expert rope climber. He made the distance with very few pulls. Miller hung the rifle on his back and quickly grabbed the rope, trying to climb as fast as he could. The wolves were now crossing the creek. Glancing back he could see their extravagantly sharp teeth as they droop disgustingly. Hong Lee knew he didn't have enough time to wait for Miller to complete his climb. It was only seconds before the wolves would reach him. Roger, Rana and Dylan grabbed the top end of the rope, adding more strength to it. Miller was still just midway down the rope.

"Come on Lee!" Dylan shouted frantically. "The rope can take both of you. Come on!"

"Jump!" Hong Shien shouted. "I catch."

The first batch of tens of wolves had just jumped out of the water. Desperate, Hong Lee ran toward the rope, jumped in the air, grabbed it and pushed on the wall strongly with his feet and let go the rope as his body leaped in the air, hands extended toward the waiting hands of his brother. In one jerk Hong Shien pulled him up. Dylan, Rana and Roger pulled the rope up with Miller hanging on it. The drooping beasts jumped menacingly in the air, growled and howled, tried to tear the stony wall down with their sharp claws. They were huge, hungry and ruthless.

Dylan quickly folded his rope. "What do these wolves eat?" He said dryly. "Look at their sizes!"

"Thanks God." Rana added. "We almost became their early morning snacks."

"Who send them?" Miller said. "Dragan? But how?"

Everybody looked at Roger. He was the subject matter expert. Roger shrugged.

"Well, in his world the difference between reality and fantasy is not very clear. Our worldly perception of objects has little meaning to him. Clearly, he has something to do with whatever we are facing on these mountains. Some of it could very well be imaginary or virtual."

"How is that possible?" Rana asked. "We just fought against the Ninjas."

"He may be using our own imaginative power against our own minds." Roger theorized.

"Then how about the wounds I got from the funky Ninja stars?" Dylan said, feeling the arm where the injury had occurred. To his surprise there was nothing unusual there. His sleeves were intact as it ever was, flesh untouched. "What the hell!"

"Are you sure you had a wound there?" Miller was doubtful.

"Come on. It's my body. I know when it gets perforated."

"I surely hope so." Miller teased.

The Hong brothers examined their fists. Usually after any serious fight, especially as deadly as the previous two battles were, they would have bruised knuckles. Their knuckles looked clean, unharmed.

"No hurt!" They echoed each other.

"I am not surprised." Roger said. "Consider this as a magic show and this rugged land as the stage. Anything that happens on this stage are planned and created to awe us. They may not be exactly what they look to be but they are still dangerous."

"Does this mean," Rana said, "that he is orchestrating this imaginary attacks on us sitting somewhere inside that castle?"

"Possible." Roger shrugged. "Or all of these could be part of his preset security system. Just like security walls, alarms etc. that we use to secure our homes from unwanted people. We don't always know who is looking over the boundary walls unless they jump over it and try to break into the house when an alarm gets turned on. I don't really know. I am just guessing."

Dylan peeked down the edge of the mountain. The blood thirsty wolves continued their futile attempt to climb up the vertical rocks, their disappointment and frustration clearly resonated in their combined howling that tore off the apparent quietness of the valley in short pulses.
"Looking at those beasts," he said confusedly, "I've no desire to verify whether they are real or not."

Roger lied down on the rocky bed. "My old bones need rest before taking another step. Let's take a short break."

Nobody objected to this. Now that they had seen the castle and were convinced that's where Farina was taken they felt just a tiny bit better. Now they could have the luxury to take a little time off and plan for the final mission. None of them had any illusion about the task that lay ahead. They didn't come there only to save Farina, but also to capture the illusionist himself. Slowly the howling and growling of the hungry wolves subsided and just before dawn broke the beasts rushed back into the woods.

Chapter 21

The Trap

Next morning Shahed woke up with a headache. The night before he'd waited for Roger's call almost until dawn. He didn't think he'd be able to sleep at all but eventually tiredness took over him. A wall clock told him it was 10 in the morning. He sprung out of the bed and rushed to Johra's room. After a few impatient knock a voice inquired, "Who is it?"

It was Johra. She'd all the kids sleep in her room last night.

"It's Shahed. " He tried to stay calm.

Johra checked him out through the eyehole. The door opened slightly, just enough for him to enter.

"Come in."

The door closed behind him quickly as he stepped inside the room. The kids were sitting quietly on the floor. A pile of dishes was waiting to be collected by the room service.

"I ordered breakfast for us. You were sleeping, didn't want to wake you up." Johra said.

"Dad, she was showing us gymnastic." Zaki exclaimed. "She can flip in the air!"

"And lot more." Musa added excitedly.

"I am keeping them engaged." Johra shyly said. "Do

you want some breakfast?"

"Have you heard from Roger?" Shahed anxiously asked. "He was supposed to call me. He never did."

"He'll", Johra calmly said, "at his earliest convenience."

"You really believe in him." Shahed couldn't help saying.

Johra smiled. "He is like a father to me. Anyway, you should clean up and get dressed. We may have to move out in a very short notice."

"Why? Are we in danger?" Shahed almost whispered, intending not to scare the kids.

Johra shook her head. "I don't think so, but I won't bet my life on it." She softly said. "The tournament has been cancelled. Teams have already started to leave." At this point she lowered her voice even further. "Remember that old man and the boy in the black? The room service told me, they disappeared last night. I think that old man was the Magician!"

"What?" Shahed scoffed. "He was here and we had no clue? What kind of intelligence Roger has? What was the police department doing? What about the mighty FBI?"

Johra shrugged. "I am just guessing. But anything is possible for him. He is extremely smart and brave. Anyway, I need to go back to the kids before they get edgy. You can stay here with us, if you want. Try not to worry too much."

Shahed returned to his room. He felt betrayed and deceived. He shouldn't have trusted Roger. This trip was a total mistake, a disaster. He felt like tearing his hairs off. How could he be so ignorant? He shouldn't have depended on Roger for security. Obviously Sygods weren't as good as he'd perceived.

Then the obvious question popped up in his mind, something that somehow managed to elude him until now. Did Roger report the kidnapping to authority? As Farina's uncle and guardian shouldn't he inform the police? Common sense said he should, however, his wisdom influenced him otherwise. He decided to hold off until he heard back from Roger. Was Sygods any match for the brilliant and mischievous Magician, he wondered. For now, he could only wait and see how things unfolded.

The morning rolled into afternoon. Shahed felt nauseous and spent most of the day in his room. Johra had ordered lunch for everybody from a nearby pizza store. Shahed sat with them but couldn't eat much. He tried to make up an excuse and return to his room but Johra insisted him to stay with them. She understood his agony and thought he'd feel better if he stayed with the kids. Shahed reluctantly agreed. Even Johra was tense; he sensed it. She tried to hide it but he could see it in her posture. Perhaps she needed some emotional support as well. Why didn't Roger call yet? The question bubbled up several times in his mind but he finally decided not to ask. How would Johra know anyway?

Hours later, Shahed was lying on a bed, messaging his forehead to ease the terrible headache that had started long ago, when his cell phone rang. As he picked it up a very thick voice spoke in broken English.

"Mr. Shahed?"

"Yes." Surprised, Shahed hesitantly replied. "Who is it?"

The kids sat in couple of rows at the other end of the room where Johra taught them how to flip in the air. She'd heard the phone ring and kept an eye on Shahed. She must have sensed something wasn't right by his facial expression. She quickly made up an excuse with the kids and walked up to him. Shahed held the phone a little away from his ear allowing Johra to hear as well.

"I am *D-r-r-agan V-v-alc-o-o-vich*." The heavy voice replied, stressing on practically every letter he said. "Some people know me as the *Ma-g-g-ician*. I called to tell you Farina is with me now." There was a pause. "If you want her back you have to do what I ask you to."

Johra was close enough to hear. She signaled to continue the conversation.

"Is she okay?" Shahed's voice shook in apprehension.

"Oh yes, she is just fine." The Magician was convincing. "I won't harm her. No w-a-a-a-y. But you must do what I say."

"Anything. What do you want me to do?"

"Step out of this room. Don't let Johra follow you."

Johra signaled Shahed to do as told. Shahed opened the door and walked into the corridor. Johra closed the door behind him.

"Walk up the corridor." The Magician instructed.

Shahed took about fifty steps down the corridor when he was asked to stop.

"Now, listen to me carefully." The voice said. "First you must get rid of Johra. Then take the kids and get out of the hotel. You'll find a rented white minivan parked in the parking lot. The key is on the driver's seat. Drive to highway 1 north. Wait for my phone call."

"Why should I believe you?" Shahed doubtfully said. "How do I even know that you really have Farina?"

There was a short silence. "Close your eyes."

Surprised, Shahed did as asked.

"Do you see Farina?" The voice became heavier,

dreamy. "She is waving at you. She is saying she is fine."

Puzzled, Shahed clearly saw Farina standing in a partly dark room. She looked worried but in good health. Her voice echoed from a distance, "I am fine, Uncle Shahed."

The image disappeared slowly.

"Was that good enough?"

"How did you do it? Can you see me? Are you a real magician?" Shahed was bedazzled.

The voice broke into a loud laughter at the other end. "I am a scientist." The man said once the laugher subsided. "The only magic I know is science. You will get to know me better, soon. Now, please do what I say. Remember, no cops, no tricks, no Johra. You have half an hour."

The phone disconnected. Nervous and confused Shahed didn't know what to do. He could do just about anything to get Farina back safely but putting the kids into any kind of risk wasn't something he wanted to consider. On the other hand, if he didn't pay heed to the Magician who knew what he'd do to Farina. The good part was he didn't sound that evil. His intentions were not clear but if he'd any plan to hurt anybody, he could have done it the previous night.

Leaving Johra behind was not an option. The Magician clearly knew how capable Johra was. Naturally he didn't want to deal with her. Shahed, on the other hand, had started to trust her very much and didn't feel it would be in their best interest to go without her. He wished he could talk it out with Johra. But the Magician might have installed spy cameras all over the place and would know about it right away. He could get mad. The last thing Shahed wanted was to agitate the guy.

When he walked back inside the room, he looked nervous and pale. Johra read him like printed text.

"I am going back to my room to take a shower." She said rather loudly, making sure the hidden microphones, if any, picked it up. "I'll be back soon."

Shahed met her eyes and moved his head slightly toward the streets, hoping Johra would get the clue. Johra walked out of the room, gave no indication of noticing the gesture. She walked into her room and shut the door behind.

Chapter 22

Where is Johra?

The proposal to get out of the hotel room was greeted with great enthusiasm by the kids. Within minutes they had slipped into their outdoor outfits and merrily raced to the elevators.

Once down to the lobby Shahed marched them out of the hotel to the parking lot. It didn't take him very long to find out the parked minivan. An eight sitter, it was painted in spotless white. He found the door unlocked and the key resting on the driver's seat as promised. Interestingly enough, the kids who had the potential to become tormenting with their ceaseless questioning climbed up the vehicle without any queries.

Of course, that didn't mean that they wouldn't bicker about sitting choices. With the older kids forcing their way to the back Zaki and Musa had to settle with the second row seats. Preeti reluctantly separated from Ivana to occupy the remaining seat on the second row while Ivana joined Stanley and Oliver in the back seat.

Shahed roughly knew how to get to Highway 1. Once everybody was tied into their seat belts he pulled out and drove his way to the highway. Nervous and unsure he felt helpless and alone. A professor of economics, what did he know about all these dangerous activities? How much he wished that Johra were with him. This was her game; she'd have known readily what to do. Did she see his signal? Would she know where they were heading?

He frequently looked at his rear view mirror, expecting to get a glimpse of Johra following in close proximity. To his great dismay, the young girl was nowhere to be seen.

Shahed feared this was going to be a disaster of grand proportion. He started to wonder if this was a bad idea to begin with and whether he should turn around and go back to the hotel. That meant defying the Magician, something that could turn out to be even more disastrous. Whatever he did he'd to do it quickly, before it was too late to return.

Suddenly Zaki leaned over and pushed a small piece of paper into his resting left hand.

"What is it?" Shahed curiously said.

"Wish list for my next birthday." Zaki said.

Shahed unfolded the paper. On it was written in large letters – 'A gymnastic show!'

Confused, Shahed looked back at him. Over the years they had developed a mute way of communication to hide things from the mother. A scratch in the middle of the head meant everything was okay; at the back of the head suggested trouble; on the left meant no information available; on the right was a refusal to share information and on the front was clear and present danger!

Zaki smilingly scratched middle of his head. Shahed knew he was trying to give him a message. Was he trying to tell him that everything was okay and he should relax? Must be.

As he looked back to confirm his presumption he now noticed that the whole bunch was smirking at him. This was good, he thought. Johra must have found a way to explain the situation to the kids. They were smart to realize that the vehicle was definitely wired and discussing about her wasn't an option.

Shahed sighed in relief. With Johra around he wouldn't be feeling half as scared. That girl knew her business. She knew how to handle these criminals. His confidence got a real boost. Thinking clear, he stayed slightly below the posted maximum speed limit, giving Johra enough time to catch up while not making the Magician suspicious. His cell phone rested on the passenger seat within quick reach.

It wasn't before another five minutes or so when the phone rang. Shahed was greeted by the same heavy voice.

"Good!" The Magician said. "Keep going until you hit highway 92. Take that and wait for my call. And please understand, I do know every movement you are making. So, don't try anything funny. Talk to you soon."

The call ended. Shahed wasn't planning anything silly anyway, not when he knew help was coming. Hopefully Johra would be smart enough to contact Roger if she'd any means to do so; or at least would leave some kind of message for him to let him know about this latest development. In case things went out of hand he could come and rescue them.

A nice and strong afternoon wind blew through the open windows of the minivan. The kids were really noisy behind him. They screamed, howled at each other, and argued non-stop. The noise of the wind absorbed most of it and made it sort of tolerable.

Shahed stole another glimpse on the rear view mirror

– fifth in less than a minute. No sign of Johra. He wasn't even sure what to look for. Did she have a car? Motorcycle? He'd no clue. All he expected to see was some kind of subtle sign, something that would stand out in the crowded highway. Clearly disappointed, he continued to drive slowly.

"Where are we going, Uncle Shahed?" Stanley shouted.

Shahed hadn't shared all the details with them yet. He assumed Johra might have given them some clues. Should he just tell them the truth? Shahed was double minded. Dragan - the Magician - had put no restriction about sharing anything with the kids. There was really no reason for him to keep it a secret from them. They were all in this together and everybody had the right to know what was going on.

He rolled up the windows and turn on the Air conditioner to cut down the external noise.

"Okay guys, listen to me carefully." He started grimly, preparing the kids before breaking the serious news.

"We are in a mission to rescue Farina." Preeti interrupted.

"We already know that." Ivana was confident.

"No we don't." Stanley barked. "Why don't you let Uncle Shahed talk?"

Preeti and Ivana exchanged meaningful glances. These boys!

Shahed took this opportunity to finish what he was about to say. "Guys, we are not exactly going to rescue Farina."

"I knew that!" It was Oliver.

"So did I!" Stanley yelled.

"Will you boys shut up?" Preeti and Ivana joined forces.

Shahed raised a hand. "Let me finish, would you? We are actually going to meet the Magician. Farina is with him."

There was a moment of complete silence inside the car.

"Really?" Zaki was the first to speak. "What if he put us into a dungeon?"

Now, that was a really scary possibility. Shahed didn't even want to get there. "No, no, he isn't going to do anything like that. I think he just want to meet us."

"What happens later?" Preeti asked.

"Hopefully we'll be allowed to take Farina and get out of there." Shahed tried to make it sound simple. It sounded rather ridiculous to him. This definitely wasn't a good idea. He could still turn back.

"Dangerous!" Stanley cried out. "That guy is cool! He is a scientist and a Magician. All right!"

"Dangerous!" The gang joined in an impromptu chorus.

It was Shahed's turn to be surprised. He wondered what went through the minds of these young kids. One moment they were all stressed, the next moment they were ecstatic. Did he used to be like that when he was a young boy? Uh, the childish innocence!

Chapter 23

The Tower

When Farina woke up again several hours had passed. She'd no sense of time. All she remembered that she was in a weird room with no doors or windows. Afraid to open her eyes, she'd to force herself to accept the inevitable. She'd been kidnapped!

Slowly and fearfully, she opened her eyes and was amazed to find herself in a sunlit room. A quick glance around the room revealed quite a few surprises. The room seemed to be the same room she saw before she fell asleep; however, one of the walls had been replaced with floor to ceiling clear glass panels allowing the sun to shine through.

She also noticed a large rectangular door with a handle stood proudly in the middle of an opaque wall located opposite to the glass panel. The door, which was securely closed, pulled her like a magnet. She walked down to it and tried to open it. It didn't move. She tried a few more times unsuccessfully before giving up and walking before the glass panel instead.

Looking outside she could not suppress her astonishment. The amazing landscape that popped up right before her eyes wasn't something she'd ever seen in such proximity. The beautiful valley with its greenery, the thin thread like creek that glittered in the sun and the mountain range that stood bordering the horizon – were simply breathtaking.

"Beautiful, isn't it?" Known voice. Flyball.

Farina looked around but didn't see it.

"I am going to land on your right ear." Flyball said. "Warning - it may tickle."

It felt like a fly. "How did the room change?" She'd to ask it. The curiosity was killing her.

"The room hasn't changed," It said. "Your access has been upgraded. Think of a computer. You can only see or do things that you are allowed to. An admin can set users up with various access levels."

How could a virtual world of computing be implemented in real world? Farina wasn't sure she totally understood what Flyball was suggesting. Perhaps it was just another visual trick that the Magician came up with. It was difficult for her to accept things that didn't make sense or defied physical laws.

"You may go out of this room," Flyball said, "if you want to. There may be some constraint but the Tower should be accessible."

"What is the Tower?" asked Farina.

"The highest point of this castle - the Castle of Illusion. Boss named it, not me."

"Is this castle built on a mountain?"

"You got it. Three kilometers above the ground."

"How did he build it?" Farina was genuinely curious.

"Beats me. I was powered up after the castle was built."

"Did you just say I could get out of this room?" Farina asked to be sure.

"You bet." Flyball said. "I've no order to stop you."

"Stop me?" Farina couldn't hide her amusement.

"You are guarding me!" What could this tiny machine possibly do to stop her? She wondered.

Flyball read her mind. "I am your guardian angel." It said. "I've no power to stop you. That was a joke. Boss controls everything. He has super intelligent machines and programmable objects. If he wants you to stay in this room he'd take away all the doors. That simple!"

Okay! It was starting to sound like science fiction. Farina thought. Theoretically it wasn't impossible, but applying such concept in real world situation seemed tomorrow's technology. Nonetheless, she believed Flyball. It had no reason to lie.

"The door is locked. I tried. " Farina said.

"It's open now." Flyball said. "I got in through a small hole, too small for you to even see. On my way in I turned on the magnetic switch that controls the door. Don't worry. I've my orders. It's fine with boss."

Farina realized trying to escape from that castle was out of question. She wouldn't even know which way to head to. Even if somehow she could make it to the valley she'd get lost in the mountain range. On the other hand she'd this strong belief that the Sygods would come for her. She needn't do anything stupid. For the time being, the best thing she could do was to explore the interior of the castle as much as she could. Just in case it came handy later.

She walked to the door and turned the handle all the way before giving it a strong push. The door, quite heavier than what she'd expected, opened smoothly and silently.

She walked out into a solitary corridor, wide and long, with spotless white wall in one side and clear glass wall in the other, displaying series of mountains extended on all sides, as far as eyes went.

After walking along the corridor for about hundred yards and couple of sharp turns later Farina found her standing behind a closed door. Hesitant, she pushed it lightly. It slid open slowly, revealing an incredible view in front of her eyes, scary yet so beautiful.

Two giant escalators hung in space, under the open sky. One moved down, as far as the eyes could see, before dropping beyond a layer of white clouds. The other moved up, reaching to a closed door at least a few thousand feet above where she stood. None had any supports whatsoever to hold them in place. The huge structures simply floated in the air, as if some invisible power was holding them in place.

Farina felt a little nauseous. She quickly took a few steps back, fearing she might fall.

Flyball was with her. "Don't be fooled!" It said. "You don't see everything, remember? Access control. What you see is what you are allowed to see."

Farina didn't question. She was starting to accept the absurdity of it all. After the initial shock was over, she gathered enough courage to take a few steps forward to the edge of the moving escalators.

"Hop onto the upper one." Flyball encouraged. "You'll be fine."

"Are you coming with me?" she was still apprehensive about all this mumbo jumbo. Such large structures got to prop on something. The access control part she understood; only if she could make her mind believe that.

"Of course!" Flyball said.

That was a little reassuring. Though tiny and invisible, it was smart and useful; especially its knowledge about the castle was priceless. Slowly, she stepped onto the small platform that joined the two giant escalators. Her feet shook, heart pounded. This was so strange. She was standing on a solid platform that just floated in the air, as if there was no gravity!

"Good start." Flyball said. "Now step on it."

Farina stepped on the escalator slowly and carefully. The moment her feet settled down on the escalator it abruptly sped up and she found her hundreds of feet high in seconds.

She could see the bird's eye view of the castle hugging the peak of the mountain below. The castle with its hundreds of minarets and domes and sections branching in all directions looked stunning yet bizarre at the background of the sprawling valley and the mountain ranges.

Her legs trembling, she felt the escalator was accelerating as the view of the castle down below became tinier and eventually got shrouded by cottony clouds. She was so scared that she sat on a step with her eyes closed. It felt like just seconds when the escalator reached the floating door up above.

Farina was almost thrown to the small platform where the door stood as the escalator continued in its rotation. She fearfully opened her eyes, tried not to look down knowing what she'd see won't be pleasant, wobbled to the mysterious door and held the knob – round and golden, still struggling to make up her mind.

"Open it." Flyball said. "Trust me."

Farina hesitantly pushed the door lightly and flinched back as it opened wide.

"Don't worry. You'll be fine." Flyball assured.

Farina took a deep breath and took couple of steps to carry her behind the open door. With sheer amazement she discovered a round, open platform at least fifteen feet in radius, with white, shiny granite floors. Just ahead, unobstructed sky hanged over protruding mountains and gliding clouds. She was never afraid of heights but the strangeness of this all shook her up well. The floor looked so glossy that she was afraid to step on it, fearing an accidental slip could result into sliding through the floor and getting hurled into the air.

"You won't fall." Flyball said.

Farina braced herself with courage and carefully took her first step onto the Tower holding the edge of the door in one hand. The floor was cold and hard, almost sticky. Her fear of slipping away was gone in seconds. The strong footing gave her confidence back. She took another small step forward and let the door go. It slowly swung back and lightly clicked to close.

"Flyball!" Farina called out.

"I am with you." It said. "It's beautiful, isn't it?"

Farina took a few more steps toward the center of the platform and stood still. Looking around her she realized that the Tower had nothing to support it beside the small section that connected it to the platform where the door was located. It got to be a hallucination, she thought.

The view from there was hypnotizing. Standing high in the sky and looking down to the beautiful green valleys, the mighty mountain ranges and the ever-flowing creek, she felt equally privileged and confused.

"Tell me this is an illusion, some sort of trick." Farina said in disbelief.

"Uh-oh! You shouldn't have said that." Flyball sounded alarmed.

Suddenly a thick cover of cloud flew from the horizon in amazing speed and surrounded the Tower making it completely dark. Farina, puzzled, could barely see her hands.

"What's going on?" She screamed.

"The Princess heard you. She has terrible anger issue."

"What did I do?"

"You used the words *illusion* and *trick*. Not her favorite words. She considers them demeaning. In future speak carefully. She has ears everywhere. A bit sensitive, I guess."

"Have you ever seen her?"

"Of course. Not that I prefer to. She is super genius. And super crazy. As I said, if she sees me I am mashed potato."

"What do we do now?" Farina asked, standing still in the pitch black dark.

"Gotta go back. Follow my voice. I know where the door is." Flyball said.

Farina followed its voice to the door, felt her way to the knob, opened the door and stepped out of the Tower to the floating platform. She noticed the escalator changed its direction and was now going down. She stepped on it.

"Flyball, can she hear you?" She asked, as the escalator dashed down.

"Fortunately not." Flyball said. "I am not in her command. Boss controls me. Her spy wares cannot decode my voice. I guess boss is scared of her power."

"Really? What kind of power she has?"

"Wait a little longer. You'll see it yourself."

On the way back to her room she noticed the glass walls had been replaced by solid opaque walls turning the brightly sunlit corridor into a shadowy passage. What kind of place was it? She wondered nervously.

Chapter 24

The Tunnel

Shahed followed the Magician's instructions to a dirt road off the highway. After driving about ten kilometers he was asked to stop. They were at the foot of a mountain – must be about a mile high.

"There is a trail just ahead of you." The Magician said on the phone. "Follow that for a few minutes until you see the mouth of a tunnel. Enter the tunnel and climb up the stairs. Go all the way up, step out of the tunnel, and walk through the woods until you reach an open field at the edge of the mountain. Wait for my call." He disconnected.

Shahed told the kids what they had to do. This was greeted with unusual excitement. Not just Musa, even Zaki could hardly suppress his urge to sprint to the tunnel.

"A tunnel! Wow! Let's go guys." Stanley yelled, as always.

"I knew there would be a tunnel." Oliver declared.

"Don't you know everything?" Preeti ridiculed.

"Don't worry about him. Come." Ivana pulled her by the arm.

The boys were already on their way to the trail. They didn't even wait for Shahed.

"Stop!" Shahed called out. "Wait for me."

Nobody slowed down. Shahed locked the car and ran

after them. These kids had no sense of danger. They didn't seem to realize this wasn't exactly a pleasure trip. He quickly rounded them up.

"No more running around." He rebuked. "We are in a mission, don't forget. Let's stay together. Okay?"

They weren't used to see him act so harshly. It worked. They shook their head in agreement. Shahed was pleased. They needed to understand the gravity of the situation.

It took them a little bit to find the trail. Almost hidden behind densely populated trees it meandered uphill through the forest. The slope was mild but was heavily packed with sprouting vegetation. At times it was even hard to move through. Clearly, it hadn't been used for a while. Shahed stayed at the rear of the pack, making sure that none of the kids fell behind. Stanley and Oliver, being the oldest kids in the bunch, led the group.

Shahed looked around to see if they were being followed. He didn't see anything suspicious. He also checked for surveillance cameras. None was visible.

He was anxious about Johra. He didn't see any sign of her while driving on the highway or on the dirt road. She might have lost them, he feared. The dirt road was hard to see from the highway and was barely used. If Johra didn't see them turning into it, she'd continue ahead on highway 92.

"What did Johra tell you?" He whispered to Ivana. Finally his curiosity won over his cautiousness.

"She said whatever happens she'll be with us." Ivana whispered back. "I trust her. Don't worry."

Shahed had every reason to worry. Without Johra this expedition could turn into a disaster. The thought of taking the kids back to the car and driving away crossed his mind one more time. He readily knew that wasn't an option any more. Nobody in this team would want to leave without Farina, not after coming this far.

After walking for another few hundred yards into the woods they came across the tunnel. The mouth was hardly visible from the trail. It was about six-seven feet tall and four-five feet wide and was mostly covered by a large boulder. Shahed carefully took a peek inside the tunnel. It went uphill in a sharp angle. Dark and cold, its rocky floor was carved into stairs. He could barely see past twenty feet inside the tunnel.

"I don't think we can climb this." He muttered.

Musa had little patience for hesitation.

"What's wrong, Uncle Shahed?" He inquired, ready to dart inside the tunnel.

"It's very dark." Shahed thoughtfully said. "I can hardly see anything."

Stanley peeked inside and agreed. "It's damn dark. Scary!"

Oliver always carried a flashlight in his pocket.

"I've a flashlight!" He excitedly reminded.

"All right!" The kids exclaimed.

"What are we waiting for?" Stanley walked into the tunnel closely followed by Oliver with his flashlight turned on. Musa and Zaki remained immediately behind them while Preeti and Ivana stayed at the back with Shahed as they steadily climbed up the narrow stairs. The kids had much easier time than Shahed did. Just minutes later he started to feel tired and suffocated. His legs struggled to rise. He stopped to rest frequently, falling behind in the process.

The kids continued to climb up as Oliver faithfully kept the flashlight focused ahead. Shahed could see the circle of light dancing through the dark walls giving it a ghostly appearance.

"Wait!" He shouted. His voice echoed incessantly for a few seconds.

"Are you okay, Uncle Shahed?" Stanley shouted back.

"Dad! Where are you?" Zaki called out.

"I am down here. Give me a minute to catch up."

He pushed against the rocky wall to increase his pace. He didn't want to fall too far behind. In case something popped up ahead the kids wouldn't know how to handle that.

Slowly he caught up with the team and signaled Stanley to start moving ahead again. This time he was determined to stay put with them. After another five minutes of continuous climbing the slope turned even steeper, making it far harder to climb up.

The kids had lost some of their excitement and were somewhat exhausted. They breathed heavily and barely spoke.

"Are you guys okay?" Shahed inquired.

"Yeah! Yeah!" Stanley somehow managed to say.

"How much further do we have to go?" Zaki asked.

"Can't be too far." Shahed tried to be optimistic. He realized the tunnel was leading them up to the peak of this mountain. The trip was far from over.

After another ten minutes the tunnel turned slightly sidewise revealing the small exit mouth about hundred feet above. The slope for this last part seemed almost vertical with steel railings installed on both sides for extra support.

"Watch your steps, guys." Shahed cautioned.

"I see the exit!" Stanley shouted in joy. "Y-a-h-o-o-o-o!"

His loud voice echoed from wall to wall amplifying the effect by several times.

"Not so loudly, Stan." Zaki yelled. "The echoes can cause rock slide."

Stanley stopped. He obviously wasn't looking forward to get quashed by rocks. Just to be on the safe side he even started to climb quietly.

Suddenly a second and larger circle of light danced on the walls of the tunnel. Curious and scared they all looked down. A pair of light footsteps was closing on very quickly. Shahed hoped it was Johra. It had to be Johra. With his heart pounding he even said a short prayer. If it was anybody else with a bad intention then they were all in serious trouble.

"Is it Johra?" Ivana whispered.

"I can't see." Shahed whispered back.

"Shut down the flashlight." Zaki said.

Oliver did accordingly though it was too late. The person down the stairs must have already seen the light.

They remained silent as the footsteps hurried up the stairs to their vicinity. The flashlight focused on them for a brief moment before moving back to the walls.

"Shahed!" Johra called out in a low voice.

"Johra!" The gang exclaimed in sheer joy.

"You made it!" Shahed couldn't be happier. "For a moment I thought we lost you."

Johra caught up with them with a few long strides.

"I'd to be very careful." She said, trying to catch her breath. "Didn't want Dragan to see me, not yet. He must have electronic surveillance on several points. Are you guys okay?"

Johra's mere presence had a clear energizing effect among the kids. "We are great!" They replied in a chorus.

"Dad was really scared." Zaki informed.

"No, I wasn't." Shahed objected weakly.

"Shhh…" Johra put her pointer on her lips. "Quiet. We are approaching the end of the tunnel."

They obeyed. Shahed found it surprising how quickly kids of this age could connect to young, amicable and exciting personalities like Johra. Youths like Johra and Farina in every neighborhood could make a great difference, he thought.

Johra overtook everybody to get at the front of the line. Shahed stayed at the back. He was exhausted, dry, and sweaty. He couldn't even remember when he last performed any physical exercise. Why couldn't Dragan build an elevator here? His legs were about to crumble. He stopped again to rest.

The kids, reinvigorated, followed Johra in quicker pace. He saw them climbing out of the tunnel and out of his sight. Alone in the dark tunnel Shahed suddenly felt scared, alone. He collected the last bit of energy that he'd left and hurried up the stairs.

Finally, after struggling with the last few steps as he climbed out of the tunnel to the rocky surface he crumbled on the ground. Johra and the kids were resting on a patch of grass near the exit.

"There you are," Zaki was relieved. "We were starting to get worried about you."

"We were about to send a rescue team." Ivana teased.

This generated some giggling.

Shahed ignored them for now. His throat was bone dry. He needed to rest a good few minutes before defending himself.

"Uncle Shahed, do we have to carry you now?" Preeti added salt to the wound.

More giggle; some laughter.

"That's it!" Shahed weakly objected. "I'll see how you do when you are fifty."

"I'll be young and pretty." Preeti replied promptly.

"No way." Stanley said. "You'll be old and grumpy."

"Watch it!"

They continued with their usual bickering.

Shahed noticed Johra looked worried as she frequently checked around.

"What's wrong?" Shahed asked.

"Don't like the location." Johra said.

It didn't take Shahed too long to figure out what she was referring to. The exit of the tunnel was carved out of a vertical surface that stood more than thirty feet high above the floor and stretched out for miles. The mountain, generally, was surrounded by dense forests with thick bushes and tall sturdy conifers.

This essentially meant their only viable way of exit from this mountain was the tunnel that brought them here.

"What's next?" Johra asked.

"We have to walk through the woods until we get to the edge." Shahed said. "He'll call. We should start moving."

He was about to stand up when Zaki cried. "The tunnel!"

"What's with the tunnel?" Shahed inquired.

"It's gone!" Zaki pointed at the cave, totally bewildered.

All the eyes turned to the tunnel and within seconds they realized what had happened. The tunnel had just disappeared. Looking at the rough rocky surface there was no way to even know just seconds before there was a large opening there.

Startled Shahed looked at Johra. "He didn't mention anything about this."

Johra shrugged. "He is a very tricky man."

The kids were curious. They keenly felt through every inch of the surface where the opening was, trying to find any kind of sign of a hidden door.

"Must be an electronic door." Zaki said. "Made to look like the rocky surface."

"We already know that, genius." Ivana quipped.

"We are now stuck in this wretched mountain, with these miserable girls." Stanley growled. "What do we do now?"

Naturally all eyes turned to Shahed. He shrugged, equally worried and repenting. "We have no choice but to go ahead."

Johra knew what he was thinking. "I'd have done the same if I was in your shoes." She said.

Chapter 25

The Pterodactyls and the Disks

Johra, Shahed and the kids advanced through the dense woods. There was a faint sign of a trail. They followed it for ten minutes. Slowly the dense woods turned lighter and eventually ended into an open field large enough to hold a dozen football fields. It slightly sloped down for about hundred meters before dropping vertically to the ground. Walking out into the openness they were stunned with the great view that greeted them - a lush green valley surrounded by hundreds of tall peaks and blessed by a lonely creek flowing across it, sparkling in the late afternoon sun.

What took their breath away was the glorious castle that stood at the top of a tall peak across the valley with its hundreds of minarets and domes piercing through the cottony clouds like a fictitious piece right out of the fairy tales. It was picturesque, unrealistic and mysterious.

"The Castle of the Magician!" Stanley howled. "Wow!"

"Farina is held inside that castle." Oliver said.

"In a secret chamber." Preeti corrected.

"With monsters guarding it." Ivana contributed.

"How are we going to get there?" Musa asked the most important question.

Shahed had no answers. The Magician was supposed

to call with new instructions. He hadn't, not yet. There was not much they could do but to wait.

Johra stayed out of sight, hiding behind a nearby tree. She wasn't expected. There was no need to reveal her presence until it became absolutely necessary. Who knew how the Magician would react once he saw Johra.

"That castle got to be more than a kilometer away." Zaki couldn't hide his disappointment.

"Doesn't matter how far it is." Ivana said. "How would we go there? We can't walk on the air."

"What should we do now?" Stanley was restless.

"Is this some kind of joke?" Oliver said.

"He definitely has a plan." Zaki muttered.

"And that is…" Preeti frowned.

"I don't know." Zaki admitted. "Don't be a prick."

"Did you just call me a prick?" Preeti was furious.

"I didn't mean it." Zaki quickly backed off. The last thing he wanted was to stir this girl up.

"You have to say sorry now." Ivana stepped in.

"Okay, okay, I am sorry." Zaki moved away.

Preeti chuckled. "Too easy."

"What is he up to, Johra?" Shahed asked.

"Dragan has a very high sense of humor." Johra replied from behind the tree. "His plans may not be very pleasant. Any of you have fear of height?"

Zaki turned pale. So did Shahed.

"I am sure we'll be okay." Shahed tried to cheer Zaki up.

"I am not scared of anything." Stanley declared.

"Are you sure?" Preeti asked.

"Of course!"

"Look, ants on your feet!"

Stanley sprung backward and shook his feet vigorously.

"Get off me! Get off me!"

Of all things he was afraid of ants.

As everybody laughed he frowned. "Ants are no joke."

Another wave of laughter followed.

That's when Shahed's cell phone rang. It was the Magician.

"Let's start the game." The voice said. "Farina is in the castle. You have to come and get her. I see Johra followed you. No problem. You can use her help. Good luck."

Shahed, confused and unsure, told the team what the Magician had just said.

Johra stepped out in the open. "I knew I wouldn't be able to fool him."

"What kind of game is this?" Ivana anxiously said.

"How can we get to the castle?" Preeti snapped. "Do we have wings?"

Shahed looked at Johra for some clues.

Johra shrugged. "He lives between reality and fiction. Expect something mind blowing."

"Hey Magician! We are not scared of you." Stanley shouted at the castle.

As soon as he'd finished something very strange started to happen. In moments the sky became dark with dense clouds, thunder bolted and roared louder than thousand tigers, large raindrops fell with vigor. It was hard to believe just seconds ago the valley and the mountains smiled in afternoon sun.

Shahed was completely shaken with this sudden change of weather. "Is this part of the game?" He asked, confusedly.

"Must be." Johra said. "It's not going to be fun. Kids, stay close to me and away from the edge."

Wet and worried they anxiously waited for the next surprise. The lightening snaked down the sky and the deafening thunders reverberated mountain to mountain. Then emerged the strange giant birds, in hundreds, from an opening in the castle and spread all over the valley in a blink of an eye. With their bodies as long as thirty feet, sharp protruding eyes, fearsome spear like beaks and large spread out wings they looked absolutely terrifying. As they flew tenaciously over the valley a few of them rushed to the visitors and   circled over their heads menacingly, filling the air with their chilling calls.

"Pterodactyls!" Zaki said. "They are giants!"

"Impossible!" Preeti screamed. "They were extinct millions of years ago!"

"Is this some kind of Jurassic park?" Stanley exclaimed. "Cool!"

"Super cool!" Musa threw his hands in the air in excitement.

"Cool?" Zaki yelled. "When they tear you off and eat your flesh then you would know what is cool!"

"Are they going to eat us?" Oliver was clearly shaken.

"Probably not." Johra said. "They are not attacking."

"That's right." Ivana said. "They are just circling over the valley."

"Not exactly." Zaki said. "Some of them are also circling above our heads."

There was no denying that.

"What do they want?" Oliver asked.

"Food. Any volunteers? Stanley?" Preeti said.

"Bite me." Stanley yelled back.

"This is no time for fight." Shahed warned them while

keeping weary eyes on the Pterodactyls.

Musa was the first one to notice the other flying objects. Nobody had seen exactly when and where they came from but with their round flat body and agile, speedy movement they soon stood out from the prehistoric birds.

"U.F.O." Musa pointed out.

"Too small." Ivana said. "They are probably just two feet in radius."

"What are they?" Stanley asked.

Nobody answered. They looked more like a round surfboard than an animal or a space ship. They moved through the birds as the tenacious animals tried to clinch them with their claws and beaks, and advanced toward the visitors.

Once a few of them successfully made it to the field where Shahed, Johra and the kids were standing they did a curious thing. Floating in the air they lined up as if to build a bridge over the valley from the mountain to the castle. Unfortunately they couldn't extend too far as the pterodactyls kept on attacking and displacing them. However, the disks kept on returning and starting the process all over again.

"They are trying to give us a message." Ivana said.

"Are they asking us to ride on them?" Zaki sounded doubtful.

"We can't ride on them. We'll fall." Oliver said.

This seemed obvious. The Flying Disks had a flat, shiny surface. If they tried to stand on them they would definitely slip out of the small surface. There was absolutely nothing to hold them.

"We can't just stand here in this storm." Johra said. "I think these Flying Disks are here to help us."

"How?" Shahed was puzzled. "Are we supposed to

surf on the air?"

"Surfing the air! Cool!" Musa jumped up. He could hardly wait.

"What are you talking about?" Zaki nervously said. "You'll fall. Don't you understand? I am not going anywhere near those silly things."

"We may not have any other choice," Johra said, "unless we want to lose the game without even trying. Dragan may not like that."

"Is he going to get nasty?" Shahed asked.

"What can be nastier than this?" Preeti was disgusted.

Johra shrugged. "Don't forget, he is a criminal. He is capable of doing really bad things. We should at least give it a try."

There was a moments silent. "Let's do it. It looks really cool!" Musa was as enthusiastic as ever.

"But the disks are constantly moving. How would we even get on them?" Stanley said.

"We just have to show interest." Johra said. "They look intelligent to me."

In the next few minutes the Flying Disks came much closer to them and dipped down almost to the ground level. From close proximity the objects looked even more surprising. They were thin with black circles on the surface and had an airy presence as if they were gaseous. They could stand still, moved around either spinning or straight and changed direction almost at the spot.

"Is this some kind of illusion?" Ivana said.

"Whatever!" Preeti muttered. "Is he nuts? We are just kids. How can he put us into this risky game?"

"Maybe it is not that risky." Oliver said.

"What do you mean?" Preeti snubbed.

153

"I don't know. It just came to my mind." Oliver was honest.

"He maybe right." Johra said. "I really doubt if Dragan would put any of us into danger. He is a bad guy, but not so bad."

"Oh, I know what you are saying." Preeti was sarcastic. "All this just looks dangerous but they are not. Okay, who goes first?"

"I'll." Musa jumped. "I can do it. I'll extend my two hands in the air and balance myself. Can I go first, Uncle Shahed?"

Shahed couldn't make up his mind. As the guardian of these kids he was responsible to make sure the Flying Disks were safe before anybody else hopped on them. But he'd insurmountable fear of height. He wanted to but couldn't make himself take a single step toward the Disks. Johra must have understood his dilemma.

"I'll go first." She said.

Before she'd the opportunity to test, Musa had already stepped on a Disk that hovered near his foot. Instantly his feet stuck to the metallic body of the disc. A pterodactyl plunged down with a terrifying scream and attacked Musa but the Flying Disk circled around it and quickly moved away safely. Musa's body turned upside down in the air but he didn't fall. After screaming a few times for dear life when Musa realized that the Disk would hold him no matter what he smiled ear to ear.

"Come on guys. Step on them." He shouted. "You won't fall. Just look how I am skating through the air."

Musa wiggled his body sidewise like a skater as the Disk followed his body movement and moved accordingly.

Both Ivana and Preeti were devoted ice skaters. Watching Musa skating through the air whatever hesitation and doubt they had, evaporated. They stepped up on two Disks and to their amazement felt an invisible force holding them strongly to the surface. As the persistent Pterodactyls attacked, the Flying Disks twitched and effortlessly dodged the sharp claws and fearsome beaks.

In minutes the girls were comfortable on their Disks and started to maneuver them. The Disks seemed to understand their wishes and allowed them to take some control. However, when attacked they took over and skillfully escaped without any harm. The girls really started to enjoy the whole experience.

"This is great!" Preeti giggled.

"It is!" Ivana cheerfully agreed.

Chapter 26

The Flying SciAngels

Stanley and Oliver must have felt humiliated as they watched the girls surfing in the air, because they casted nasty looks at each other.

"Why don't you go?" Stanley barked.

"Why don't you?" Oliver retorted.

"I want to make sure you go up safely." Stanley reasoned.

"Don't worry about me. Go ahead. Go on." Oliver insisted.

There childish bickering could have been too much for a pterodactyl that flew right at them and flipped over Stanley with one of its long wavy wings. Unable to stop, Stanley rolled on the ground several times and eventually was thrown over the edge. Oliver dived reflexively to catch Stanley but missed him by inches.

Shahed and Johra had both seen Stanley falling down and ran to help him but it was already too late.

"Stanley!" Shahed screamed, petrified.

Johra dashed but didn't make it on time. "Stanley!" She shouted, horrified.

Screaming his lungs out, Stanley desperately scratched the rough mountain surface to hold onto anything. The small plants that he could grab weren't strong enough to bear his weight and were instantly uprooted. Suddenly to his absolute relief and amazement a Flying Disk dived down in lightening speed and managed to take Stanley on its back. Stanley, feeling his strong footing on the thing, gave away a scream of joy. "Thank you God! Thank you! I'll be good from now."

The Disk flew up with him and rose over the mountain. Oliver was ecstatic seeing him alive and kicking.

"This thing saved my life!" Stanley shouted at him.

"Oh God! I thought you were dead!" Oliver laughed frantically.

"Come on!" Stanley called out. "This is really fun!"

Oliver quickly picked one of the flying Disks nearby and jumped onto it. Soon he joined Stanley in the air.

Both Shahed and Johra breathed out a deep sigh of relief.

"I was expecting the worst." Shahed admitted.

"Looks like I was right about Dragan." Johra said.

"You really believe he won't harm the kids?"

"Yes. However, not all of us are kids."

"You mean, we are not covered – you and I."

"Exactly. You should ride with Zaki. You'll be safe."

"What about you?"

"I doubt if the Disks will work for me. Let's try it out."

Johra walked to one of the Flying objects and saw it dart away. She tried a few others but they all refused to take her.

"I can't ride them." She said grimly. "Dragan doesn't want me in the castle."

Johra looked around, searching for alternatives. There was nothing else but the giant birds.

Shahed didn't like it at all. This was bad news. The last thing he wanted was to leave Johra behind.

"What now?" He said, clearly nervous.

"I could try to ride one of the birds." Johra said thoughtfully.

"How?"

"I carry ropes. I'll make up a lasso and try to slip it through one of them when they come close to the ground. Don't worry about me. Move on. You need to lead the kids to the castle. I'll find a way to catch up with you."

Shahed knew he'd to go. Five kids were up in the sky all by themselves. He held Zaki closely and moved to the nearest Disk. To his relief the Disk held still almost urging them to step on it

"This doesn't look scary. Step on." Shahed encouraged Zaki.

"You first, dad." Zaki dryly said.

"Okay, let's go together."

Zaki agreed. He held his father strongly as Shahed, legs shaking visibly, slowly stepped on the Disk. The Disk behaved very well. It gave them a few seconds to get used to it before shooting up, causing the dad-son duo screaming at the top of their voices. However, as the Disk fluidly moved around the dangerous birds and there was no apparent risk of falling down, both regained some of their confidence soon.

"Whatever you do don't look down." Shahed cautioned.

"I am not." Zaki said. "I know the fear is in the mind. I just have to forget that I am so high in the sky. Right, dad?"

"Yes, of course." Shahed tried to sound assuring. He'd to find the other kids, group them up and move toward the castle. Real or fantasy, they now had no choice but to play along. They had to save Farina from that crack-head scientist.

Johra made a noose with her rope and threw it like a lasso at any bird that flew within thirty feet of the ground. Her intention was to slip it through the neck or claw of a pterodactyl and then climb up the rope to its back. Once there she'd have to find a way to control it. But she was not having much luck. The birds moved too frequently and the noose seemed a little too small. She kept on trying. Determination and persistence were part of her nature.

"I can do it." She muttered, repeatedly.

Chapter 27

The Castle

Above in the sky the kids were having time of their lives. Once they were comfortable on the Flying Disks and learned exactly what kind of maneuvering they were allowed to do, the whole thing became a blast. They didn't care how high in the sky they were hovering. None of them were scared anymore.

The pterodactyls had continued their rivalry and attacked them whenever they felt like it. But the kids had already figured out how easy it was to get away from the attacks. Quick change in heights and a few sharp turns were more than enough to discourage the prehistoric birds.

Accidents happened though. While facing a similar attack Ivana was slow to move and soon discovered herself shoved away by the long wings. Her Disk spun a few times in the air, avoided clashing with another oncoming bird by moving down and finally came to a halt. Ivana, shaken by the experience, was uptight on her feet. Preeti quickly flew to her.

"Are you okay?"

"I guess. But you know what? I don't think these birds are really trying to hurt us. If they wanted they could have tear us off by now."

Musa, flying past them somersaulted twice on the air.

"Did you guys see that? Let me do it again." He followed up with a few more somersaults.

"I can do it too." Preeti said.

Soon she found out it wasn't as easy as Musa made it look like. Her Disk spun perfectly in any way when it wanted but to make it do what she wanted was a different story. After a few futile attempts she gave up.

"Not working?" Ivana came to her.

"Nope." Preeti said. "This thing doesn't want to do it."

Shahed and Zaki had just flown close to them.

"We must go to the castle, girls." Shahed shouted.

The rain was still falling and the lightning continued to strike sporadically accompanied by the belated howling of the thunders.

Shahed had to shout again at the top of his voice to get the attention of Preeti and Ivana. Once they got the idea, Shahed then moved to fetch romping Musa. Even dad-son's combined screaming failed to get his attention. Annoyed, Preeti flew after him and was able to give him the message. Musa came down flying.

"What's going on guys? Zaki, come with me. It's miraculous."

Zaki wasn't in a mode to enjoy this unwanted air trip. Though not as scared as he thought he'd be, he couldn't totally forget the fact that they were so up in the ground that the creek looked like a thin thread. "What are you doing?" He scolded. "We have to go to the castle. Remember, we are here to save my cousin."

That worked, sort of. Instead of flying all over the place he now limited his maneuvers close to the team. They carefully advanced toward the castle, making sure not to bounce into the monster birds.

Shahed looked around for the older kids – Stanley and Oliver. It was hard to see too far as the large number of pterodactyls hovered around, each covering quite a bit of space. After gliding forward by a quarter of a kilometer they found the two boys together. The boys had seen them first and flew at them.

"We couldn't go too far." Oliver said.

"The closer we got to the castle," Stanley added, "more and more birds came at us. We have been stuck in this area for minutes now."

"What are the birds actually doing?" Shahed asked.

"Nothing." Stanley said. "Just won't let us through. We tried going down, shooting up, nothing worked. They just followed us and blocked us."

Shahed looked around. The boys made sense. He could clearly see the presence of the pterodactyls grew denser near the castle.

"What do we do now?" Ivana said.

"We need something bigger and powerful to cut through their defense line." Zaki said. "These Flying Disks are great but too light."

"We have to move forward." Shahed insisted. "Let's stay close to each other and try to push through them."

Holding hands, the team advanced in a semi circle. However, the monster birds showed no mercy and menacingly flew too close to them. This feat worked perfectly to scare off the humans and the Disks as well.

Frustrated, Preeti said, "Where's Johra? We needed her now. This plan is not working."

"The Disks wouldn't take her." Zaki replied. "She is down there on the mountain."

Shahed was helpless. He didn't know what else to do. He looked back at the mountain behind searching for Johra.

She wasn't there. Where did she go?

Johra must have tried a few dozen times before she finally got the lasso to slip through a Pterodactyl's neck. The bird gave up a chilling shriek and took off frantically trying to get rid of the unwanted noose. Johra was pulled right into the air, holding the other end of the rope for her life. The bird flew erratically as the noose pressed against its throat supporting the full weight of Johra. Deafened with its intense screams, Johra started to climb up the rope.

After a few agonizing moments she succeeded in pulling herself up on the back of the pterodactyl. She grasped the bird by its long feather and tried to guide it. Not consenting, the giant bird shook its long wings vehemently, trying to throw her off. Johra held on to the feathers and flattened her body against its back to reduce resistance to air. No matter what she wasn't about to let go as that would mean falling all the way to the valley - over a kilometer below.

After a little while things started to get better. The monster bird seemed to realize that she was not any serious threat to it and slowly calmed down. Another few minutes and it even started to respond to Johra's slight pulls on the neck feathers.

"Y-a-h-o-o-h-o-o!" Johra couldn't resist herself from giving out a victory cry.

Now she'd to look for the rest of the team. She doubted they could have gone too far. The castle was clearly well guarded by the birds. She'd to fly around a little bit before she spotted the team, literally stuck inside the circle of defense by a group of persistent pterodactyls. She built up some momentum by making her bird fly in circles and beamed through the defense. Her sight was a definite blessing to the frustrated team.

"Johra!" They screamed so loudly that even some of the monster birds startled away.

"Look like they are taking their jobs pretty seriously." She said gleefully.

"Where were you?" Stanley complained. "We have been looking for you."

"I was catching a bird for dinner!" Johra smiled. "What do we have here?"

"They are just trying to restrict us." Ivana said. "Seems like a video game. The higher the level the tougher it gets. We are half way down to the castle but can't go any further because of this dense barrier that these monster birds have created."

Johra examined the barrier for a long moment. The fearsome monster birds circled the sky in front of them in tremendous numbers, almost obstructing the view beyond them. The way they swung their wings and kicked in the air that was more than sufficient to discourage even an elephant to try to penetrate the defense wall.

"We need to ride the birds like Johra." Zaki said.

"And how are we going to do that? Beg them?" Preeti sharply said.

"Why don't you all climb up on my bird?" Johra said. "There's enough room for all of us."

She tried to hold the bird still in the air as the kids attempted to sit on the back of it. The bird didn't like the idea at all and quickly shook away anybody else who sat on it. Johra had to abandon that idea and come up with another.

"Gang, make up a single line holding each other's hand. Shahed, please stay at the front of the line because you'll have to hold one of the feet of my bird. I'll try to fly through the barrier. If I am successful it'll create sufficient room for all of you to squeeze through. Stay very close to me and don't lose your grip. Ready to go?"

"Yes!" came the screaming answer.

With Shahed and Zaki at the front, the rest of the team lined up keeping as close as possible without banging into each other's Disks.

"Hold hands." Johra shouted. "Tightly, so that none of you are thrown away."

They did accordingly and looked like a string with beads.

Johra flew ahead of the line and took her bird close to Shahed so that he could grab one of the toes of its giant feet. This was a little scary for Shahed as the toes had sharp knife like nails. A little jerk could cut his hand off. After a few tries he was able to safely grab one of the toes.

Johra gently slapped on the back of the bird signaling it to move ahead. It seemed to understand what she wanted and flew ahead in full speed. As it pushed through the dense wall of birds it created a passage large enough for the team to slip through. While they were able to penetrate a little deeper into the defense line, Johra knew the barrier close to the Castle was too dense to negotiate. There were just way too many monster pterodactyls to push away.

She quickly changed direction and shot up at the clear sky, rising until they passed the last group of hovering birds. They were now flying way above the Castle and the guarding monsters.

"I don't think those birds would follow us this high." Johra said.

"I hope not." Shahed said, apprehensively.

Unobstructed the team now flew quickly toward the mysterious castle.

As they came close to the castle they were truly mesmerized by the extravagant beauty of it, especially the mixture of elegant medieval architectural style with slick modern style. In the midst of tall stony minarets and large domes there were complex rectangular shapes and rooms with clear glass fronts, something that can only be seen in the modern high tech buildings. As they flew over the castle to a nearby peak where they intended to land, out of the reach of the monster birds, something got their attention. They noticed someone standing behind a glass panel watching them. They readily recognized the lean frame behind the glass.

"Farina!" The kids screamed in sheer joy and waved vigorously.

Farina, stricken by pure astonishment, even forgot to wave back as the team flew past her quickly to avert being crashed by a group of rushing pterodactyls.

Chapter 28

The Medieval Ship

Since Farina returned from the Tower she didn't dare to think that she'd see the beautiful picturesque view anytime soon. Her wall-to-wall glass window had turned into an opaque wall. But when suddenly the glass window returned, she was surprised. It wasn't clear whether it was the Princess or the Magician who had the heart to do so. She'd just cautiously stood near the window when Flyball whispered into her ears, "Doesn't sound very good."

There could only be one meaning of that. The tiny machine thought the window returned because somebody wanted Farina to see something unpleasant.

Nothing unusual happened for a little while. Everything looked nice, quiet and normal. Then all on a sudden hell broke down on the valley. The sunlight disappeared, clouds rolled in, lightning rocked, thunders boomed and finally the rain fell heavily. It was unexpected, unusual.

Farina knew right away something was brewing and it couldn't be anything good. Soon, from a passage somewhere in the castle, poured out tenacious looking monster prehistoric birds, pterodactyls - she readily knew; hundreds and hundreds of them.

In minutes they literally filled out the sky ahead of

the castle, relentlessly circling in small groups. It was obvious that they were guarding the castle.

A little later, a much smaller disk like objects that spun around its own axis poured out and zoomed away from the castle. She couldn't figure out whether they were just gadgets or some kind of strange looking animals. If pterodactyls can be revived than why can't a disk be alive? A little observation revealed that the birds and the Disks were not exactly on friendly terms. The tenacious birds attacked the Disks whenever they came too close. The slick looking Disks were quick and effortlessly moved away from the attacks, unhurt.

Few minutes later, she noticed an increase in movement among the bird shield. She couldn't see much but hoped this had nothing to do with either Roger or Uncle Shahed and the gang. In her mind she really hoped that the kids had gone home with Uncle Shahed. That was the only rational thing to do, taking them away from any danger.

Just when these thoughts were crossing her mind she saw the unbelievable - a group of humans flying high in the sky, higher than the birds and the castle. She briskly walked as close to the window as she could without pressing her nose on it, to see the flying figures. As the kids saw her and waved she was shocked and ecstatic both at the same time.

What were they doing up in the sky? She wondered. Why would Uncle Shahed bring them here? It just didn't make any sense.

"What's going on?" She asked Flyball.

"Looks like boss wanted them here." It replied. "Don't worry. They should be fine."

"Fine? Is that what you call fine? Surfing desperately on a disk like object so that the monster birds can't tear you off?" Farina felt truly angry.

"I guess one might question boss's judgment." Flyball whispered.

Farina saw the team follow a pterodactyl to a nearby peak. Was it Johra sitting on the bird? It was too far to see clearly, as the team had moved on far ahead. She'd no clue what was happening. Sygods she expected, Johra being one of them didn't look out of place. But where were the others of the Sygods? Where was Roger?

She saw Johra landed her bird on a flat section of the peak right next to the one where the castle was located. It was at least half a kilometer away from where she stood. The rest of the team safely landed near Johra. This was a relief to Farina though she'd no clue how they planned to enter the castle. Even if by some miracle they found a way to get in, how Uncle Shahed, Johra and a gang of clueless kids were going to rescue her?

Johra climbed down her bird and allowed it to fly away. The rest of the team was still on their Flying Disks. They were standing on a small rocky platform near the castle. This was part of the same mountain where the castle was built. The descent was steep but doable.

"I think that's as far as you can use the Flying Disks." Johra said. "If you try to fly it anywhere near the castle the birds are going to attack."

"Do we have to walk to the castle from here" Ivana asked.

"That's the only option we got." Johra said.

Looking ahead they could see the sprawling castle, quiet and mystic – just a few hundred meters away. There were no boundary walls, fences, gates or any visible entry point. It looked like as if the whole castle was carved out of the mountain.

"Where is the entrance?" Zaki said.

"I don't see any." Stanley replied.

"It's weird." Oliver remarked.

"There got to be a way to get in." Ivana said.

"May be it's on the other side of the mountain, the side we can't see from here." Preeti chipped in.

"I can go and check it out." Musa couldn't wait to fly on his Disk again.

"No!" Johra warned. "Don't forget the birds."

"We have to take a decision quickly." Shahed said. "We can't stand here too long. We might get hit by the lightning."

"The pterodactyls may come chasing us too." Zaki said.

Johra quickly browsed through the area. "Let's climb down first." She said. "Then we'll look for an entrance. Don't forget, Dragan wanted us here. He has to let us in."

"I was expecting to hear from him by now." Shahed said. "We made it to the castle. The game should change now. This weather is a killer. We are all soaked."

"He must have other plans." Zaki dejectedly said.

"Let's move on." Johra rushed them. "There's no use standing here in rain."

Shahed and the kids gently stepped out of their respective Flying Disks. The objects seemed to detect their intention. They released the invisible grips allowing their riders to detach from them.

"I wish I could keep mine." Musa said, with a deep sigh.

"Me too. They were like really fun." Stanley roared.

Once released the Disks quickly flew away from them.

"We are on our feet again." Zaki was relieved.

Johra had just taken a few steps down the hill when something really unexpected happened. A roaring sound approached them fast. It seemed like coming from the clouds above head, a sound of deluge or rushing water. They looked at each other.

"What's that?" Stanley yelled.

Nobody needed to reply because they just saw it pouring over their head – a large column of water! Before they could even totally figure out what it really was the flow of the rushing water had moved the ground from below their feet and carried them to the edge of the peak and then beyond, dropping them to the ground - way below. Terrified, they frantically screamed their lungs out.

When Farina saw an outlandish flash flood throwing the gang of the mountain into a very long fall, she was utterly socked and speechless. This was not something that she'd even imagined. Falling from such height would definitely kill everybody.

"Don't worry." Flyball knew what was going on in her mind. "They'll fall into a wooden ship, unhurt. The ship is steering through a rocky channel on rough water. They'll have to pass through it without being smashed by the rocks."

Farina noticed with amazement that the outside view have changed dramatically. Instead of the usual valley and mountains she was now seeing a large medieval wooden ship, rocking dangerously in the midst of a stormy sea as the howling high waves crashed against its body. Just ahead of it was a tiny passage among a series of submerged rocky boulders, just enough for the ship to slip through.

"What's happening?" Farina was surprised.

"Consider this glass panel as a large screen." Flyball

replied. "This is what boss wants you to see."

She could see Shahed, Johra and the kids, safe and sound, standing on the deck of the ship, staring ahead with total disbelief as their ship rapidly advanced toward the submerged rocks.

Farina panicked. "None of them have any experience in handling a ship." She grumbled. "What kind of game is this? What's going to happen if the ship hits the rocks?"

"No idea. But accidents are bad - real or imaginary. This is a tough test. This must be the Princess's idea."

"I've some experience with small sail boats." Farina was desperately looking for a way to help the hapless team. "If I could join them I might be able to help them. Do you know of any ways to get there?"

"On that ship?" Flyball said hesitantly. "Well, I do. Let's check if I've any restriction in my memory." He paused for a moment. "Nope. You are in luck."

"Can you hurry up, please?" Farina almost yelled at the poor machine.

"On our way to the Tower there was a second escalator going down, remember? Take that." Flyball whispered.

"That'll take me to the ship?"

"Yes."

"Sorry, I screamed at you."

"You are a sweet girl. Go now."

"Are you coming?"

"Only up to the escalator." Flyball said. "I do not have permission to leave the castle. The Tower is considered part of the castle but not the ship."

"Damn! Let's go."

Chapter 29

The Deadly Sea

Farina didn't waste any time. She burst out of the door and ran through the corridor. She'd no idea what game the weird scientist was playing but she just couldn't stand there and watch something horrible happening to those kids.

It felt like mere seconds before Farina stepped out of the corridor and stepped onto the hanging platform where the two giant escalators moved on opposite directions. Looking at the one moving down Farina could see very little as it disappeared beyond a dense layer of fog. It looked scary, illusive. But Farina knew she'd to win her fear. Flyball would not lie to her. It had no reason to. Not to her knowledge.

"Trust me." Flyball confirmed. "This will take you to the ship. It looks scary but you'll be okay."

Farina took a deep breath and stepped on the escalator.

Instantly the escalator sped up, forcing Farina to sit down to keep from falling. In a blink of an eye she'd passed through thick layers of fog and discovered herself on the deck of the wooden ship. She didn't even realize exactly when the escalator disappeared from under her feet. Everything happened so quickly that it almost felt like a dream.

However, once on the deck of the ship, the raging sea around her quickly revealed a clear truth - this wasn't a visual magic. The ship, the sea and the tormenting waves all were real, at least felt as real as it could be. It was obvious that either the Magician or the crazy princess had set this strange game up for them. She felt angry. There was no sense in putting a group of young kids through such risky and traumatic experience. Shouldn't a scientist have more sense than this?

It took Farina a little bit to get accustomed to the constant rocking of the ship. She couldn't figure out how such large waves appeared suddenly in the middle of nowhere. Standing at the middle of a three mast medieval ship, she wasn't sure whether she should be surprised or panicked. How did the Magician make this possible?

She didn't get much time to analyze the situation. The ship shook dangerously as a huge wave slammed onto it. Farina quickly held a rope nearby to secure her.

Once safe and settled she looked around to find the rest of the team. It didn't take her too long as they were just yards away, still in very much shock after the long fall into the medieval ship surrounded by monstrous waves. None of them had ever been on a ship leave alone a wooden one. Scared and panicky they grabbed the nearest ropes that they could find and hanged onto them amid the nauseating rocking of the ship and the spilling waves. When Farina appeared there like magic, their eyes popped out.

"This is some kind of scientific magic." Farina said, shouting over the howling waves. "I believe it's an illusion."

"How did you get here?" Shahed grinned even in such disastrous situation.

"On a giant escalator!" Farina replied. "This whole place is weird."

Johra was standing near Shahed. She happily waved at her.

"Great! We won't have to rescue you anymore." She said.

"What's all this about?" Preeti sounded mad.

"Where is this ship taking us?" Ivana bitterly asked.

Farina shrugged. "I've no clue. I assume it is part of the game."

"Game! This is a game?" Stanley roared. "Magician, you suck!"

"You suck beyond imagination." Oliver added.

"Do you know how to operate this ship?" Johra asked. She looked restless, keen to do something.

"No. I've a little experience with sail boats." Farina replied.

The ship bruised past a sharp edge of a protruding rock. They could hear wood cracking below. The deck tilted dangerously for a few long moments before leveling up. The kids screamed at the top of their voices.

"We are going to drown! Oh God, we are going to drown!" Stanley cried out, shaken.

Ivana pointed at the water passage ahead dotted with sharp tips of submerged rocks, strong enough to tear off any ship - metal or wood. "I think we are going to smash into those rocks." She shouted.

It was inevitable. They had at most a few minutes before that happened.

"We could dive into the water and swim away." Musa suggested.

"I can't swim." Oliver's voice shook as he spoke. "Beside how are you going to swim in this crazy water?"

Farina tried to assess the situation quickly. The oars and the masts were all in place and intact. Only the main mast had a loose piece of sail. It was necessary to tie it back in. Nobody was at the steering wheel either. Shahed noticed it about the same time.

"I'll take the steering wheel." He said. "Which way should I turn?"

"Away from the rocks." Farina said. "Hurry up, Uncle. Watch your steps."

Shahed walked as fast as he could, laboring to keep his balance by holding anything that he could reach to. A stream of water gushed over the deck, right under his feet. One bad step and he could get swept away into the dancing waves.

Once he reached the steering wheel, he tried to turn it clockwise, away from the rocks. It gave no indication of moving, even a tiny bit. Looking forward he trembled in fear. The strong current was pushing the ship toward the rocks even faster than before. If the ship hit the rocks the outcome was crystal clear – a shipwreck. The whole thing was bound to break into pieces after such impact.

He tried once more to move the steering wheel with every bit of strength he'd in his body, but to no avail. He shook his head in pure frustration.

Farina didn't expect too much. When the ship continued in its course she knew the steering was jammed. Now the only way to steer off the rocks was to use the sails.

Johra must have read her mind. "We can try to change the direction of the main sail." She said.

"That's not an easy task. This is a big sail." Farina knew the situation was helpless. They could barely take a step without fearing to be swept away, how would they maneuver the sail?

Zaki, pale and shaky, stood nearby holding a rope tightly. "Farina, did you notice that torn sail?" He said.

"We can't fix it." Farina said. "It's too late. Nothing

can help us now."

Preeti panicked. "Are we all going to die? Is this really happening? Can we actually die in magic?"

Everybody looked at Farina, expecting answers. Farina scrambled to find a suitable answer, something that would soothe the kids, but she simply didn't know what to say. Only the psycho scientist and his crazy daughter knew their fate.

Suddenly Musa started to climb up a rope.

"Where are you going?" Farina cried out.

"I can tie that sail back on." Musa replied.

"That's no use. Come back. Musa!" Farina screamed.

Musa didn't stop; he continued to climb up the rope like a skilled seaman. Farina threw her arms in desperation. The ship was rocking heavily on its sides. One loose grip and Musa could get thrown into the turbulent water.

Shahed came back after giving a few more useless thrust to the steering wheel.

"It is jammed." He said to Farina. "We can't escape the collision. Let's stay close. If we stick together our chances of survival will be better."

Oliver and Stanley crawled toward them. Johra helped Ivana and Preeti. Everybody held onto the closest ropes. It was only matter of a minute now before the obvious happened.

"Musa is on the mast! Call him down." Farina said to Shahed.

Shahed looked up. Fifty feet up in the air, hugging a pole in one hand, the skinny boy was desperately trying to get hold of the loose sail that waved like a flag in the stormy wind.

"Musa!" he shouted. "Come down. Quick! We are going to crash."

Musa couldn't possibly hear him in all the noise. He was still trying to grab the sail when suddenly his other hand slipped. To stop his fall he scrambled to grab anything that came on his way. After failing a few times he was able to hold on to a rope to break his fall. As his body dangled in the air like a pendulum everybody on the deck below shrieked fearing something terrible was about to happen.

Before anybody else could react Zaki did a very unusual thing. He started to climb up the thin ladder that was hanging from the main mast.

"Where are you going?" Farina yelled. "Come down. Zaki! Stop him, Uncle Shahed. He'll fall."

"I must help him." Zaki shouted back, trying to concentrate as he climbed up as quickly as he could.

"He is never going to make it." Shahed anxiously said. "I'll go after him. You and Johra stay with the kids."

"I can climb very well." Preeti said. "I am going with Zaki."

She was about to jump on the ladder when Johra came forward and stopped her. "I'll go." She said calmly. "All of you just hang on to your ropes."

She sprung out of the ground and was on her way up the rope. In seconds she caught up with Zaki, said something to him without slowing down. Zaki hesitantly started to come down. Shahed went up a few rung to bring him back on the main deck.

The ship was hurling toward the rocks, just seconds away from smashing into them. Farina hugged the kids and closed her eyes in anticipation of the big crash. Shahed looked up one last time to find out that Johra had helped Musa to a wooden platform.

"Hang on!" He yelled at the top of his voice.

The ship was now moments away from the rocks.

"I love you guys." That was the only thing Farina could think of saying.

The ship floated up on a high wave and as the wave moved away from underneath, it came down heavily right on the deadly rocks.

Chapter 30

The Wild Ride

A few second before the crash something very bizarre happened. A dense fog blew in and shrouded the ship completely. It was so dense that they couldn't even see their own hands.

Everybody aboard the ship was ready for a thundering crash but nothing happened. The ship shook as it rode another rising wave and simply sailed through the fog. Slowly as the fog thinned they noticed with sheer amazement that they have somehow made it past the rocky terrain, unharmed.

"We didn't crash!" Stanley cried out. "Oh, God! I'll definitely be good now."

"What just happened?" Preeti sharply asked.

"Who cares?" Ivana said. "Just be happy that we are still alive."

"It's a magic. We are not going to die." Oliver screamed.

"Land Ho-o-o-o-o" Musa cried out from the mast.

Confused but relieved that they had just averted the deadly shipwreck Farina didn't want to waste time wondering how it happened. She was more interested in knowing exactly what was ahead. The fog had thinned but didn't totally go away. It hung like a sheet of powdery cloud ahead of them.

"I can't take it anymore." Zaki said grimly. "I am getting seasick."

"Try to relax. You'll be fine." Farina comforted.

"Do you see anything, Johra?" Shahed called out. Johra was still up on the mast with Musa.

Johra leaned forward as far as she safely could laboring to see through the sheet of fog.

"Nothing. More waves." She shouted back. "Dragan just spared our lives."

"Spared?" Preeti snared. "That guy is a psycho. I hate him."

Ivana shushed her. "Do you want to get us into more trouble?"

"Just take it easy, Preeti." Zaki begged. "I want to get out of this ship alive."

"You are not going to throw up now, are you?" Preeti cautiously asked.

"If you do," Stanley said, "do it that way. Please!"
He pointed toward Preeti.

Oliver giggled. "Yes, please!"

"It goes in the direction of the wind." Preeti smirked. "And the wind is flowing toward you boys."

Stanley and Oliver paused for a long moment.

"She is right." Oliver muttered.

"Zaki! Don't puke." Stanley begged. "Please! I'll give you ten bucks. I swear upon God."

"I see something." Musa shouted excitedly.

"What is it Musa?" Zaki asked, praying for this torturous journey to end.

"Hang o-o-o-n! A...." Musa said something but his voice was drowned in a sudden gust of wind which also swept away the fog clearing the view.

Looking ahead what they saw ahead was so terrifying

that their tongues froze in their mouths. A WHIRLPOOL! It was massive with a radius of at least hundred feet and looked eager to gobble up just about anything that went near it. Its gigantic size, deafening howl and terrifying spin was so overwhelming that the kids even forgot to shriek.

"N-o-o-o!" Stanley cried out, once he returned to his senses. "We are dead!"

"S-o-o-o dead!" Oliver screeched.

"I knew this was coming." Preeti sobbed.

"I think I am going to pass out." Zaki murmured.

"Be strong, Zaki." Farina pressed his shoulder.

"I am trying." He replied back, his stomach twisting dangerously.

The ship bounced off a few high waves and helplessly headed right into the whirlpool.

"There we go!" Johra shouted. "Hold tight, guys. Be ready for anything."

"I am!" Musa replied with a grin on his face.

Farina watched the giant spinning pool of water faintly hoping this wasn't the end of them. It couldn't be. After all, this was supposed to be a game. Wasn't it?

The ship drifted quickly toward the eye of the whirlpool. She could hear the kids screaming in fear. She knew she'd to say something. She collected all her strength and shouted: "Don't be scared. Remember, this is a ...."
Her words were stolen by the deafening sound of the water. The ship spun helplessly as the whirlpool pulled it right into the center and started to sink in the dark, deep ocean.

Nobody was sure exactly what had happened next but they felt the ship melting away from under their feet. Then, all sound ceased and they were thrown into a space that was soft and airy with unexpected tranquility. They drifted slowly, somewhat dreamy and distant, deeper and deeper into it, as if for eternity.

Suddenly the sleepy calmness was shattered by a glowing sun and they found them thrown into air with the ubiquitous blue sky hovering over them curiously. Fully alert the kids quickly realized they were in a free fall – all the way to the ground. Screaming in mortal fear as they dropped in an incredible speed a thick, white cloud appeared magically and acted as a cushioned buffer to break their fall. Relieved for a split second the team again sensed water around them as they were sucked quickly into a series of giant, near vertical water slides.

Sliding down in lightning speed they did the only thing that made them feel better – screaming and more screaming. There was no time to think or talk. They spent all their energy just to be on their back, balancing through the curves and drops. To Farina it seemed like a never ending journey as they kept on sliding down and down.

As they speared through the final sheets of cottony clouds that hung lazily underneath them the misty land down below with large patches of green dotted with gray lines became visible. Not knowing where the rides ended all that came to their minds was that they were going to crash right into the ground.

Petrified, Farina tried to put her attention away from the obvious. Clearly this was another visual illusion. All she'd to do was to make her mind not believe it, she thought. She looked around to find others. They were nearby, screaming in pure horror.

"Don't look down!" She shouted at the top of her voice. "Close your eyes. This is just an I-L-L-U-S-I-O-N!"

Her words were lost in the thundering water that rushed down the slides. Farina fought her urge to look down. No matter what, she wasn't going to be fooled.

A few long moments passed by as she waited for something to happen, not sure what. Suddenly she saw a heavy, cool mist rushing up spreading in all direction. As she is driven into it she felt she was slowing down. Her vision blurred she continued to fall, clearly decelerating at a high rate. For couple of seconds everything turned dark and quiet, right before she plunged into a shallow pool of water. Gasping for air she swam up instinctively. She could see bright light reflecting on the surface just above. With a few strong kicks she rose above the water. Pulling in lungs full of air she briskly checked around and discovered in utter amazement, she was inside an enormous indoor swimming pool. The slide that brought her here was clearly visible and went right through the roof of the huge facility that housed the swimming pool.

She looked for others. Nobody else was there. Before she'd time to worry they came sliding down in packs and plunged into the pool. Farina helped the kids out of the water to the shiny granite floor. Shahed pulled himself out of the water and crashed on the floor. He looked shocked.

"Where are we? This is now starting to boggle my mind."

"Starting to?" Preeti snapped. "I am about to lose mine."

"I can't take it anymore." Stanley dejectedly said. "My mind is already blown up."

"I can't even feel my head." Oliver added.

"That's exactly what Dragan wants." Johra said as she suspiciously looked around. "He likes to impress."

"That was cool!" Musa didn't lose his grin yet. "I wish I could do it one more time."

"You are a nut." Zaki muttered. He was fully drained.

"That was a great ride, admit it guys." Musa insisted.

"Yeah! It was one hell of a ride." Stanley agreed.

"It was really scary. I thought we were drowning and then I saw the sky!" Oliver chipped in.

"I want no more of this." Preeti said. "Thank you very much, Mr. Magic man."

"I'd enough too." Ivana said exhaustedly.

"I am so hungry that I can eat a full cow." Stanley declared.

"Can you guys keep quiet please?" Zaki said wearily. "Why are we here? Where is the Magician?"

Good question. They looked around, inquiring. Nobody was there.

Right at that moment a large door at the far end of the hall room opened up silently and a man of average height with unusually wide shoulders walked in. His rough face and powerful steps clearly showed his strength. Once he came close enough he spoke in a soft voice. "I am Gombu. I am an associate of the Magician. Come with me. Everything is ready for you."

"Nepali Sherpa!" Zaki whispered. "World's toughest people."

"Looks like a gorilla." Oliver muttered.

"If he hears that he'll tear you off." Stanley cautioned.

"Will you boys keep your mouth shut?" Preeti barked.

"Don't be so bossy." Stanley objected.

Gombu gave them a hard look. This worked like a magic. All talking ceased. They quietly followed him to the change rooms located at the other end of facility.

"You'll find your lockers inside." Gombu said. "They are labeled. Once you are ready Diego will take you to the dining room."

Farina could not hide her amazement. "Dining room!"

"Boss is a hospitable man." Gombu said in expressionless voice. "A big feast has been prepared for you."

He gave them no more opportunity to ask any additional questions and quickly walked out of the room. The door shut down behind him, quietly. They didn't even hear his footsteps.

"He looks dangerous!" Stanley whispered.

"Like a big tiger!" Oliver consented.

Farina felt relaxed. "The food sounds just terrific. After all these juggling and shuffling my appetite has just soared."

"There must be something else that he didn't tell us." Johra was even more suspicious now. "We have to be careful."

"What's the use?" Shahed said. "We can't stop anything. He is just playing with us."

"Are we going to change now?" Stanley was impatient. "I am really hungry. I can't wait for the feast to begin."

Everybody was hungry, no denying that. The change rooms were gender based. They divided and walked inside. There was a locker assigned to each of them with their names written on it, just as Gombu said. Inside the lockers they found brand new outfits.

Strangely enough, each of them got their favorite outfits. Zaki had the Spider Man, Musa Batman, Stanley Power Ranger and Oliver Star wars villain Dark Vader. Only Shahed received a traditional pant and shirt.

"Why did I get so unlucky?" He said in fake disappointment. "Once upon a time I wanted to be the Superman."

This drew some giggle.

On the other change room, Ivana received a princess's dress, Preeti Bat woman, Farina an Angel and Johra of a Cheetah.

Johra turned her dress around and checked carefully. "You can't be sure about Dragan. He is always scheming."

The other girls had already gotten themselves into their dresses and thought Johra was being too psychotic. When they came out the boys were already impatiently pacing up and down the hall room.

"What took you so long?" Stanley impatiently said. "I am so hungry! Oh, my God!"

"Oh, shut up!" Preeti retorted. "We already heard that ten times."

Chapter 31

The Scheming General

Seattle. General Bowman's seaside villa. A few very high-level government representatives have gathered here for a highly classified meeting. Among the guests were a few influential senators and congressmen. They sat silently around a round table in a completely isolated room. This was done to ensure their full safety. General requested his guests to help themselves with drinks and foods that he'd arranged and excused himself from the room with the promise that he'd be back in no time. Most didn't have any appetite for liquor for the time being. The Magician alias Dragan Valcovich was a serious issue and nobody wanted anything to influence their thought process when discussing about him.

General, sitting in his study, was quickly finishing up a conversation with his trusted associate Colonel Don Blake.

"What's your situation, Don?"

"I am fully ready sir." Don Blake strongly said.

"Did you find Dragan's location?"

"Roughly. He is a very clever man. He used some new technology around his camp to bluff the satellite cameras. That's why our searches in the Coast Mountains area revealed nothing." Colonel sounded excited.

"How did you find him then? Did you follow Roger?"

"Negative. Roger is a careful man. It would be very difficult to follow him without being detected. So I came up with an alternative plan. We implanted a small transmitter into Farina's skin when she went visiting the hanging bridge."

"Yes, I heard about the stunt." General sounded a little annoyed. "Your men were followed. Are you dealing with capable men?"

"That was a minor setback." Colonel tried to downplay it.

"Who were they? Many eye witnesses told the TV reporters there were three men who came chasing the two attackers." General wanted to get deeper into it.

"Don't know Sir. Could be anybody." Colonel briefly said.

"They were not with Roger, right?"

"Not those three, no." confirmed Don Blake.

"Good. He does have the power to jeopardize our mission. So, what's the plan now?" General was unhappy but decided to move on.

"Well, following the signal from the transmitter we now have an idea where Dragan took Farina." Colonel Don was happy to get out of the grill. "Once I get your blessings I am going to go right in."

"The Senators and the Congressmen are here. I don't think it would be hard to get their approval. They'll inform the President and also take necessary steps to get permission from our Canadian counterpart." General said.

"Convincing the Canadians shouldn't be a problem. Just mentioning the name 'Dragan' brings hiccup to any government. I am sure they'll be more than eager to kick him out of Canada."

"Listen Don," General paused for a moment. "Make

sure he doesn't escape. That would be disastrous."

"No question of that, sir. Failure is not my options."
He hesitated for a tiny second. "What about Roger?"

General was quiet for a few seconds before he spoke
again. "Do whatever is best, Don."

Don Blake knew what that meant. He coldly said,
"Don't worry, sir. It'll be taken care of."

General put the receiver back on the cradle. He
picked up a file. He was going to present some vital
information before his influential guests. One of his main
pressing points was the fact that Dragan did not keep his
promise with American government. He'd signed an
agreement with the government agreeing to jointly
implement the new technology that he was working on,
which he named MEGANANO.

America funded his doubtful but potentially
enormous research projects on nanotechnology with
hundreds of millions of dollars. But once his research started
to show some solid results he simply disappeared. Just
thinking about the audacity of such treason irritated the
General. How dare he?

He also had a few other irrefutable points in his
collection to present including the possibility of a nanobomb,
which may be sold to the enemies of America along with
Meganano. Also, he'd mention that Dragan attempted to kill
a possible eyewitness who was in a coma and tried to kidnap
the only daughter of the eyewitness, an outstanding chess
player, a jewel of America! He was confident his guests
would have no issues in agreeing with him that they had to
take drastic measure against the crazy thug. They must. Don
had already taken all the measures to attack. There was no
turning back.

Chapter 32

The Mirage

The Sygods found themselves in a visual maze. They could see the castle at the top of the mountain quite clearly, however the more they advanced the more it looked distant. They had rested a few hours in the morning and believing it to be safe to move ahead climbed down from the rocks where they ended up when chased by the horrifying wolves. Roger didn't want to wait until the nightfall fearing the wolves might return and limit their movement seriously.

They walked for hours, past the creek and across the plains. To cut the overall distance to the castle they moved diagonally through the plains. However, the castle seemed to remain as far as it ever was, like a mirage.

Patiently they continued through giant grasses and bushes and dense woods. The good part was that there was virtually nothing to challenge them. The only living things they saw were squirrels and chirping birds. The day was warm and sunny. Everything seemed peaceful. No more attacks of any kind. They weren't sure whether it was good or bad. Obviously, Dragan had the knowledge that they were coming. If he decided not to stop them on their way to the castle then he must have had other plans. What was it?

Finally around noon they made it to the other end of the valley, to the edge of the series of mountains. From here they would have to walk uphill through a linked forest to the foot of the mountain that held the castle at the top. Next they would attempt to climb up to the castle.

As always, Hong Lee and Hong Shien led the group, the rest followed closely. Dylan, staying at the end of the group, frequently grumbled about this never-ending journey.

"What's the meaning of this joke?" He finally spoke up. "How can he even make a whole mountain keep moving backward on us? There got to be some trick to it. Why doesn't he face me in the ring? I'll put him to his senses."

"Watch it! He may be hearing you." Rana cautioned.

"I am not scared of him." Dylan whispered. He definitely didn't forget about the horrific experience with the ferocious wolves and definitely didn't want to start another two legged vs. four legged frenzied running competition.

Miller looked impatient as well. His hands touched the rifle often. Clearly he was much more interested in shooting at something than just walking for hours after hours.

At noon Roger had the team stop for a brief rest. Walking up the mountains was no easy task. They could now see the castle sitting proudly on a peak of the mountain. Finally they were cutting down the distance. Somehow the mirage effect of the castle had waned off. Perhaps, whatever technique Dragan was using was more effective from a distance, thought Roger.

Rana was still holding the GPS device in his hand. He noticed the signal got stronger as they continued to walk toward the castle. This was a temporary relief for Roger. At least they knew where Farina was. Most of all, he knew where Dragan was. He probably should have called Shahed to give him some update but after pondering about it he decided not to. If Shahed had already filed a police report they could try to trace Roger's calls and find his location. He didn't want that, by no means.

After a light meal consisting mainly high calorie dry food the team took off again. They had already spent more time than planned and didn't want to delay any more. Advancing in the daylight increased the risk of being spotted but they didn't worry about that anymore. Dragan obviously knew they were coming. As always, they walked carefully, keeping as much cover as possible.

The sun continued its drop in the west, the warmth slowly decreased into a comfortable coolness. It took the team another couple of hours before they finally came to a point from where the foot of the *castle mountain* was within twenty minutes walk. Standing inside a lightly populated woods Roger looked ahead across the plains to the castle mountain. To reach there they must get out of their cover and walk through open fields exposing them to possible attacks.

Roger knew it was too risky. They would be within the range of a gunshot from the castle. Dragan could simply have his snipers sit in the comfort of the castle and blow the Sygods off, one by one. Perhaps that's why he didn't even try to stop them. He knew where he could get them easily. He was just waiting patiently.

"I know what you are thinking." Rana said.

"We are going to be easy targets." Roger said thoughtfully.

"Even if we make it to the mountain," Dylan said, "how are we going to get up there?"

He was pointing at the Castle up above.

"That got to be over a mile high," Miller said.

"We have to climb." Roger said.

"Of course! How silly of me." Dylan was sarcastic. "A

vertical surface - only a mile high. Piece of cake! Miller, what you have to say?"

Miller cleared his throat. "Don't they have an elevator?"

"Nay, they have flying unicorns." Dylan joked.

Roger chuckled. "I didn't come here unprepared."

"Oh, I know," Dylan said, "Some of Orenda's ridiculous gazettes. I am not stepping on any of them. None of her antigravity things ever worked."

"This one does. I tried it." Roger said smilingly. "Now, let's cook up a quick plan. I don't feel comfortable attempting to climb up in clear daylight. We'll be too exposed. I suggest we wait out rest of the daylight and attempt it after dark."

"Beautiful!" Dylan mocked. "Doesn't that sound really good?"

The Hong brothers loved the idea. They didn't like the uneventful day and suspected the scheming scientist was up to something very serious.

"You scared!" Hong Shien teased Dylan.

"You no like dark. Hah! Hah!" Hong Lee was uncharacter-istically jocular.

"Great!" Dylan rolled his eyes. "Now even the Hongs are making fun of me. Which way did the sun rise today?"

"You are a funny guy."

"Very funny."

The brothers chuckled together.

"There are still a few hours of sun left." Rana said. "We should seek better hideout. This part is too sparsely treed. We won't get good cover if attacked."

The brothers agreed readily. They pointed at a dense forest just past the next hill. "Good! No see."

"Yeah! Good. No see." Dylan taunted.

They walked carefully around the hill and took shelter inside the densely populated pine forest. Here they would wait until it was dark.

Chapter 33

The Deadly Hunters

At the approaching of dusk they left their hideout and started for the base of the castle mountain. Things had been awfully quiet, something that started to worry Roger. He couldn't be sure anymore exactly how things were being unfolded. Was Dragan still in the castle or he decided to abandon it?

Rana's handheld GPS monitor went mum for a while now. This could mean only two things. One, Drgan found the bug planted in Farina's stomach. Two, he'd already moved out of here taking Farina with him. They should have probably waited until it was darker but Roger simply couldn't wait any longer. If Dragan was really gone he wanted to know it as soon as possible. Dylan was particularly happy about the early start. He was not a willing climber and preferred to do that at least when his eyes worked better.

Minutes later as they walked past a few huge boulders they found themselves staring at a group of fearsome warriors menacingly rushing toward them. The warriors consisted of three different groups of fighters - samurais, stick fighters and kick boxers.

"Oh God! They haven't forgotten about us." Dylan sighed. "Can't we have a little peace on this green planet of ours?"

"Fight first; peace later," Miller said. He seemed happy. Finally some action.

"This is not looking good." Rana was apprehensive. He wasn't sure if they were strong enough to hold this army.

"Amen to that." Dylan said.

"He is still here." Roger was relieved. This was a good sign. The last thing he wanted was Dragan disappearing taking Farina with him.

There was less than five seconds to prepare for the battle. The razor sharp blades of the samurai swords cut through air in unbelievable speed, looking for victims. The attack was vicious, ferocious. The blood stained eyes of the enemy looked traumatizing. Being the focus of the samurai attack, Hong Lee and Hong Shien sprung into air and separated forcing the samurais to divide into two groups. It was clear that the warriors planned to take care of the brothers first using their most effective group while the rest tried to subdue the other members of the team.

The Samurais were quick and determined as they used their weapons with maximum force and skill, cutting through thick branches and leaves like papers while chasing the two brothers deeper in the woods.

Hong Lee knew it would be difficult fighting against a dozen expert samurais. Instead of directly involving into a face-to-face battle he went for a more strategic approach. He tried to run swiftly into increasingly denser woods hoping to divide the pursuers into even smaller groups by confusing them about his exact location.

His plan didn't go very well. His pursuers, the mighty Samurais, were just as fast. They quickly surrounded him. Left with no other choice Hong Lee did what he did best. He fought back. Attacked by several samurais he quickly moved aside to avoid a swishing sword and simultaneously grabbed another attackers arm, dislodged it from its socket with one forceful jerk and effortlessly took his sword away.

Now the scenario changed quickly. With a sword in hand he was now blazing. Within moments he ran havoc on his attackers. His sword moved around him in a freakish speed. He mercilessly attacked his enemies, cutting through their defense easily and forcing them to either retreat or ending up in a bloody defeat. Soon, he was the only one standing with a sword. Now he ran to check on his brother.

Hong Shien had a vigorous fight as well. However, he liked bare hands than a samurai sword to limit him. With his extremely agile and fast movement he made it impossible for his enemies to touch him, with their fist or swords. In between changing places he threw deadly punches and kicks in flashing speed. The hapless samurais who attacked him soon became completely disorganized and ended up accidentally slashing each other. When Hong Lee reached his brother the battle had already ended with several warriors on the ground while the rest fled.

They didn't waste time congratulating each other. Winning battles like these were expected to them. Any other outcome would be extremely disappointing. They now rushed to help rest of the team.

Miller, Rana and Roger were trying to stop the stick fighters. Even though they were equipped with guns and blowpipe they looked sort of helpless against the half a dozen attackers who spun their sticks with such power and speed that even bullets were being reflected. Slowly and surely the stick fighters were gaining on them as they steadily closed on.

Just tens of yards away Dylan alone fought bravely against another half a dozen kick boxers. As a boxer he excelled but his kicks were no better than a foolhardy donkey throwing its hind legs. So, Dylan mostly tried to stay away from any attacks and threw deadly punches only when his attackers braved to come too close to him. That was his best friend, the punches. One good punch could knock down just about anybody. Unfortunately the kick boxers were no fool themselves and kept a safe distance only except when they attacked. Yet, Dylan didn't do too badly. With two knocked down he only had to deal with four more of them. The remaining four barely gave him time to rest. They continuously attacked him from all four sides, trying to confuse him and weaken him. Dylan hanged on, subjecting his opponents with barrage of curse and abuses.

"Come, come closer, you nasty good-for-nothings. I'll kiss you with my fist. Not the kicks! That's so unfair. You just soiled my shirt! You beasts!"

The Hong brothers analyzed the situation quickly and decided Dylan could hold on for a little longer. They picked up couple of sticks from two fallen enemies and attacked back the stick fighters. They spun their sticks just as skillfully and forcefully as the stick fighters and met their resistance with even vigorously. The sticks clashed against each other, swished dangerously in the air and often found their way to the flesh and bones, mostly of the mysterious attackers. To the rest it seemed like just a few seconds before the brothers cornered the stick fighters and with a combination of sticks and lightening kicks easily set their opponents in a fleeing spree.

The kick boxers didn't seem interested in staying behind all by themselves. They turned around and joined their fleeing comrades.

"Does Dragan have a fighter manufacturing facility somewhere in here?" Dylan said, messaging his knuckles.

"Sure sounds like that." Miller said. "Some of these creeps were reflecting bullets with their sticks!"

"Do we keep moving?" Rana asked.

"We have no choice." Roger said. "They know we are coming but at least they can't see us very well. We have to use the darkness of the night."

This time they moved very carefully, checking every turn and every suspicious movement.

Not even ten minutes had passed they were attacked again. This time it was a group of hunters on horses. Carrying modern long range rifles the hunters galloped out of the woods in fearsome speed. This was way more dangerous than anything the Sygods had faced until now. They ran; ran as fast as they could; back into deeper and denser woods, making it difficult for the hunters to follow them on horseback. The hunters persisted on their tail for a little longer but eventually had to give up and retreat.

Once the hunters were nowhere to be seen the Sygods stopped. Suddenly everything had turned very quiet. There was no other sound but the murmur of the leaves as a gentle breeze flew through the woods.

"Where did they go?" Dylan asked. "I hope they didn't turn into ghosts."

"Nothing is impossible here." Miller said. "I just don't want those wolves back."

"I suspect these hunters are just trying to delay us." Rana said. "They didn't shoot any shots."

"They have long range rifles." Roger said. "We can't be sure what their order is. We shouldn't rush until we know their exact intentions. Hong Lee, please display your climbing skill once more."

Hong Lee effortlessly climbed up an oak tree, soon disappearing among branches. He returned in a few minutes. He didn't see anybody around.

Roger frowned in disbelief. "They must have some other plan. Could be hiding behind some rocks."

"Like an ambush?" Miller asked.

Rana pointed at the end of the woods where the land descended gently and merged into the plains. They must cross a section of the plains - a few hundred yards in length - to reach the base of the castle mountain. "That's practically our only way to the castle from here." He said. "These hunters know that."

Dylan was more concerned about climbing the mountain than the deadly hunters. "I can't climb that." He said. "I weigh two hundred twenty pounds, for God's sake! No antigravity device can hold that much weight."

"Don't worry." Roger assured him. "The *jumpies* – that's what Orenda named her new flying shoes - are pretty powerful. It can support up to 300 pounds."

"Not another flying shoe." Dylan joked. "The last one couldn't even lift twenty pounds more than ten feet."

"This one does. It lifted me easily." Roger said.

"How does it really work?" Miller asked curiously.

"Well, it doesn't really make you fly." Roger said. "Each shoe contains a small but strong engine that will be able to support majority of your weight, if not all."

"Majority?" Dylan was unconvinced.

Roger shook his head. "Trust me. It works."

"You are not two hundred and twenty pounds." Dylan muttered.

"Let's leave that aside for now." Roger said. "Let's worry about the hunters."

"Yes, the hunters! More pain in the butt!" Dylan

grumbled.

After scrapping a few ideas they finally came up with a workable plan. There was still considerable risk but they had to do something. The plan was this - Miller, the shooter, would hide inside the woods with his guns ready while the rest would dash out of the woods, get to the plains and run toward the base of the castle mountain. Assuming that the hunters were hiding, they would come out to prey on them. This is when Miller would get another opportunity to prove his shooting skill. Hopefully, he'd be able to do some damage to the hunters, forcing them to retreat.

"You sure you'll be able to do this?" Dylan looked doubtful.

"You keep on talking I may let the hunters have some fun first." Miller said, innocently.

"I was just kidding. Don't get all worked out, brother."

"Kung fu masters, wolves, samurais, hunters, God knows what's next." Roger muttered. "This guy never runs out of ideas. Anyway, we got to go now. You guys ready?"

"I was born ready." Miller was already lying on his chest, his rifle aimed at the plains, finger on the trigger. He was ready.

"Just don't shoot my ass." Dylan murmured.

"Let's do it." Rana said.

"Go!" Roger signaled.

Hong brothers went first; then Dylan followed by Roger; Rana held the end. They shoot out of the woods, bending as low as possible, ran down the slope to the plains and darted toward the base of the mountain ahead. They ran in a zigzag course, frequently wiggling their bodies – a general practice to make it difficult for sharp shooters to hit target.

Nothing happened for the first few minutes. They had covered more than half the distance and still nobody came chasing after them. Did the hunters already left? Roger had just started to wonder when he heard the sure sound of galloping horses – closing on to them. They were right! The goons were indeed hiding, looking for an opportunity to attack.

"Take me God! Take me God!" Dylan sped up. "I am not going to be a shooting duck."

"Keep low! Keep low!" Roger warned.

"Why isn't Miller shooting?" Rana shouted.

"Don't know." Roger started to worry. The hunters were on their tail more than five seconds now, and there were no bullets fired.

"If he messes this one up, I am gonna kick his butt." Dylan swore.

"If you live that long." Rana reminded him.

"No talk. Run." Hong Shien yelled back as he tried to catch up with his brother.

Miller saw the hunters on their horseback emerging out from behind a rock the size of a four storied building and galloping toward his running mates. For a second he wanted to get crazy with the trigger. But then he calmed down and allowed his judgment take over his impulse. This was something he'd been working on with the guidance of Roger – to control his impulses. Just years ago he'd have definitely start shooting at the first sight of the hunters. Which would have been a mistake, as the hunters would be able to retreat safely behind their hideout and try their luck from long distance.

He followed the galloping goons with the tip of his

rifle, watching them carefully. There were a dozen men in the group, each carrying powerful rifles. They were about three hundred yards away from Rogers' and continued to accelerate. They were not shooting yet, obviously wanted to get close enough before letting the guns loose.

Miller waited a few more seconds allowing the galloping hunters to move away from the rocks that could be used as temporary hideouts. When they were out in the plains, clearly visible, he looked for the leader. Every team had a leader, he knew. Lying low on the ground - his guns ready to rattle, he glanced through the chasing men, trying to keep his mind cool. He'd less than a few more seconds before he'd to act. But he needed to act right.

Then he saw him. It would be hard to miss him - a big man, riding a black mustang, one of the front liners. Miller knew there was one last thing he'd to consider. Kill or wound? He wasn't a humanitarian, not like Rogers. He believed bad endings for bad people.

The bullet went right through the heart. Thrown from his horseback the lifeless body slammed onto the ground. It took couple of seconds for the hunters to realize that they have been attacked. To Miller every second was worthy. He helped two more riders out of their saddles on a rough fall. Nevertheless, scattered and bewildered the hunters charged ahead as they shot back at the general direction of Miller, indiscriminately. Miller kept his cool and continued to pick and shoot, hitting every time. Keeping your head cool does work, thought Miller.

Roger heard the gunshots and saw four or five hunters fell from their horses. He'd hoped the rest of the hunters would be galloping back to their hideout. That didn't happen. The hunters slowed down but still continued to approach them. It was clear that Miller did well but yet the plan didn't fully work.

Roger took out his gun and started to shoot. Hong brothers took out their throwing knives. Normally they would rarely use knives but there were time for everything. It was amazing how skilled they were with those small looking weapons. They could hit their target from as far as fifty yards away. The proof became evident when two unfortunate hunters looked at the knives hooked into their hearts in awe before slipping down their horses.

Miller left his position and ran out of the woods as he continued to shoot, hitting a couple more. Finally the hunters had enough; the few - exactly four – who were still unhurt, quickly turned around and galloped away from them, disappearing beyond bushes.

Now it was Miller's turn to run, before the hunters reinforced and returned. There was no doubt in his mind that they would come back. He made it safely to the base where the rest of his team was already preparing for the journey up.

Roger had his backpack opened and a few shoe like objects lied on the ground.

"*Jumpies*." He declared. "Nothing fancy but works. All you have to do is to stand on them. It would automatically hug your feet. A strong thump on the heel would start the engine. Don't worry. You are not going to fly away. You'll just feel a lot lighter. Using them we should be able to climb up this mountain quite easily."

Dylan picked a pair up in his hand, checked them out distrustfully, and then carefully stood on them. He kicked the ground hard with his heal. The shoes started to vibrate mildly with a low buzzing sound. A few seconds passed by, nothing happened.

"This jumbo-mambo doesn't work." Dylan shook his head in despair. "I still feel like two hundred twenty. Please don't tell Orenda. I don't want to hurt the good lady's feelings."

"You sure you don't feel different?" Roger asked, concerned.

To his amazement, Dylan started to feel light, as if something is pulling him up, giving him a hand. The vibration and the buzzing was nothing desirable but the thing was doing something.

"Okay, it is kicking me a little bit up." He admitted. "But she gotta get this shaking gone."

Roger smiled. "Say it to her yourself, when you meet her."

He quickly put on a couple of jumpies and effortlessly started to climb up the mountain using his fingers to grip jutting rocks or small cracks to push him up and used his feet to press on the near vertical surface only to balance him.

Dylan observed him go for a few long moments before trying himself. It took him some practice but once he got the rhythm of it, things started to move for him. Rana was lighter and had little difficulty getting used to his jumpies. The Hong brothers, however, carefully tucked their jumpies under their garments and climbed using their bare hands and feet – as always.

"This is too much!" Dylan muttered. Perhaps a little embarrassed.

Chapter 34

The Floating Dinner and The Amazing Reef

As Farina and the gang waited outside the change rooms impatiently the large entrance door opened silently once again and a young man in his late teen - average height, slender, light brown skin – walked in.

"I am Diego. Please come with me." The young man said gently, in a slightly thick accent.

"Where are you taking us?" Stanley anxiously asked, rubbing his belly.

"In a very nice place." Diego smilingly replied. "You will love it. Trust me."

After a short walk through a specious corridor they pushed open a second large, heavy door to enter a huge hall room – no smaller than half the size of a soccer field with no pillars to support. The dome like ceiling must have been sixty feet or more high at the center. There were no other doors or windows. The room was lit in dim blue light giving it a mysterious but pleasant hue.

In one corner a large dining table was placed with ample chairs for all of them. The sitting arrangement was predetermined. Diego helped them take their respective sits. Farina was surprised to notice that the kids were placed in one part of the table, Shahed and she at the middle - just one position away from facing each other and Johra at the far end.

Diego left quietly giving them no opportunity to ask questions. After all the flying, tumbling, soaking and dropping not just the kids, even the adults were hungry as hyenas. However, there were no sign of any attendants, food or drink, or even cutleries. At first the kids sat patiently, but when several minutes had passed and nothing happened they started to get a little restless.

The insurgency started with Preeti. "This is unacceptable." She declared. "After all the crap we went through, this is what we get? Sitting in a stadium, no light, no food, no drinks! Where is the Magician? He could at least give us some appetizers."

"Yes!" Stanley approved. "Go on sister. Let the Magician know who he is messing up with."

"Watch it." Ivana warned. "Don't forget he is not a good person."

"I am not scared of anyone." Stanley howled.

Encouraged, Musa jumped on the table, looked for something suspended to climb on. Fortunately nothing was around. Little disappointed, he raised his hands in the air like the wings of an airplane and declared, "I am the Batman."

Suddenly the huge door opened again and a cold gust of air breezed through the room. A big Caucasian man wearing a colorful long gown – interlaced with red, blue and yellow stripes – walked majestically into the hall room. In his well-trimmed goatee, a slim moustache with twisted edges and a crown consisting collections of valuable stones that glittered even in the dim light; he looked proud, powerful and strangely interesting. Right behind him was a wheelchair bound teenage girl, dressed all black with a veil partly covering her face. Diego pushed the wheelchair gently to the table.

The first thought that crossed Farina's mind was that she might have seen the duo – the man and the girl – before, but where? Could they be the old man and the strange wheelchair bound boy from the science tournament? It was difficult to picture the big, proud man as the fragile, soft-spoken elderly man she saw but a little make up and wigs could go long way in deceiving looks. Even Diego could have been one of the other kids who sat quietly by the veiled boy.

Three large men – clearly bodyguards – followed Diego inside. One of them was the Nepali Sherpa who received them at the pool. He was accompanied by a heavyset Chinese man and a big, blonde Caucasian man.

The crowned man elegantly walked toward the center of the table, stopped, looked at the guests, one by one, holding a slice of smile sneaking through his lips.

"I am Dragan Valcovich - *the Magician*!" He threw his hands dramatically in the air and announced in lively, thick voice. "Welcome to you all in my *Castle of Illusion*. I ask for your forgiveness for all the trouble you had. It was a good game - to watch, of course. "

Here, with equal dramatic gesture, he introduced his company on the wheelchair.

"This is Aretha, my dear daughter. We have twisted sense of humor. Like father like daughter. Ha… ha… ha…"

He laughed out loudly and cheerfully making no secret how much he enjoyed their plight.

"I hope you have enjoyed it as well." He said, smirking. "Now, let me take the pleasure to introduce my team. This young man is Diego. You have already met him. He is the friend and round the clock company of Aretha. Behind him ", he pointed the three men who stood in a row at the center of the hall room, "are my three associates cum bodyguards – Gombu, Kongsi and Damien. Gombu is a Sherpa. He holds unbelievable strength and can easily beat a Gorilla. Kongsi is from China. A highest master of Karate he can literally smash rocks in one strike of his hand. Damien is Russian, a famous Savate fighter. He is the master of street fighting."

The Magician glanced through his guests with a smile of satisfaction. It was quite clear he was happy to have the kids here.

Farina suspected she'd seen the three bodyguards before and was digging into memory. Finally, after some strenuous effort Farina remembered where she'd seen Gombu. The suspension bridge! Gombu was chasing the two men who attacked her. She could not remember his companions as the attackers took most of her attention. Nevertheless, it meant only one thing - the Magician had everything planned. Another team got in the middle and had to be chased away. What was going on? Farina wondered.

Dragan sat by Shahed and shook hands with him respectfully.

"It is a pleasure meeting you, sir."

"Same here, sir." Shahed was surprised with such courtesy but didn't want to say too much fearing one wrong expression might tip the powerful man off.

Aretha sat at the right side of her father, facing Farina. Once Diego helped her to a chair she moved the veil to show her face. She'd a very pretty face and a pair of eagle sharp eyes. Farina had her doubts gone by now. It was definitely Aretha who she saw during the tournament. The girl, sitting face to face with Farina, stared at her inquisitively, showing no interest at any other guests. Farina waved at her smilingly. Aretha didn't even blink. She kept watching her with a face expressionless as a white paper.

Diego pulled up a chair and sat on the other side of Aretha. Gombu, Kongsi and Damien didn't sit; instead they moved back a little and stood about twenty feet behind Johra. It was quite evident that they didn't trust Johra much. Dragan, still on his feet, announced once more with his dramatic gesture: "We have plenty more magic to see. But, let's have dinner first. We must be hungry. Hello gang! You hungry?"

The man looked kind of weird in the beginning, but his fun loving nature and dramatic manners had the kids starting to like him already. "Yes!" They shouted.

"Dinner." Extending his hands in the air, the Magician ordered.

To the amazement of the guests a three by three feet door opened up in the center of the ceiling and large dishes of well-arranged finger leaking foods floated right inside. Curiously, the dishes gave an impression of being intelligent. They didn't float down and land on the dining table. Instead, they continued to float around the room in random direction. The appetizing aroma of butter rice, roasted chicken, fried breaded shrimp and a dozen other dishes filled the room quickly.

The Magician, showing his excessive hospitality, bowed majestically and invited them to eat. The kids looked at each other, scratching their heads. Shahed, Farina and Johra quickly exchanged glances as they watched the floating dishes with certain degree of amusement. All the dishes were hovering way above their reach. Exactly how were they supposed to get the food? Musa spent no time thinking. Up on his feet he jumped vertically a few times.

"Look, I can't get them. They are up in the sky."

"Stop it Musa." Zaki warned. "You are making a fool

out of yourself."

"Won't be the first time." Preeti gloomily taunted.

The Magician was caught smirking. Aretha observed with witty eyes and solemn face. Even the bodyguards smiled through their pressed lips.

Johra snapped. "I am hungry as a pig. Could you please stop this joke?"

"What a farce!" Preeti added. "Do we have to pick our food like picking coconuts from a tree?"

Dragan found this funny and cracked into a loud laughter.

"On your feet and focus." He advised.

"What will happen?" Stanley howled.

"You'll find out. Soon."

The kids, hungry and tired, did what he said. As they stood up and looked hard at the floating dishes something wonderful happened. Stanley's heavy body started to lift up in the air, slowly. Terrified at first, Stanley soon started to love the effect. He extended his arms in the air and laughed nervously. "I am flying! I am flying!"

The rest of the kids followed him gradually. Their sheer excitement, amazement and happiness quickly filled the place.

"I am not scared! Look dad!" Zaki shouted.

"There's nothing called fear in my Castle of Illusion." The Magician proudly said. "Come on Shahed, let's eat. Farina, Johra, come along."

Watching the kids flying in the air right before his own eyes, Shahed was already freaked out. Obviously it was some kind of illusion but how was it done?

The Magician and Aretha went up effortlessly, grabbed empty plates from a stack of floating plates and started to pick food of their choice. Farina and Johra followed them too. They definitely didn't want to miss the party above.

The kids were chasing around the constantly moving and dodging dishes, happily of course. The place turned into nothing less than a playground with the kids romping around.

Shahed scratched his head. There was no doubt that the Magician fellow was a mental case. The food should be eaten sitting around a table like civilized people, not flying and chasing around dishes.

Seeing him still sitting on his chair Dragan came down and pulled him in the air by his arm. To his utter surprise Shahed noticed his body turned as light as a piece of cotton. Dragan smiled. "Feels great, doesn't it?"

Shahed had no way to deny it. "But how?" He asked.

The Magician chuckled. "You came in the Castle of Illusion. What else do you expect? Let's eat."

The dining experience turned out to be more enjoyable than appetizing, at least to Shahed. The dishes were really smart. The moment somebody tried to catch them they slipped away. Chasing them he collided with others a few times, got thrown at the wall twice. That didn't hurt though. He just bounced back slowly as if the walls were made of soft cushion.

Farina and Johra had already become friends. They stayed together. Aretha watched them from a distant but didn't join them. Later, Farina approached her.

"Aretha, do you play chess?"

Aretha looked at her with shiny eyes but didn't reply.

Johra joined them too.

"Your dad is a genius! He must have found a way to neutralize gravitational force." She said.

Aretha didn't reply her either. Suddenly Dragan

excused himself from Shahed's company and flew toward the three.

"My daughter isn't really a social type." He said apologetically. "Come on sweat heart, stay with me."

He literally grabbed her and took her away. Farina and Johra exchanged glances. What was that about?

The kids cheerfully bumped into each other, rolled in the air and bounced back and forth to the surrounding walls. This, Aretha found very humorous and broke into giggles. She surely was enjoying the childish acts.

"Sick?" Johra whispered.

"Some kind of abnormality." Farina whispered back.

"There's one thing I've noticed." Johra said. "You two have strikingly similar eyes."

Farina didn't comment. Looking at Aretha always gave her a strange feeling. She could feel the incredible force that was hidden inside that cripple girl. She wondered if she also had such forceful presence.

After another half an hour when the guests had finished their meals Dragan made his next announcement. "Listen! Who wants to visit a wonderful water world?"

"Me!" The kids shouted.

"You mean, we!" The Magician corrected.

"We!" This time it was even louder.

Startling everybody the walls of the hall room disappeared in a blink and was replaced with clear, almost undetectable glass. Awed, they found themselves merged into water, like a submarine. Gliding ahead they discovered themselves right next to an amazing coral reef - filled with corals of all kinds and colors. Numerous fishes and invertebrates of various species and characters swam over the reef. The beauty of this strange underwater world

214

captivated them in moments.

"Great Barrier Reef!" Shahed mumbled. "Are we in Australia?"

Dragan gently placed a hand on his shoulder.

"This is one of my favorite places. It's so calm and peaceful!"

"It is stunningly beautiful." Shahed managed to say as he observed the breathtaking views, a world so different and yet so attractive.

Their strange vehicle moved slowly along the reef. Every crevice, every turn revealed new colonies of corals and other life forms, amusing the visitors with their eye popping beauty. Even the kids were glued on the reef, forgetting their usual silliness. Nobody even realized how tens of minutes had passed by.

A little later, Dragan coughed to get their attention. "There's more. You want it, gang?"

"Yes!" The kids cried out.

"You got it! Next - Isle of Paradise." He declared with extended arms and a big smile. "Watch out kids. Now the real fun starts."

Chapter 35

The Isle of Paradise

Almost instantly a nontransparent material surrounded the exterior of the hall room. With a sudden jerk, it started to accelerate very fast, throwing away the unprepared riders from their sits to the air. Once they floated back to their seats unhurt, the blue hue that lit the hall room slowly turned into a grayish tone, limiting their vision greatly. Sitting quietly in the semi-dark they could feel the room continued to accelerate for a few long moments before settling down to a speed. If there weren't this slight vibration on the floor it would be impossible to know that the ship was actually moving.

The lights didn't return. There was no new announcement from Dragan. Inside the hall room, everything was quiet, ghostly. The kids, perhaps the first time in a very long time, stayed totally silent, as if they didn't dare to utter any word, in case, just in case the words turned into something really scary. Farina, Johra and Shahed exchanged glances, wondering what was coming next.

Another few seconds later the shield disappeared revealing the star studded deep dark sky that surrounded them.

Oliver nervously scratched his head. "Are we in space?"

"What does it look like?" Preeti teased.

"G...great!" Stanley nervously laughed.

"Holly Christ!" Oliver exclaimed.

"Are we dreaming?" Ivana said. "Can you pinch me, Preeti?"

Preeti did as asked.

"Not that hard!" Ivana cried out in pain.

"Was it too hard? Now you know all of this is real, don't you?" Preeti smirked.

Ivana returned the favor with an equally tangy pinch.

"Ouch! You went overboard!" Preeti objected.

Aretha broke out into another long giggle. There was something unusual about that outburst. None of the kids joined her. They went mum until she stopped.

Farina felt almost guilty. Obviously Aretha had some kind of communication deficiency. Such a beautiful, intelligent girl but yet so unfortunate!

"Are we even moving?" Zaki asked.

"We are." Replied Dragan, smilingly. "Twenty five miles per second."

"Wow! That's like very fast." Stanley said.

"Actually," Zaki said, "the stars are so far that at this speed it would take us thousands of years to get to any of them."

"That's right. We are barely moving." Preeti backed him up.

"You kids are good." Dragan said. "However, our destination is not a star. We are not going that far."

Shahed looked out. The ever-blinking stars stood stationary, as if somebody had embroidered a black piece of cloth with glittering bids and gently spread it out over the sky. It looked like a framed picture. Everything was far, far away. He wasn't sure what Dragan was referring to.

"Where is Isle of Paradise?" Shahed asked.

Dragan pointed ahead in the sky. "There. Have patience."

"What is it?" Johra impatiently said.

The Magician smiled. "Patience is not one of your virtues, is it my lady daredevil? Wait. Everything in due time."

Johra frowned. Obviously she wasn't ready to get impressed by this crazy scientist.

Not even five seconds had passed when a tiny, star like dot quickly started to grow on them, first into a bright tennis ball and then in no time into a round moon. It was now quite obvious where they were heading.

At this point the makeshift spaceship slowed down considerably as it entered the atmosphere – undisturbed - and passed through the dense phases of clouds. Looking out, they simply didn't have the words to describe the absolutely gorgeous natural view that greeted them warmly.

In the middle of a deep blue sea that extended to the horizons was a small round shaped island with parts of it covered in dense forests and the rest turned into an extravagant children's park. Every possible playground instrument that a kid of any age could dream of had found its way there. In addition it included all the adventure rides that the world had ever experienced. At the center of it all, a series of roller coasters - enormous, complex and unique, were the heart and soul of the mind-blowing exhibition.

The kids stared at this astounding display with a mixture of distrust and delight. They in fact forgot to blink.

"Oh dear Lord! What am I seeing? Is this real?" Oliver muttered.

"As real as your clueless mind." Preeti taunted.

Ivana chuckled. "You are too mean."

"Just confirming I am still the same person." Preeti gravely said. "Don't let all these illusions get to you."

"Illusion? This is not illusion." Stanley readily objected.

"Definitely not." Zaki supported. "I want to ride the roller coasters, all of them."

Several eyes rolled.

"Are you sure?" Musa said, clearly surprised. "You won't be scared?"

"I don't feel any fear." Zaki excitedly said. "My fear of height is gone, totally."

"What else you expected, gang?" Dragan interrupted in his characteristic dramatic way. "This is the Isle of Paradise. No fear has any place in this world."

"I'd wait until I see it." Preeti said. "Even a kiddy swing is too high for him."

"N-o-o-o." Zaki objected. "Don't exaggerate."

Oliver chuckled. "Admit it. She is right."

"Which team are you on?" Zaki demanded.

"We are all in one team." Ivana stepped in.

Dragan left the kids to their arguments and joined Shahed.

"I built it for my daughter, Aretha." He almost whispered. "Challenged with movement; no siblings; this is the only place that charms her. None of the general laws of the world applies here. "

"How do you mean?" Shahed was inquisitive.

"It is a place free of earthly limitations. You can do whatever you believe in, anything. Zaki can leave his fears behind. Aretha can walk on her legs. There are infinite possibilities."

"Are these all magic?" Shahed had to ask.

"Are you magic?" Dragan asked back.

Shahed nervously smiled. He never believed in magic. Either they were tricks or illusions. However, anything that he'd seen today how could he explain them? Science? Black magic? Wizardry? Obviously the Magician wasn't going to divulge any of his secrets.

The spacecraft slowed down to a full halt few thousand feet above the sea. Gombu pushed the large entrance doors open. This was not something the guests had expected.

"What's going on?" Johra inquired. "Aren't we landing this silly spaceship?"

"What are we supposed to do now?" Stanley was puzzled.

"Jump. Please. Take your buddy with you." Preeti said.

"Get off my back." Stanley yelled.

"Mine too." Oliver added.

Aretha, who was quietly sitting on her wheelchair, suddenly stood up, spun slowly around herself in the air and then flew out through the open door. With her hands spread out like a bird she dived toward the ground, bottom of her long black dress waved like a tail against the wind. As she neared the ground she slowed down and gracefully glided through the air to a sky-high monster roller coaster that had a formation of several interconnected gigantic circles and carefully landed on a seat. She looked back and waved at the kids to join her.

The kids observed her go with exploding eyes.

"She was flying like a bird!" Musa exclaimed. "Can I

do that?"

"Anything is possible here." Dragan nodded. "You just have to believe."

"I believe. I am going." Musa ran toward the open door.

Farina tried to stop him, almost reflexively, but Musa dodged. He stood hesitantly for a brief moment before following Aretha's footstep. With his hands spreading on his sides he threw his body into the air, screaming as he fell down sharply. Then, seconds later, his fall slowed down, air uplifted his body slightly and allowed him to fly down, just like a bird.

That did it for the rest of the team. With a scream, one by one, they dropped out of the spaceship, right into the air and miraculously flew using only their hands to guide them.

"Are you coming?" Farina didn't see any reason to miss this unique opportunity. But she wanted Johra to come with her.

"Why not?" Johra shrugged. "Let see what this mad man has done here."

The two of them jumped together, side by side. The initial fall was scary, at one point Farina started to think this wasn't going to work for her, but then she felt the uplift on her body. She was flying, controlling her direction simply by twisting her body and moving her hands. The kids were still flying around, maneuvering in the air, and enjoying every bit of this one-of-a-life-time experience. Farina and Johra joined them.

"Let's join Aretha. She wants us there." Farina said.

"Let's go!" Stanley shouted. "Come on guys."

They started to fly toward Aretha but in the midway Musa and Zaki drifted away toward another roller coaster, a wavy framework that promised an unforgettable ride. It had two different tracks connected at the bottom. At the peak of the first track, way high above the ground, a trusted mechanism ejected the passenger cars in the air only to be caught by the second track hundreds of feet below.

Rest of the kids followed them, same way they followed each other everywhere. Farina and Johra were in a dilemma. They didn't want Aretha to be left alone but at the same time felt leaving the kids all by themselves was not a viable option.

Farina gestured Aretha to join them. The girl watched them impassively. She stayed where she was.

Farina shrugged. "She is familiar with this place. She'll be okay."

"She doesn't look happy." Johra said.

"We'll deal with her later." Farina said. "Let's go check on the silly bunch first. It takes them seconds to mess things up."

She flew after the kids with Johra following her.

The team boarded the coaster at the second track where the moving cars automatically stopped to allow them to climb up. Each car had two seats located side by side. Once they were all on board the roller coaster rushed ahead rapidly and silently.

Aretha observed this with pure sadness. Diego noticed it and quickly flew to her. Aretha didn't pay any attention to him. She continued to watch the kids in the other roller coaster, the combined screams and the occasional cheerful laughter slowly started to turn her sadness into anger. It wasn't easy to know exactly what was going into her mind but Diego sensed her contempt.

"Aretha, listen to me. They are just little kids." He

spoke softly. "They love you."

"They left me alone!" Aretha spoke in perfectly good voice.

"That's how kids are. Their minds drift away."

"Why didn't Farina come?" Her voice was sharper, tenser. The anger was sitting in.

"She'd to look after the kids. Remember?"

Aretha didn't reply. Diego clearly felt she was about to be taken over by her notorious rage.

Chapter 36

Aretha's Rage

Dragan flew down with Shahed on his side to a shiny, spotless snow-white yacht floating near the shore. They softly landed on the deck and sat on the cushioned chairs in the sun.

"When I come here I do not feel like going back on earth." Dragan said, his eyes closed, a divine smile hanging between his lips.

"All the stuff that I heard about you doesn't fit you at all." Shahed said with admiration.

"You must have heard that I am a fearsome devil."

"Many do foster that impression of you."

With a simple gesture of his hand, Dragan made two glasses appear in front of them. They contained colorful drinks.

"I apologize but my faith does not allow me to consume liquor." Shahed humbly said, careful not to sound insulting to his host.

Dragan smiled. "I know. This is just grape juice."

Shahed wasn't surprised. The man did his homework. He must have had collected all the information he could before inviting them here. He accepted his drink and sipped. Whatever juice it was, it tasted better than anything he'd ever drank.

"Good and evil are very relative things." Dragan spoke softly, thoughtfully. "I am a scientist who refused to give up to the greed for arms and dirty earthly politics. I refused to hand over my inventions to the government so that they could build deadly weapons. Instead I chose to decide who I'd allow to use my inventions.

"Wherever I went I tried to balance the forces; the forces that build up a country, culture and community. I tried to make sure opposing ideologies survived. There's nothing more unacceptable than a stereotyped society."

"I must say, with due respect, there are people who believe that you have supplied weapons to rogue guerilla groups to fight against their own governments." Shahed said politely. This was a serious allegation.

Dragan shook his head lightly. "I can't deny that my foresight have failed me in several cases. Sometimes I'd strengthened the *weak* thinking I was helping the commoners. Unfortunately today's weak becomes tomorrow's murderer. I am a human. I do fail but I am not a monster. Never was, never will be. I am a scientist who loves the magic of science."

"How long can you continue like this?" Shahed felt the passion of this strange scientist. "The powerful countries are looking for you. What happens if you get caught?"

Dragan laughed. "They can't catch the Magician. I am not real. I am just a segment of their imagination." He stopped for a second before starting to talk in a more serious note.

"I know how to handle the bloodthirsty - give them the taste of blood. Consider the Americans. They act as if they would chew me alive - if they find me. Truth is, I promised to give them Meganano and they gave me hundreds of millions of dollars, no question asked. With that money I helped the poor, bought them food, gave them education, and taught them to be self-sufficient. Imagine that!" He chuckled.

"What is Meganano, if I may ask?"

"Let's just say it is a new technology using nano sized particles. They have the power that you can only imagine."

All on a sudden a caravan of dark, heavy cloud appeared from nowhere and wiped out the smiling blue sky that hung over just moment earlier. With it came gusty wind and towering waves.

Baffled, Shahed stood up anxiously. "What's happening? Is there going to be a storm?"

Dragan jumped out of his seat. He was not laughing anymore. "Aretha." He said gravely. "It's not a good thing when she is angry. She was born with unthinkable power."

He gestured Shahed to sit back. "Don't worry. I'll be back in a blink."

Extending his arms up, he effortlessly lifted in the air and flew toward Aretha. She was still sitting at the same place, her eyes closed, face expressionless. Diego, sitting right next to her was softly speaking to her. Obviously his attempts to calm her down weren't working. Dragan sped up but was only halfway down when all hell broke down.

The wind picked up speed quickly and blew in excess of hundred kilometers per hour, the clouds roared and the lightening accompanied by the deafening thunders came down in plentiful. Almost instantly came pounding a heavy rain, blinding the vision completely. Then the high tide came rushing toward the land in a mad dash.

To Shahed's amazement not a single drop of rain fell on him as the yacht remained as steady as before as if the storm had no impact on it or anything on it. However, the kids were in serious trouble. Crumbling into their cars on the roller coaster they hung onto their seats hoping that the seat belts would hold them against the storm. Shahed, not knowing what to do, observed the kids battling against this sudden rage of nature with total horror.

And then, when the chaos was about to multiply, the storm ceased just as abruptly as it started. In moments the Isle of Paradise was again flashed with bright sun. Looking up Shahed saw Dragan flying down with Aretha in his arms, followed by Diego. He landed on the deck softly.

"She is very emotional." He said affectionately. "It's not easy to be her. Growing up alone in a speechless world isn't much of a fun."

He sat on his chair, still holding Aretha dearly to her. "I thought perhaps having the kids here would make her happy. Young minds need other young minds. She never had a normal social life, doesn't understand a lot of normal humanly things. Anyway, we should head home once their ride ends. What do you say, pumpkin?"

Frowning heavily, Aretha was observing the kids on the roller coaster that continued through her wrath. She was clearly very upset.

"I hate them!"

Chapter 37

Sygods and the Three Giants

The Sygods had made good progress as they climbed up the mountain and were just about a hundred yards away from the edge of the castle after about half an hour.

As always the Hong brothers were ahead of the pack. They had put on their jumpies, perhaps realizing that there was no need for straining their muscles. Dylan, Miller, Rana and Roger climbed slowly, staying close to each other. With the exception of Roger the other three had barely ever done anything that qualified as rock climbing. Even Orenda's magical shoes couldn't help them move faster.

Far below on the ground there was some noise. As they looked down the danger became crystal clear. The hunters had reinforced and were coming back. There were at least fifty riders galloping toward them, shooting at will.

"What the hell?" Hearing bullets ricocheting on the nearby rocks Dylan screamed in disgust. "Don't these idiots have other things to do? Why do they keep shooting at us? We have a secret assignment, for God's sake!"

"Look for a cave, quick!" Roger said. "I think a bullet just touched my left earlobe."

The Hong brothers realized the danger and were scrambling to find a place to hide from this quickly approaching onslaught. The surface of the mountain was relatively bare with few trees and occasional shallow caves. They passed a few of these small caves knowing that they won't be deep enough to save them all from the deadly bullets.

After climbing up another fifty feet Hong Lee first noticed the mouth of a cave that promised a lot more than a small cavity. He signaled the rest to move toward the cave. As they frantically raced to reach the cave the bullets followed them closely, missing too narrowly for comfort. Everybody knew they were quickly running out of time. Once the hunters closed in a little more there would be no way out of this. They would never miss from such short distance.

Hong Shien moved swiftly, often leaping in the air like a monkey and was the first person to reach the mouth of the cave. Hong Lee remained right on his brother's tail. The rest struggled behind them but were able to make it before the hunters reached the foot of the mountain and started to blast the rocks up above their heads with rapid shots.

As the bullets started to find their ways into the cave the Sygods ran deeper inside. The cave, about five feet wide and six-seven feet high meandered through the mountain body for about fifty yards before ending into another enormous cave that was at least a hundred feet high and could easily hold a dozen full size soccer fields. There were numerous smaller hills, caves and a creek that dotted the large cave.

"Is this some kind of secret government project?" Dylan quipped.

"Does look like one." Roger said. "However, I am sure this was Dragan's idea. This must be his quick escape route."

"That suggests there must be a connection from here to the castle above." Rana suggested.

"I see something like a tunnel on the far end." Miller

said, pointing at an opening on the other end of the cave - hundreds of yards away and ten fifteen feet above the ground.

The rest noticed it as well however nobody made a move. Before rushing to the other end they wanted to make sure that they were not stepping into a trap that Dragan had set up for them. For the next few minutes they carefully checked around for booby traps.

"I don't see anything suspicious." Rana said. "But there can be danger anywhere. With Dragan, you can never be sure."

Miller stepped ahead with his rifle ready. "What's the use of wasting time here?"

Everybody agreed to it. They had to move forward. Forming a half circle they advanced quickly in long leaping steps with the aid of the jumpies.

Halfway down, they saw the first sign of trouble. A herd of bison – long, sharp horned and fiery eyed - rushed out from behind a hill and dashed toward them with thundering noise. Their smashing hooves stirred up a dusty fog.

"Is this some kind of 'Cows gone wild' show?" Dylan managed to say before sprinting across the cave.

The rest followed, as fast as they could with their jumpies on. This wasn't exactly the situation where you waited to analyze your options.

"They are not bison." Roger informed. "They are mountain goats."

"Impossible!" Rana said with utter disbelief. "These things are at least twenty times bigger than a regular mountain goat."

Miller shot at the herd a few times but that didn't seem to bother the rushing terror in the least. He could swear that he did hit a few.

"Goat or not, they are invincible!" He said in total disbelief. "How did they turn so big?"

"Good mountain food!" Dylan remarked bitterly. "Another of Dragan's mischievous magic."

"There's no magic in it." Roger said as he jumped over a small hill with his jumpies. "It is pure science. Dragan was working on nanotechnology. He must have done some experiment on the mountain goats that roamed this area."

"What nanotechnology has to do with mountain goats?" Dylan was in disbelief.

"He must have built tiny robots of nano scale and inserted them into the bodies of these animals." Roger replied. "With these nanorobots he could then control the proteins and hormones of a live body to control its various characteristics. Many scientists have already thought about it but nobody actually succeeded in building anything like it."

"I thought it would take scientists at least another twenty-thirty years before they could even come close to building something like nanorobot." Rana was purely surprised.

"I compare Dragan to Einstein." Roger couldn't hide the shade of respect he'd for the person who he distasted otherwise.

They hopped their way across the cave in the general direction of the mouth of the distant tunnel as the monstrous mountain goats chased them like possessed animals, showing no sign of slowing down.

"How come even bullets can't stop them?" Miller was clearly baffled. He'd continued shooting at the herd and not a single one had stopped.

"Got to be the work of the miraculous nanorobots." Roger said. "They are healing the bullet wounds so quickly

231

that the goats can't even feel them. Incredible! Dragan did it! Deep inside I hoped he'd fail."

Suddenly the herd picked up speed and ignoring the desperate Sygods, who frantically tried to jump out of their way, rushed away to the other end of the cave and soon disappeared behind a series of hills.

The Sygods stopped and were about to relax on their feet when the real threat revealed itself. Three giant men walked out of a tall cave and stood in front of them, completely blocking their way. They were at least nine feet tall with wide shoulders. Their incredibly muscular bodies and angry faces promised deep trouble.

"This must be the outcome of another experiment." Roger said.

"You mean another experiment gone bad?" Dylan bitterly said.

"May be not. This could actually be just the opposite." Roger replied, carefully observing the giants.

"You mean that's what he wanted to make?" Miller said.

"I definitely think so. Dragan doesn't play with science. Hong Lee, Hong Shien, can you guys beat them up?"

Miller didn't believe the brothers who looked like two flies before the giants had any reasonable chance of disturbing their peace. This was a situation that could only be handled with a gun. He raised his rifle and shot at one of the giant's leg.

The giant didn't even flinch. Blood gushed out of his body, flooded the floor, before slowing down in about five seconds. Within fifteen -twenty seconds the bleeding completely subsided and the wound started to heal right before their eyes. A few seconds later what was left was nothing but an almost invisible tiny scar.

Roger was stunned. "If I didn't see it in my own eyes I wouldn't have believed."

Rana consented. "Neither would I."

The giants shook their heads in annoyance and came charging at them.

"Look Miller, what you have done." Dylan cried. "They are mad now."

Miller shrugged in despair. "How would I know?"

"Learn from the goats."

One of the giants reached for Dylan, effortlessly picked him up in the air and threw him. Dylan flew in the air for a little while with his hands searching for something to grab before thumping down on the ground.

Miller raised his rifle to take another shot but it was quickly snatched away by another giant, who folded the barrel of the gun and threw it hundreds of feet away. However, Hong brothers weren't ready to concede defeat just yet, even after such display of pure strength and power.

They heroically attacked the giants, forced them to step back as they overwhelmed them (the giants) with their deadly kicks and hammering punches. Unfortunately this proved too insignificant for the three mountains of men. Once they became familiar with the pattern of attack they moved ahead boldly ignoring the barrage of onslaught.

"Like rocks. No human." Hong Lee declared frustratingly.

Hong Shien agreed. "Ghosts. Like ghosts."

Roger quickly took out a small glass tube out of his backpack. "Don't breathe," he said. "Orenda's famous and reliable gas capsule. Works like miracle."

He smashed the capsule on the floor. Within seconds a heavy gas with a tangy smell filled up the air. For a few moments the giants showed no sign of distress and walked

233

through the gas toward the tiny invaders. However, a few steps later they suddenly stopped and crumbled down on the ground, their bodies motionless.

Roger signaled everybody to walk ahead. Once they moved to a safe location they gasped for fresh air.

"I don't know how long it's going to hold them." Roger said. "It may not take the nanorobots very long to find a way to nullify the effect of the gas. So, we need to get out of here. Run."

"Isn't that all I am doing since I got here." Dylan muttered before brushing off dirt from his cloths. "Run! Run! Run! I am getting sick of it".

Chapter 38

The Mosquitoes

They raced across the cave to the tunnel without any other incidence. The mouth of the tunnel was higher than they had thought. It was at least twenty feet above the ground on a perfectly vertical surface. The jumpies came in handy once more. Using its uplift they sprung up to the mouth of the tunnel and crawled inside, one by one.

The tunnel was just large enough for one person to walk with his head bent. Dark and cold, it meandered through the rocky mountain, gradually going up, often steeply, and consisted several staircases with hundreds of steps.

"This does look like an escape route." Rana said.

"It better be." Roger said. "If it doesn't lead us to the castle, we are in trouble."

"God knows what kind of creeps are waiting for us there." Dylan grimly said.

Nobody spoke. There was no way to know what the dreaded Dragan Valcovich had in his sleeves for them. The miracle gas might have saved them from the fearsome giants, but it surely won't be able to save them from everything that would come their way.

They walked into the dark for the next half an hour,

frequently turning their flashlights on to get a quick glimpse of their surroundings, before finally finding a heavy steel door bolted on the side of the tunnel.

Roger examined the door carefully. "This is good news." He said. "We are still below the castle. This door may lead us to it."

"We break?" Hong Li asked, impatiently.

The Hongs were all ready to smash into the door with their dynamite flying kicks when Rana, trying to feel the strength of the door, curiously gave it a push with both of his hands. To all of their delight the door opened up silently allowing them to have a glimpse of a smooth, spotless white marble elevator lobby, about fifty feet long and ten feet wide. Two elevators stood side-by-side, doors closed. There were no call buttons visible on the wall.

"Push before kick." Dylan teased the brothers.

"You scared dark!" They laughed back at him.

"Stop saying that, please." Dylan frowned.

"Should we get in?" Miller whispered.

Rana took a step inside the lobby to examine the door. "Electronic. It couldn't have opened by itself."

"Somebody wants us in there." Roger thoughtfully said.

"That must be our sweetheart Dragan the psycho scientist." Dylan scoffed.

"We go?" The Hong brothers said, impatient as ever.

"What else can we do?" Miller said. "If he wants us there, let's get there. We can handle him."

Rana shrugged. There was nothing in that lobby that even remotely posed any threat to them. "Just be very careful. Watch before you take a step."

Slowly and carefully they entered the lobby, one after another, very watchful, ready for anything.

"If we see anything suspicious we are back into the tunnel." Roger said.

Dylan stood in front of the elevators, perplexed.

"How do we get these things to work?" He said. "By brain waves? Hello? Can you hear me Mr. Elevator. Open your door, please. I beg you."

"Quiet!" Rana warned. "They may have voice or sound activated alarm systems."

"So? The big guy wants us in here, doesn't he?" Dylan countered.

"True. But we don't know why. Not yet." Rana looked around for surveillance equipments. None was visible. Naturally. These things have gotten so tiny now, it would be impossible to see them.

"There are no other ways out of here." Miller stated. "No doors, no stairways."

Roger had noticed that too. "These elevators would be our best way into the castle." He said. "The tunnel would take hours, considering it goes there. Let's see if we can pull the safety doors open…"

Suddenly one of the elevator doors opened, silently, revealing a specious dimly lit interior.

"Now what?" Dylan asked. "That thing is waiting for us."

"It is definitely a trap." Miller said.

"Didn't you say you could handle him?" Dylan teased. "Get in that thing. Handle."

"Wait!" Hongs stepped ahead. "We check."

"Great! You check you die. I run." Dylan taunted.

Hongs gave him a cold look. This was no time for joke. They carefully peeked inside the elevator. It looked like a regular elevator without any surveillance camera. There was nothing to imply any kind of danger.

"No fear." They declared.

"Perhaps the guy finally realized what a creep he'd been all his life. " Dylan said as he walked into the elevator. "I guess he is trying to make it up to us."

Roger took one step inside the elevator, quickly looked around and jumped out of it pulling Dylan with him. He pointed at the ceiling of the elevator where a group of tiny mosquito like animals sat innocuously.

"Those can't be what they look like." He whispered.

"What else can they be?" Rana whispered back.

The mosquitoes started to move. Slowly they lifted off the ceiling, neatly lined up, producing a constant low buzz.

"Guys, turn around slowly and run back to the tunnel as fast as you can." Roger said. "These are robots. They could be poisonous. Remember the monsters we saw down there? I believe these robots are here to stop them from going up to the castle. Now do the calculation."

The robot mosquitoes were now flying toward them – the intruders. They frantically rushed out of the lobby into the dark tunnel. Hongs cleared the door last and closed it split second before the tiny devils reached it. Standing outside they could hear the mosquitoes issuing a loud warning buzz before becoming silent.

"Have they gone back? " Dylan said. "Even the mosquitoes are kicking our butts. Nobody must know."

"Should we continue through the tunnel?" Miller inquired.

"The elevator would be good." Roger said. "But we may not have any choice."

"How about using electromagnetic signal scrambler? We could blind them up for a little bit. That would give us enough time to board the elevator without being detected."

"Let's fry the tiny creeps." Dylan was enthusiastic.

"There is a problem." Roger said. "Did you notice there were no buttons inside the elevator? This thing is remotely controlled. Even if we fool the mosquitoes and board the elevator we won't be going anywhere."

"Who says we have to go inside?" Miller said. "We could climb up the elevator roof and climb up the walls."

"No problem. Easy." Hong brothers quickly said.

Dylan shrugged. "Yeah, easy. You guys will be pushing me up."

Roger nodded. "Not a bad idea. We may even surprise Dragan."

"That's my kind of thing." Dylan grinned. "Surprise with a jab, knock out with a hook."

Chapter 39

Meet the Magician

After the eventful dinner, Farina and the guests were led to her room. Flyball knew they were coming. It didn't say anything but Farina somehow believed the tiny robot also knew everything about her experience since she left on the escalator. She assumed Flyball was wirelessly connected to a central server and was being fed with regular updates on certain proceedings.

She saw no computing equipments on her way up to the room but she barely saw anything but barren passages. She knew by now that a lot of things were kept out of their views. What a strange, unearthly place!

The kids were delighted to meet Flyball, who allowed them to chase him around for a little while. Later, he revealed, "We have the world's best games room in this castle. Anybody interested?"

"Interested!" Stanley roared.

"Lead us the way, o' little thing." Ivana was dramatic.

"You better! Or…" Preeti threatened.

"Let's go!" The rest shouted.

Shahed really wanted to lie down on his back and rest for a little bit. Good luck! He was swept on his feet and pushed toward the only door. They simply weren't going to take a no for an answer, not this time. This was too good to pass on.

They followed Flyball to the corridor. The glass panels along the corridor were not visible. All they saw was spotless white walls. Farina and Johra went with them as well; none of them felt comfortable leaving the kids in the hands of Flyball. They couldn't be totally certain about the role of this tiny robot.

As the team advanced through several corridors and doors, Flyball kept the young followers entertained by changing shape, color and size of its body. By using air bubble it could become as big as a peach and as colorful as a saltwater fish.

A few minutes later they stopped at the end of a corridor guarded by a heavy steel door. After a short wait the door slid open, silently.

Looking inside what they saw was simply mind blowing. It was an exceptionally big hall room with high ceiling, filled with gazillions of video, Nintendo and other electronic games, arranged neatly in specious rows. The kids watched the exuberant display with exploding eyes.

A few moments of pure awe was followed by frenzied attempt to try out as many games as they possibly could. Soon they found out that the games weren't just regular Nintendo games. With whatever magical prowess was in effect, it took them to a level of reality so vivid and intense that it was no more possible to differentiate reality from virtual reality. The characters in the games jumped out of their virtual existence and became so lively that they could almost feel them and talk to them as if they were made of flesh and blood. This wasn't something that any of the kids ever imagined that they would experience.

Shahed, quite tired, was observing the kids swiftly maneuvering the joysticks with absolute devotion. All he really wanted was to crash on a bed. Flyball noticed it and invited him to a strange looking machine. On it was carved in large letters 'World travel'.

Now, that was something he really didn't mind going for. No matter how eager he always was to go on a world tour, it just never became reality. But the machine promised good time and he just couldn't pass it.

After putting his head into the super sized weird looking helmet he pressed the 'Select Country' button to settle on Bangladesh and then clicked 'OK'. In an instance he was taken to a beautiful green village that looked just like the one he'd left behind many years ago. He'd none left there, not anymore. Even before his parents had passed away all their children had long left the village, first for education, later for pursuing carriers.

Shahed missed his parents - an ordinary village couple, who had sacrificed so much to give their four children a chance to succeed in the modern world. As he walked on the dirt roads it felt so real that a slew of youthful memories flooded him, fogging his eyes in nostalgic feelings. Oh, the sprawling paddy fields, the bamboo forests, the banana groves and the mango gardens!

Johra and Farina stayed away from the games and kept eyes on the kids. Johra was restless.

"Are you okay?" Farina asked.

"The Sygods should have been here already." Johra replied. "I am really worried now. God knows what kind of hell they are going through."

Farina was convinced that the whole castle was wired. She didn't think it was safe to discuss this. She shook her head, asking Johra not to say anymore. Johra got the message readily. They walked around the hall room, carefully checking out for hidden cameras. None was visible.

"There's only one door!" Johra was a little surprised.

This was a huge facility. Having just one entry and exit point was not normal.

"We don't see everything. Computer controlled." Farina said.

"Magic? Tricks?" Johra asked.

"Advance science. Intelligent walls, doors, windows. Each is programmable and can change their properties like visibility according to access level of the visitors."

"Really?" Johra was dumbfounded. "But how?"

"I've no clue." Farina shrugged. "But I assume they are made with special material that can control its light absorption abilities. Just a guess."

"Is the whole castle like that?" Johra couldn't stop herself from wondering.

Farina shrugged. "Unlikely. I think only some interior parts are intelligent."

They noticed Diego entering the room through the only visible entrance. He walked to them. "Farina, father wants to see you."

"The Magician?" Farina wanted to be sure.

"Yes. I grew up with Aretha. I call him father as well. Come please." Diego was calm but insisting.

Farina exchanged glances with Johra. Shahed was too busy with his world traveling. Farina wasn't sure what to do. Could she refuse to see the big man? Was it an invitation or order?

"I am coming with you." Johra said.

"I don't think the boys would allow that." Diego gently warned.

Farina didn't want any more trouble than they were already in. She silently gestured Johra to stay back and followed Diego out of the hall room to the corridor.

The three bodyguards - Gombu, Damien and Kongsi stood there quietly. Gombu followed the two through a new set of doors onto a different corridor. At the end of this corridor there was another heavy metal door. A simple knock on the door caused it to slide sidewise, silently. Looking ahead Farina noticed there was yet another door about ten yards away.

Diego motioned forward. "Go. He is expecting you alone."

"I'll wait here." Gombu coldly declared.

"Father can defend himself." Diego didn't try to hide his disapproval.

Gombu frowned at him but remained quiet. It was clear they were not in best terms.

Farina walked to the door ahead, slowly pushed it open and carefully stepped inside. It was a specious, rectangular room with floor to ceiling clear glass windows on two adjacent sides. It was decorated contemporarily with little furniture and a sense of fine art. It had dozens of built in shelves, each was overwhelmingly loaded with books, hundreds and hundreds of them – science, economics, magic – covering just about everything. A big man in a flashy colorful gown was leaning over a book placed on a wide table loaded with more books. The man raised his head and looked back at her, smilingly.

"Come dear. How did you like this evening's trip?" He sounded loud but cordial, if not affectionate.

"Scary!" Farina said honestly. "And thrilling. You are a genius."

He blushed. "Oh no, don't call me that. I am just a scientist. Please sit."

He looked around to find a chair. There were a few

around but each had a tall column of books on them. Disappointed, he pointed at the small twin bed at the corner of the room.

"Please sit on the bed. I need more shelf space."

Farina didn't move. She wasn't expecting to see such a mess.

"Don't be scared. I am not so bad." Dragan softly said.

"Are you sure?" The words slipped through her mouth.

There was a trace of clear sarcasm in her voice. The Magician didn't miss it. He gave her a quick inquisitive glance before looking out through the glass windows and looked down to the beautiful valley below.

"What have you learned about me?" He calmly asked.

"Horrible things." Farina said, fearfully. She didn't want to agitate him but couldn't pass on the opportunity to speak her mind before this extremely talented but highly irresponsible man.

"I admit I don't know a whole lot about you but a little search in the Internet revealed many of your criminal acts. In the name of balancing power you had supplied dangerous weapons to the terrorist groups in the developing countries. Not once, but several times. As a result innocent civilians, many women and children, were killed. Your attempts to save the so-called 'Suppressed' backfired and created anarchism. In the end all you did was to create killer armies. Asia, Africa, South America – you spared none."

Pausing, Farina tried to arrange her thoughts before she spoke again. "At the same time you sold formulas for deadly weapons to the developed world. Many have successfully built the weapons and gained major advantages against their rivals. At the end, you just created more bullies. I am sorry to say this but I can't think of anything that you did had a good impact."

Without moving his eyes from the mountain range and the valley, Dragan sighed. "If we always knew right from wrong, we would become God. Wouldn't we?"

"Don't know about God but evil is what I am referring to." Farina bitterly said.

Dragan spoke after a few moments of quietness. "My dear young lady, the world is not an easy place. Not when you want to change it- in a good way. Think about the numerous nations, races, tribes, religions! There's no end to differences. Today's abused are tomorrow's dictators. Today's friends are tomorrow's foes. All my life I tried to help people, often without realizing full outcome. I've done mistakes, too many times. Sometimes I sheltered the hyenas of future, not knowing of course. But my dear, be assured, never was I evil, never will I be. My intentions had always been good."

"The thousands of lives that perished untimely, all your good intentions can't bring them back." Farina softly said.

The Magician shrugged. There was a clear sign of bite of conscience in his face. "Perhaps, I built my life on a dubious ideology." He almost whispered. "Perhaps this wasn't what I really wanted to turn into. Hatred had governed my life, made me do things that I wouldn't do otherwise. I must say I am truly remorseful for all my blunders."

"Remorseful! Then why am I here? Why are the SciAngels here? Why are you hiding in this rough terrain? What game of destruction are you hatching now?"

His eyes flickered teasingly. "Brilliant as you are, how

come you haven't figured it out yet?"

Farina was thoughtful for a few seconds. "Did roger had anything to do with this?"

He smiled. "You are on the right track."

Farina looked puzzled. "He must have used me as bait, didn't he? The question is why? What do you got that he wants? A new invention? Most importantly, why would you even care about me?"

Dragan slowly walked to her and held her hand affectionately. "I brought you here to answer that question. I've been looking for you for many years but Roger and the General kept you hidden from me. Come with me, you'll get your answer in no time."

Chapter 40

The Truth about Aretha

Farina followed him through a hidden door to a second room. This one was much larger, very lightly decorated and was filled with hundreds of toys, scattered all over the place. Careful not to step over the toys they walked to a giant toy house – about ten feet wide on its sides and nearly six feet high.

Dragan gently opened the door of the toy house and lowered his head to step inside. Farina followed him. What she saw was highly unusual but not surprising. On a small pink bed slept Aretha, all curled up. Her wheelchair was parked by the bed. A few strings of her long hair fell on her beautiful, innocent face as she slept deeply, like an infant.

Dragan sat by her on the ground and caressed her head, almost with motherly softness.

"She is an autistic savant." He said calmly. "From outside they look sick, less than perfect. However, they are born with one or more incredible talent. Aretha's level of maturity is no more than a six-seven year old girl but she has a brain with unusual mathematical power. She can beat the fastest computers of our time easily. Don't ask me how because I don't know. I first found out about her power through chess. She has beaten all top rated computers in the world. Can you imagine?"

Now it all made sense; the weird behaviors, the uncontrollable screams and the unusual quietness. Farina had mixed feelings. She was sympathetic but at the same time somewhat jealous knowing what unworldly power this girl held within.

"Is she your daughter?" She was curious.

"No, no, not so." Objected the Magician. "She is not my daughter. Many years ago I was the researching professor of a university. I'd two assistants, one was your mother Rajia and the other one was Amena, an Egyptian. That was my first experiment on nanotechnology. We all worked very hard. In the course of time two of them had become like sisters. They would do practically everything together.

"Strangely enough, both became pregnant almost about the same time using donor sperm from the same person and quit the project. An army general named Derek Bowman and his close associate, nobody else but our Roger, had been showing extraordinary interest into my research work. I just didn't trust them. So, I packed up and left before the general and his men could get me. Later I came to know that Amena gave birth to Aretha and Rajia to you. But I was on the run and didn't have the opportunity to see either one of you.

"After five years I found out that Amena died in an accident and her abnormal daughter was living a painful life with a relative. I took her up as a foster child. I looked for you for years however had no luck. Just a few days ago I came to know that you were coming in the science tournament. Somebody had spread the news that Rajia's daughter was participating in the tournament. Anybody who knows me knows her as well, as one of my talented assistant scientist.

"Later I found out Roger was coming too. Immediately I knew he'd planned all this. The question was why was he presenting you to me after all these years?

"In spite of the doubt, I took the risk, primarily for Aretha. I wanted to introduce her to her only sister. Look at her face. Can you see the similarities with you?"

Farina wasn't shocked. She felt the connection the first time she'd seen Aretha. She just didn't realize how true her feelings were. The similarities between them were not striking but detectable. So, this was her half sister? A genius! She thought, somewhat proudly.

"You can touch her." Dragan said. "She cannot sleep normally. I've to drug her to put her to sleep."

Farina knelt down by the bed and brushed Aretha's long, dark and smooth hairs with her fingers, gently. She'd similar silky hair. Aretha suddenly threw her hands in the air with a sharp cry and slowly changed side. Startled, Farina stepped back quickly.

Dragan pulled her gently out of the dollhouse. They walked back to the previous room.

"Aretha knows you are her sister." Dragan sat on a stiff wooden table and spoke softly. "She has grown immense feelings for you, even before meeting you in person. My fault. I thought this might improve her social drives. You surely understand why she reacted the way she did in the Isle of Paradise. That is another side of her - absolute anger. Her powers and her anger together are not anything pleasant."

Farina was overwhelmed. Never did she even dream of having a half sister so strange and powerful. Yet, she knew this was the right time to get some answers from her captor.

"It's been a great pleasure meeting you and Aretha." She tried to put it the best way possible. "However, I must ask how long do you plan to keep us here?"

He smiled. "Once Roger shows up with his Sygods I'll hand over all of you to him and move out of here. We have been here for long time. We need a change. In addition, the general and his goons are closing on. Roger had implanted a tiny device on you. That's how he knows where to find me. Unfortunately, the General would also find my location by following Roger.

"I'd have known it before; a little oversight on my part. I've taken care of the bug but it might have already been a little too late. We'll see. But the fact is I don't want to get caught. They could trade the world for my inventions."

There was no reason for Farina not to believe him. She thought of asking where Roger and the Sygods were but later decided against it. Obviously he wasn't very pleased with them. She was also very curious about his inventions but scraped the idea fearing it might annoy him. In the end she tried to be patient and allowed him to talk uninterruptedly. He mostly spoke about Aretha, about her loneliness and hardship.

Farina understood his emotions. For a man of his status it definitely had been very difficult to raise a kid like Aretha.

Another half an hour later before allowing Farina to return to her friends he reached his pocket and took out a ping-pong ball size crystal.

"Safety crystal. I affectionately call it *Blue Dragon*. It has some distinct electro-magnetic properties that can interrupt the signal flow among nanorobots. Don't ask me for any details. Just keep it with you, all the time. You never know when you'll need it."

Farina curiously examined the crystal. It was perfectly round, cold to the touch and had a light blue hue, but nothing special. She put it in her pocket without any further question. Something told her she could trust this strange man.

Just when she was stepping out of his room he called out.

"Farina! I've to tell you this. Aretha loves you very much. But she doesn't control all her faculties." He sighed. "Be aware of her."

Farina knew readily it wasn't something she could take lightly, not when the Magician himself warned her. She wasn't sure exactly what the large, blue crystal would do but yet she felt it unmindfully.

On her way back Diego was friendlier. Clearly, he knew the truth about Farina and Aretha and looked somewhat excited about the fact that the two sisters had finally met.

"Aretha has this unearthly power." He almost whispered. "You'll never believe unless you see it in your own eyes."

"What kind of power?" She asked.

"I can't explain. If you are unfortunate enough you'll see it." Diego said. He was quiet for few seconds and looked a little dejected before he spoke again. "Aretha really liked it here. We all did. I just can't believe we have to go back to Chile again."

"Chile? Is that where you from?" Farina asked.

Diego nervously looked around to see if anybody was listening. Gombu had left earlier; possibly realizing Farina was no match for the heavyset scientist.

"I didn't say this to you." Diego whispered. "Father used to have a secret laboratory there. My dad worked as his supplier. After my parents were killed by the street gang father picked me up from the slum and raised me as his own."

Farina was about to press Diego a little harder to gather some more information about the scientist, when a series of sharp battle cries abruptly broke the sanctity of the silent corridors.

Farina and Diego both ran, fearing the worst. As they burst through the last set of doors into the passage to the Sports room they found Johra engaged in a fierce battle against the three bodyguards. One moment she was in the air throwing swing kicks, the next moment she was on the ground - somersaulting.

The display of her fighting maneuvers and free hand combat skills was simply astounding. The three bodyguards were focused on defending than attacking. They all had visible signs of minor injuries from the ceaseless kicks and punches that Johra kept on raining on them, but yet they showed great patience and held back.

"What are you doing Johra? Stop!" Farina shouted.

Johra issued a blood shivering high pitch karate scream but stopped. "Oh, you are here!" She said, relieved.

Gombu was annoyed to the max. "Is she crazy or something? We don't want to fight her."

Kongsi backed him up. "That's right. All I said that she shouldn't go out of this door and she just went nuts."

"I was worried." Johra fumed. "It has been a while that you were gone. I was just going to look for you. These three odd balls wouldn't let me go. Anyway, are you alright?"

Farina smiled. "I am just fine. Are the kids still busy with the games? I think we should head back to the room and take some rest."

"Good idea." Gombu said.

"Shut up!" Johra barked at him. "One more word and

you are doomed."

Gombu frowned but kept silent. Farina chuckled. A woman weighing barely hundred pounds threatening a human gorilla – one must see to believe.

They didn't have much luck with the kids. Even Shahed refused to leave.

"Just got in Egypt." He briefly mentioned. "I am not leaving before I see the pyramids."

Helpless, they stood aside away from the guards.

"Did you get any information?" Johra whispered to Farina.

"Some." Farina whispered back. "The Sygods are coming. Don't know where they are. He won't say that. But, apparently he has no intention to harm any of us. He is planning to flee."

"Really? What about his experiments?" Johra looked surprised.

"I think he is done with it."

"Too bad."

"Why?"

"It's dangerous. I just hope Roger show up before Dragan escapes."

"He'll wait." Farina grimly said. "He has plans. I could feel it."

Johra looked worried. "Make no mistake. He is a mad man."

Chapter 41

The Sygods Vs the Body Guards

The Sygods had managed to confuse the mosquitoes using electromagnetic scrambler, drove them into the tunnel and closed the door behind them. The elevators had no buttons, so they kicked out the ventilator in the ceiling and climbed on the elevator roof, as planned.

Next they used spider-gloves in addition to their jumpies to climb up the vertical walls. The gloves provided them with a comfortable grip on the concrete surface allowing them to walk up almost like a spider.

They climbed about five hundred feet before reaching the next elevator stoppage. Hong Lee pulled the safety doors open just enough to take a peek inside. He saw a long corridor with closed doors at both ends. There was no sign of any guards or electronic surveillance.

"What do you see?" Rana inquired.

"Nothing." Hong Lee said.

Roger checked it out as well. There was nothing suspicious, not even mosquitoes. This could mean one of two things. Dragan didn't think there was any need to guard it. Or he'd other plans and didn't bother to guard it.

"Somebody tell me something." Dylan said. "I can't just hang on here like a monkey. I weigh too much for these funky gloves and these pair of worthless non flying shoes"

"This gotta be it." Roger said thoughtfully. "There's no more stoppage up there." He pointed above their head. "This means we are on the right place. This must be Dragan's castle. Come on."

They climbed up on the platform quickly.

"What's now?" Miller asked.

"We have to find his lab." Roger replied.

"What about Farina?" Rana asked.

"We'll find her first, of course." Roger was embarrassed.

Everybody understood his eagerness to find the laboratory. That was the heart of Dragan.

Standing in the middle of the corridor Dylan looked both ways. "Which way are we heading? There are two doors in opposite directions, as usual."

Rogers shrugged. "My guess is as good as any of yours. I say let's form two groups and follow two different directions. Hong Lee, Rana and I are going east. Rest of you head west. Let's hurry. We must find Farina before Dragan finds out about our presence."

"You mean if he already doesn't know." Miller said grimly. "He is waiting for us, trust me."

They knew that was a strong possibility. Dragan could be simply leading them to a trap. Nobody argued. Roger was already halfway down the east door. His enthusiasm was understandable. He'd spent too many years and too much effort chasing this mad man. Being so close he could hardly wait. Hong Lee and Rana shrugged and ran to catch up with him.

Miller, Hong Shien and Dylan ran toward the west-end door.

There expedition was halted prematurely. After carefully passing through the first set of heavy metal doors they found themselves in a corridor leading up to another door. The door had opened with a slight push of the hand. Carefully they walked into a large oval space with sky-high ceilings, neatly painted walls in bright white and shiny marble floor. The room had no other doors, no windows and was completely empty, not a piece of furniture, no light fixtures, nothing.

Once they walked in, the door behind them silently closed and disappeared in thin air. Shocked and awed they browsed around the room only to find out there was no other way out. They were completely boxed into a strange white and shiny space.

Dylan threw both his hands up in the air. "I give up. Do you hear me Dragan? Let me go. Take these two."

Miller raised his gun reflexively.

Dylan stepped back acting scared. "Easy! Easy! I was just kidding. I am still your man."

Miller frowned. He didn't appreciate humor much, especially not at a time like this.

Just seconds later something strange happened. An invisible power snatched the gun away right from his hand and threw it at the far corner of the room. Hong Shien stood still, his muscles tensed, eyes sharp, ready to spring up in the air if attacked by the invisible thing.

"Hey Magician," Dylan whispered, "Forget about what I just said to Miller. I am actually yours. Just don't hit me. Please!"

Right before their wide-open eyes a door just popped up on the oval wall and walked in three men - Gombu, Kongsi and Damien. They advanced boldly to the three visitors, stood face-to-face, smirking.

"We have been waiting for you guys." Gombu said. He pointed at Miller. "You are mine."

Kongsi pointed at Hong Shien and made a really threatening notion, something that suggested he was about to tear him off.

Hong Shien tried not to show any expressions but his excitement was hard to miss. He'd sensed a good challenge and could hardly wait to fight.

Damien stood nose to nose to Dylan, who quickly stepped back. "Oh, no! I am not into violence. I am a peaceful man."

"I am going to beat the crap out of you. " Damien said in broken English. "My name is Damien. I am the x-Russian Savate champion."

"Look," Dylan shook his voice in dramatically, "I am already shivering. Can you not smile like a devil, please?"

Damien was advancing aggressively when a deep voice spoke over a hidden microphone: "Be patient Damien. I don't like unequal battles. After all, balancing forces is my specialty. Let's bring the rest of the great Sygods and their crown jewel. We can't just start the party without them."

As soon as the voice stopped they could hear the sound of raging water, rapidly advancing in their direction. Moments later, one of the walls collapsed and came rushing in a monster tide, hissing and slamming as if to destroy just about anything that came on its way. In a blink the water level rose over ten feet and promised more.

"Are you out of your mind, Dragan?" Dylan yelled as he tried to swim up. "Fight like a man. Don't drown your opponent."

That's when they noticed the water had brought in three guests - Roger, Rana and Hong Lee, floating completely helplessly. In a few seconds the surging water started to recede, disappearing faster than it had appeared. Soon there was absolutely no sign of water anywhere. The crushed wall that allowed passage to the water just reappeared in its place, undamaged.

Roger, Hong Lee and Rana stood up quickly; they looked lost, baffled. Strangely enough they were all bone dry as if the water had never touched them.

Hong Lee was the first one to act. He quickly somersaulted several times covering more than twenty feet and stood beside his brother.

Seconds later, a new door popped up at the far corner of the room. The man who stepped in was the great Dragan Valcovich himself. He wore a golden decorative long gown with high straight collars, glittering pointed shoes and an authentic looking crown. He walked with an air of self-importance, a credible mixture of pride and confidence.

Roger had never seen the man face to face before. Deep inside he was excited but outside he maintained a straight face.

"Dragan Valcovich!" He muttered. "Finally we meet."

Dragan extended an exceptionally large hand toward Roger. "I am honored to meet you Mr. Roger. Who ever imagined a man of your caliber would dedicate your life to chase me."

Roger kept his hand to himself. "I respect your intelligence but can't shake the hand that caused death and sufferings of so many innocent people." He coldly said.

Dragan took his hand back, unbothered. "I understand your feelings. I am not specifically proud of everything that I've done. Creating a good balance of power in this truly unequal world isn't easy. I might have failed a few times but who haven't?"

"Whatever!" Roger tried to keep his voice controlled. "Let go the past, let's talk about now."

"Why don't we do so?" Dragan patiently said. "What

is that you want to talk about?"

"I want to talk about Meganano. What you are planning to do with it is a blunder. It will have catastrophic outcome." Roger said, strongly.

"Blunder? Who says so? You represent the first world – the privileged. I could care less about your opinion." Dragan was disdainful.

"You know very well what I represent." Roger said bitterly. "It's called common sense, something that you don't have."

Dragan frowned gravely. "Don't lecture me on common sense. Where's your common sense when the superpowers invades the little countries and cause mayhem, making mockery of everything sensible. Define common sense for me now. Not so easy, is it? I call it t*he game of the mindless.*

"Anyway, you took a lot of futile risk. Too bad, you have to go back empty handed. But, before that," he smirked, "we are going to have a memorable match – a fighting match. Your team against my team. I'd call it a fair fight, wouldn't you? Oh, I forgot about the kids. I can't have them miss out such a wonderful show."

He raised his hand in the air and moved it into a circular motion. One of the sidewalls of the room disappeared and was replaced by clear glass panels. Behind the glass panel stood the kids along with Shahed, Farina and Johra. Johra was visibly excited at the sight of the rest of her team and waved jubilantly.

"Sir, let her stay where she is." Gombu cautiously said.

Dragan guffawed. "The girl is a good fighter. She gave them some hard time. I'll leave her alone. Now, let's start the fight. Roger, I am a fare man and would like to offer you a spectator's seat right by my side."

"I prefer to stay with my boys." Roger boldly said.

Dragan smiled. "Great! I knew you are a man of honor. Let's bet something. If you win this fight the castle is yours. If you lose you'll be my prisoner forever. Huh...huh...huh. That sounded better than I thought. Prisoner forever! Huh...huh...huh. Start the fight!"

Chapter 42

The Big fight

Gombu wasted no time; he came rushing at Miller, grabbed one of his hands, lifted him up in the air in one quick pull and threw him on the floor.

Falling flat on his back Miller could hardly breathe for the first few seconds. He realized the only way he could possibly beat this gorilla was using his gun. Unfortunately, it was at least forty feet away from him. Even if he ran very fast he'd never be able to make it without being caught up by the gorilla. He could only imagine what was going to happen to him in the next few minutes.

Gombu hurried toward him, his hands formed claw like grips. Miller waited until Gombu came too close to grab him before rolling away. For the time being the only way to survive was to play hide and seek.

Dylan had no better luck with Damien either. Damien threw him on the ground with lightning speed and brutal strength and hammered his every attempt to stand on his feet with a barrage of ugly kicks.

Rana came to help him and was easily captured in a nasty lock and later thrown on the ground as well. This started to look like something out of a horror movie.

Kongsi stood boldly before the Hong brothers. His exceptionally broad shoulders and unbelievably muscular arms made the two brothers look tiny and weak. However, it was never easy if not impossible to intimidate the Hong brothers. They glanced at each other as if to prepare a battle plan silently.

"What's the meaning of this farce?" Roger cried out. "Stop it Dragan. You know we are not the government, or the army. We are civilians. Let's stop this madness and discuss it like gentlemen. There's no need for blood."

Dragan found it very humorous. He burst into laughter. "Actually, Roger, I've another idea. Everything has a fitting environment. This is not looking right. How about we make this match even further exciting?"

He raised his arms in the air and rotated them slowly, like a rehearsed magician. Almost instantly the hall room became pitch dark. A few long moments of pure silence was followed by a flood of bright lights, filling up every spot with day like energy. With the light came deafening noise that almost sounded like gazillions of cheering spectators.

Once their eyes adjusted to the light they noticed with utter surprise that they were standing at the center of a very large roman Coliseum like stadium and the noise that they thought were cheering people were exactly what it sounded like. The stadium was filled with people, tens of thousands of them. Soon the crowd started to chant, first incoherently, later in roaring harmony.

"Gombu! Gombu! Kongsi! Kongsi! Damien! Damien!"

It wasn't just the Sygods who were startled by this extravaganza; the three bodyguards seemed just as shocked. Miller, Dylan and Rana took this opportunity to get back on their feet.

Dylan quickly stepped back from Damien. "Have mercy!" He begged, pretending to be scared. "Why embarrass me in front of the whole world. Let's be friend. Give me a hug."

"None of this is real." Roger yelled. "It's holography."

"Looks damn real to me." Miller said bitterly.

Dragan was seen sitting high on a podium in a royal armchair, waving at them, grinning.

"The royal guests get royal reception." His voice echoed in the powerful microphone. "Roger, in the last few years you and your Sygods have given me quite a bit of headache. Many of my smaller projects were interrupted by you and were cancelled. I understand! You were doing it for the good of humanity. Let's say, this is my way of saying thank you. Huh...huh...huh!"

Roger shouted something back but he couldn't even hear his own words in the loud jeering of the crowd that followed. Dragan raised his arms and signaled everybody to be quiet. In seconds the whole stadium turned so quiet that one could even hear a pin dropped.

"Roger, you were saying...?" Dragan said.

"I am asking you to reconsider your plans about Meganano. Please listen to me." Roger shouted.

"You are still worried about Meganano?" Dragan smiled patiently, as if he was listening to the last wishes of the death row convict. "If I were you I'd be worried about my life."

"I've much bigger thing to worry about – the world."

"The world? What is it that you are so concerned about?" Dragan frowned, acting confused.

"Don't act naïve. " Roger said calmly. "The buzz was there for years but now we all know that you have built something phenomenal. We also know you have offered to sell it to a handful of countries. That's a blunder. You are forgetting that if you sell Meganano selectively to a few third world countries in the name of balancing world power, it would only create more chaos and trouble. No real good can come from it.

"The powerful countries like America, Russia, China, India, German, Japan who you don't want to sell it to, would never allow them to live in peace. Consider the gasoline of the Middle East. It brought in good and evil both in equal parts. The third world countries with the new technology cannot expect to have a fate any different than that if not much worse."

"I'd rather destroy this technology before I hand it over to the super powers." Dragan said with disgust. "Enough is enough. They have already caused more mayhem than I possibly could in a million lives. It's payback time."

"Why don't you understand?" Roger almost pleaded. "Meganano would do more bad than good to them. It would in turn bring wars to them, resulting into shattered economy and millions of unnecessary deaths."

"That's a ridiculous exaggeration. I've no reason to believe anything like that is going to happen. On the other hand, what choice do I have? Give it to America? Russia? Not in their wildest dreams."

"I don't suggest that." Roger said. "I want you to give it to everybody. Let every country in the world use this technology and be benefited."

Dragan shook his head strongly. "No, I cannot do that. I've no desire to give the powerful yet another weapon." He seemed impatient, clearly annoyed. "What makes you think that your judgment is better than mine?" His confidence seemed wearing off. "In fact I don't even think you should worry about that now. Let me see how you use your *good judgment* to save your own life. Huh…huh…huh!"

"Princess! Princess!" Suddenly the crowd chanted in roaring reception.

Looking up they saw Aretha sitting on a flying golden chariot, her face glowing in excitement as he flew next to Dragan.

Once seated on a high back chair right by her father she raised her right arm above her head and waved it in an airy motion.

She'd barely finished when magically the kids, Johra and Shahed discovered themselves inside the arena, standing by Roger and the team. Only Farina found her sitting on a golden chair located on a high podium built right beside the center field. They had hardly any time to respond to this completely unexpected twist because about the same time a large iron gate had opened and came rushing out three raging monsters.

Now, this was something to be worried about, thought Roger. These were the three monsters that they had put to sleep just a short while ago using the gas. Their belligerent attitude made it quite clear that they were not in a friendly mode. Obviously the memory of being gassed was still very vivid in their minds. Things looked very bleak, he admitted.

"Well! Well! Well!" Dragan shrugged helplessly. "Isn't exactly the way I planned it but I guess I can live with it. Roger, just a word of caution. Don't try to use the same gas on the monsters. It's not going to work. They have nanorobots inside their bodies. You know about the tiny machines, don't you? After the first attack those machines have already worked out a protection plan against it."

"Great! Wonderful! How do you expect us to beat them? Pinch them? Tickle them?" Dylan scorned.

"Take the kids and stay back." Roger instructed Johra. "We'll take care of these circus punks. Don't know how but we'll find something. Shahed, please stay with Johra."

"I want to fight." Shahed tried to be brave but his trembling voice gave away the truth.

Johra held him by the arm and pulled him away with the kids. Shahed didn't object. He knew he'd just be a burden to the others if he joined them to fight.

Johra gathered the kids in one place, moved them as far away as she possibly could within the arena. Interestingly, the kids didn't seem to be scared at all. They rather seemed quite amused.

Farina, to her dismay, soon found out that somehow she was actually stuck to the chair and couldn't move herself up.

"Don't struggle." She heard Flyball whispering in her ear. "Just take it easy. You won't be able to get out of this chair on your own."

"Isn't there any way to save them, Flyball?" Farina asked helplessly.

"Don't worry." Flyball calmly said. "The kids will be safe. I won't let anything happen to them. It's my responsibility. However, I can't do anything about the others. That's beyond my power."

"How are you going to save the kids?" Farina asked with disbelief.

"I've many powers." Flyball confidently said. "You might find out soon."

Chapter 43

The Secret

Roger formed a half circle with Dylan, Miller, Rana and the Hong brothers. Facing them stood Gombu, Kongsi, Damien and the three foaming monsters, less than twenty yards away. With the roaring crowd backing them up, the six men advanced toward the Sygods in short, confident steps.

"If you can provide safety to the kids," Farina was thinking loudly, "Johra can give a hand to Roger. With her in the team, they'll have better chance to survive."

"I surely can. Have faith in this little guy." Flyball sounded excited. Clearly it was looking for an opportunity to show Farina some of its powers.

"But how can I let them know?" Farina said, helplessly.

"Hello! You are ignoring me." Flyball cried out. "I can help."

"How?"

"Simple! I've telepathic power, weak but works within short distance. Thanks to the big guy. I pass him information over the brainwave. In English, I can get you connected to anybody in that arena."

"You can?" Farina was doubtful. "Give me Roger, then. Hurry up, please."

Just moments later Flyball announced, "Done! You

and Roger should be able to talk now. Just think what you want to say. A word of caution, all information will be passing through me."

"Roger! Can you hear me?" Farina spoke in her mind.

Roger looked at her, surprised. "Yes! How...? Are you okay?"

"Yes, I am fine but stuck." Farina replied. "Anyway, I think I can help. I've clear view of the battle ground from here."

"Great!" Roger said. "This is your opportunity to use your skill of chess in real world situation. Give me some ideas, quick."

Farina was thinking fast. "Get divided into smaller teams. The kids do not need Johra. They have guaranteed safety. Dragan has ensured that. Just trust me on this. Call her back to defense line. Keep moving around the field, continuously. Don't let the enemy focus on any one of you." She paused to clear her thoughts.

"Don't allow the Hong brothers to get involved into direct fight. Instead they should resort to quick counter attacks. They are no match in strength against these opponents but with their skill and speed they can do damage to the enemy line. They are your primary weapons.

"Miller doesn't have his guns but he still has exceptional ability to hit a target. Give him some Ninja stars and throwing knives. He might be able to do some damage."

Roger quickly instructed the team accordingly. Johra was apprehensive in leaving the kids in the care of Shahed alone but at the end decided to join the fight. Shahed was asked to take the kids as far away as possible from the battle ground and stay close to them. His initial fear had worn out to some extent and adrenaline pumped into his body. He quickly drove the kids to the outer edge of the round arena, to a safe distance.

Roger divided the team into four groups. Each group was asked to change locations frequently and to avoid direct conflicts. Everybody understood flashing counter attacks were there only way out of this deadly situation.

Their sudden change in strategy initially surprised and later confused the aggressors. The ceaseless movement of the smaller groups was soon able to disintegrate their opponent as they aimlessly chased them around the field.

"It is time for counter attack." Farina suggested. "Gombu is the brain of the group. He must go first. You have to make it quick and precise."

In a slight gesture of Roger's finger the four groups suddenly teamed up and attacked a puzzled Gombu. As he tried to put up a defense against the combined attack, Hong Lee took full opportunity of the situation and delivered a ferocious flying kick right on his neck followed by Hong Shien, who delivered a double leg low flying kick right on his sturdy legs. Gombu fell heavily on his back. At that point Dylan dived over him and hit him right on the chest with a fierce elbow. Gombu screamed in pain. Kongsi and Damien rushed to help him. The Sygods quickly spread out again. After a few futile attempts to stand on his feet Gombu gave up.

"One less, five to go." Roger muttered.

"Next Kongsi. Back off and allow him to get aggressive." Farina said.

Roger signaled the team to step back and regroup. "I knew I could rely on you." He said to Farina.

"Is that why you used me as bait?" Farina could not hide her contempt.

"When I heard that Dragan was about to sell his

MegaNano I became desperate." Roger confessed.

"You risked my life. It wasn't right."

"I didn't say it was. However, I knew Dragan would never harm you. He must have already told you everything."

"Watch out!" Farina warned.

Kongsi was becoming impatient. Realizing Roger was the driving force he attacked him. Roger rolled out of his reach. Johra threw a knife at Kongsi. He moved out of its path effortlessly.

Rana used his blowpipe on Kongsi almost simultaneously. Kongsi saw it coming a bit too late and tried to spin out of its way. The poisonous pin missed him by millimeters but in the process he lost his footing. Hong brothers took it up from there.

Hong Lee held Hong Shien by his hands, spun him around once and released him, who flew right at Kongsi with a kick that hit him like a bullet. Kongsi's muscular body were lifted in the air and slammed right back on the ground. He didn't move. The Sygods spread out again.

"Yes, Dragan told me everything." Farina picked up from where they left. "Aretha and I share the same father. How did you know this?"

"Let's say I know him for very long time. Now, did he tell you who your father is?"

"Some donor." Farina could sense something fishy.

"Strange! He hid it from you?" Roger sounded unsure.

Farina needed a long pause before she could gather up the courage to put her fear in words. "Are you suggesting he is our father?"

"According to your mother's journal - yes. Both you and Aretha."

"You knew my mother?"

"Yes, to some extent." Roger answered somberly.

Farina sighed. She'd so much expectation and dreams about her father. Who knew this mysterious, mad man was her dad! She wondered why he'd lie about his paternity. If he didn't want to reveal his true identity, then why even bother to bring her here? Did he suddenly realize how low Farina thought about him and how disappointed she might be if she found out he was her father?

Looking at the crowned man sitting on a high back heavily decorated golden throne, she could barely find any resemblance of the friendly, affectionate man she'd spoken earlier that day. It was obvious he'd things to settle with Roger. He made no attempt to hide his true feelings as he joined the roaring crowd in cheering his men against the Sygods. "Hit! Hit! Hit!" His loud voice echoed every corner of the enormous stadium.

Chapter 44

The Thrasher

"Next Damien." Farina said.

"Yes, of course." Roger agreed.

Damien must have noticed a pattern and guessed he could be attacked next because he held on his aggression and became more vigilant. However that strategy didn't work very well. The Sygods ignored the three giants totally and ganged up on him.

Attacked on all fronts Damien could put on very little resistance. He looked for help from the monsters but they showed no interest in him. Clearly they were not in good terms with the bodyguards and made no attempt to come to their rescue.

In less than ten seconds Damien discovered himself on the ground struggling for air as a result of Hong Lee's sweeping kick followed by Dylan's dangerous diving elbow. Dylan was pretty happy with this new move. In boxing there was no concept of crashing on others with your elbows. It felt good. He even wondered if he should take up wrestling.

The three monsters looked pleased with the fate of the three bodyguards. They boastfully waved at the cheering crowd; their unbelievably muscular arms could intimidate even the toughest opponents. They roared, slapped their chests in a show of strength and then boldly advanced toward the Sygods.

Farina knew it wasn't going to be easy to defeat these monsters. Roger had no illusion either. He asked the teams to regroup and stay in safe distance. The last thing he wanted was to attack immaturely and obtain unnecessary injuries if not loss of lives.

The kids had been merrily running around the outer skirt of the field, bursting into celebration after each spectacular counter attacks by the Sygods. Then suddenly, for some strange reason they decided to ignore Shahed's commands and moved closer to the giants, as the Sygods looked in disbelief.

Farina was alarmed and annoyed. No matter what the tiny Flyball claimed, she still couldn't see how it could save those kids if one of the beastly giants attacked them. Roger and the rest of the team tried to scream some sense into them but in vein. With childish fearlessness and perhaps a sudden rush of adrenaline they continued to advance toward the center of the arena.

"What are they doing?" Farina asked Roger.

"No idea. Hopefully they won't come too close. How do you think we should handle these monsters?" Roger asked.

Many ideas crossed Farina's mind but none looked perfect. Sudden counter attack wouldn't work very effectively against these large bodied extremely strong humans. The Sygods would have to wear them down slowly.

"Use the jumpies." She suggested. "Those would help you to spring away from their reach."

Roger instructed the team accordingly. Everybody put on their jumpies and spread out to create a half circle around the three giants. The giants looked eager to attack.

Farina noticed the kids were now close enough to be on harm's way.

"Flyball, they'll be safe, right?" She asked anxiously.

"Of course!" Flyball answered readily. "They are brave."

"Brave and stupid! Anyway, I am counting on you." Farina knew she'd no other choice but to rely on Flyball.

"Farina?" Roger called out.

"Yes, I can hear." She replied.

"Any more ideas?"

"I do. No matter how big they are they must have at least one weak point. I believe it's their eyes. We have to interrupt their ability to see. Then we'll have to use their own weight against them. There's only one way to do that. Trip them over."

"Good plan." Roger said. "Though, they seem to be very quick and alert. How are we going to destroy their eyesight?"

They didn't have time to think; the giants roared in rage and attacked them with full force. The ground shook below with the vigor of a small earthquake.

"Oh boy! There they come." Dylan was truly scared.

The giants rushed toward them with their hands spread out, clearly intending to squeeze their opponents to death.

"Watch out!" Roger cautioned.

Everybody jumped frantically to get away from the path of the three.

The crowd chanted: "Fight! Fight! Fight!"

"I feel like slapping the crap out of this crowd." Dylan tartly said. "You wanna see fight? Come down here, pals. I am going to break every bone in your bodies."

"Don't worry about their bones," Johra said, "Save

yours from getting mushy."

"As long as I don't become their snack, I am okay." Dylan muttered. Joking or not, he'd no delusion about the graveness of the situation.

The three giants recovered and wasted little time before attacking again. As they came rushing the Hong brothers locked their eyes briefly, planning their next move. It was clear they weren't going to be chased around, not any more.

This time instead of jumping away from the monsters like the rest of their team members, the brothers sprung over the giants and landed behind them. The monsters took their bait and two of them turned around and came after them (the brothers) while the third one stood nearby, driving away any of the Sygods who tried to come forward.

Hongs were in no hurry to deal with them. They continued to move around, leaping several feet over the giants' heads. They seemed to enjoy the marvel of the jumpies.

The two giants had little patience for this game. They jumped up in an attempt to grab the elusive enemies. This is when the brothers attacked back. Before the two giants had time to fully regain their balance the Hongs leaped in the air again, this time only half as high, spun in the air and then delivered two perfect flying kicks with brutal force right on the faces of the two giants.

For a few seconds nothing happened. The brothers jumped away to prepare for the next attack. The giants stood stubbornly as blood gushed out from their noses and mouths and streamed down their bodies, soaking their cloths in thick, red fluid. Then, they took couple of steps forward, shaking heavily on their feet, before slowly crumbling to the ground like two lifeless sacks of sand, unconscious.

Suddenly there was pin drop silence in the stadium. This was not something that anybody had expected. There was a slow gasping sound that traveled through the crowd, almost in a rhythm.

The third giant, visibly shaken, went to check on his mates. As he knelt down to examine his friends Roger knew it was the right time to take him down. He signaled rest of the team to stage a synchronized attack. The giant must suspected something like this might happen because he quickly turned around and faced them boldly. The initial attack had little impact on the gigantic man as he brushed them off with sweeping arms as thick as a tree trunk.

The Hong brothers came back in the attack with another set of powerful flying kicks. The giant guarded his face with crossed arms but was pushed back by several yards and suffered visible bruises on his arms. Agitated and hurting he roared like a wounded tiger.

Roger decided not to allow him any time to recuperate and put up a serious fight. He spearheaded another attack on the weakening giant, who growled in anger and hastily tried to shove them away. He looked nervous, vulnerable.

The kids must have believed that this was an appropriate time to get some real action. They disregarded all the warnings and moved too close to the giant, who snatched away the opportunity by capturing Musa in one quick movement.

Musa, leading the pack, was quite surprised when the giant suddenly grabbed him by the waist and was raising him above his head with the clear intent of slamming him hard on the ground. He screamed at the top of his voice, terrified to death.

That's when something very strange happened. A narrow but intense blue laser beam hit the giant on the hand like a sharp spear. He flinched in excruciating pain and allowed Musa to slip down. There was a clear sign of burn on his hand - an electric burn. Still in pain, he looked down right at the source of the laser.

"Flyball, I assume that was you?" Farina anxiously said.

"Of course." Flyball proudly said. "That's one of my powers. However, it is not strong enough to completely stop a mountain like him."

As if to prove it right the giant shook off the pain and advanced toward them in long, determined strides.

Farina was alarmed. "Flyball, is he going to attack us?"

"He can't see me. He probably thinks it was you. Don't worry. I'll take care of it."

"You better. He looks mad!"

Flyball hit the advancing giant with a few more laser shots, which slowed him down but proved to be insufficient to totally incapacitate him. Suffering and furious the giant rushed toward Farina with some serious agenda, Farina could tell.

Realizing what was about to happen, the Sygods frantically ran to intercept the giant but he reached the podium where Farina was seated a second earlier than them. The jubilant crowd backed him up with a thundering approval as he raised his arms in the air before hammering them down on Farina, definitely crashing her to her death.

Then, something really bizarre happened. In a blink of eye the sky turned dark and an enormous spinning twister appeared from nowhere along with startling lightening and cracking thunders. Before anybody had a chance to realize what was happening it issued several tentacles like smoky spinning arms which coiled around the giant like group of raging snakes.

Just seconds later the twister picked the giant up effortlessly, pulled him up tens of feet high and slammed him on the hard ground with such power that even the gigantic stadium shook in the impact.

"The Thrasher! The Thrasher!" The crowd whispered.

Shaken but temporarily relieved, Farina looked up at the Thrasher, an entity at least a hundred feet high and fifty feet wide at the base, continuously spinning, as hundreds of arms protruded out of it like flames of a fire.

The Thrasher picked up the immobile body of the giant a second time and smashed it against the ground forcefully. The giant must have died the first time, this time his body was damaged beyond recognition.

Chapter 45

Castle under Attack

The Thrasher paced inside the stadium in unstoppable rage for a few more seconds, as if it was looking for something to destroy, to smash into pieces. Farina looked at Dragan and noticed he was holding Aretha close to his body.

Aretha, her eyes closed, face twirled, sat into his lap motionless. Was the Thrasher Aretha's creation? Farina wondered. Was this what Diego referred to earlier? Was she being protective to her?

As the crowd roared "Thrasher! Thrasher!" the twisting gaseous monster started to calm down slowly, its spinning decreased, the flame like arms started to subside, when a thundering blast shook everything, the stadium, the mountain, even the Thrasher. A series of aftershocks accompanied by more deafening blasts followed closely. Then, for a few long moments everything was quiet. The roaring crowd was mum in complete shock.

Then, on a loud speaker a mechanical voice announced: "The Castle of Illusion has been attacked! The Castle of Illusion has been attacked!"

The words echoed relentlessly as the blasts returned in dozens, shaking the earth beneath in close intervals.

Dragan, grave and angry, slowly stood up, raised his arms in the air and muttered in total disbelief, "So quickly?

How is that possible?"

"You brought this upon yourself, Dragan!" Roger shouted.

"No, you did." Dragan shouted back. "All I wanted is my daughter."

"And all I wanted is you to share the Meganano." Roger retorted.

"You'll never see the face of it." Dragan replied angrily.

At this point the crowd started to disintegrate into sparkling dots before completely disappearing. The stadium was the next to fade away in thin air along with several walls and fancy partitions leaving Roger and the rest of the visitors in awe as they found themselves standing in a large, continuous cave, with a series of glass windows dotting the outer edges offering views from the mountain range and the valley.

"So, this is the original castle?" Roger muttered. "Just a big cave? Everything else was just illusion!"

Looking out through the windows they saw a few dozens of modern special powered helicopters hovering around the castle.

"You stinking devils! I am going to take care of you soon." Dragan warned pointing an angry finger at the invaders.

Moments later the giant, tenacious pterodactyls poured out through an opening in the castle and attacked the helicopters.

Unfortunately they had no chance against the modern weaponry. The soldiers mercilessly fired upon them with automatic machineguns. Bloodied and busted they perished in large numbers.

"Are they real?" Farina asked Flyball, pitifully.

"Reality is relative." It grimly replied. "They are made of a special class of nanorobots - very small particles with specific attributes. They did look and feel real."

"They sure did." Farina breathed out deeply, relieved.

Another strong blast shook the castle vehemently. For a moment it felt as if the whole mountain was about to crumble down to the ground. Dust and smashed rocks gushed into the castle, making it so murky that they could barely see anything.

It took minutes before the dust started to settle down. Once the vision became clear they noticed one part of the castle had been blown away opening up the sky above. The attackers must have thrown a small missile. The loud roar of an approaching chopper made it apparent what the invaders had in mind. They were planning to land it right inside the castle.

"This must be that worthless Colonel." Dragan growled in absolute anger, his eyes red as blood. "Does that idiot have any idea what this mountain holds?"

"Don't just stand there." He yelled at Roger. "None of you will be spared from the stupidity of this insect. Follow me. I'll make sure all of you get out of here safely. Quick! Gombu! Kongsi! Damien! What are you waiting for - a kiss in the forehead?"

The three bodyguards struggled on their feet and rushed to catch up with Dragan, who was already on his way to the escape route.

"Come quick." Dragan shouted at Roger again. "There's no time to waste. Farina, bring the kids. Quick!"

Dragan picked Aretha up from her wheelchair and briskly ran toward the far end of the long cave. Exhausted and anemic, Aretha leaned on his chest like a little girl. The Thrasher had calmed down and disappeared but it had obviously drained all her energy.

Farina knew deep in her mind Dragan would not knowingly hurt her or the kids. She waved at the kids to come with her as she followed Dragan. Roger hesitated for a few seconds. At the end he knew he'd no other choice. They couldn't stay in that open cave. They would get shot at and possibly killed.

"Hello? Roger!" Dylan called out as they waited for Roger's decision. "Just want to be clear. We are waiting here until they shoot us dead, right?"

"We got to go." Rana said, ready to run.

"Let's go." Roger said. "After them."

"We'll find the lab later." Rana said as they dashed at the other end of the cave where Dragan and the rest had gathered.

"This idiot colonel is going to destroy everything." Roger said. "We'll never find the lab."

"Live today, lab tomorrow." Dylan said, running as fast as he could.

Dragan stood before a solid wall and made a quick gesture with his hand that looked almost magical but Farina assumed it was some kind of electronic authentication. In seconds the stony wall cracked into two sliding doors revealing a narrow, stone staircase running down steeply. Dragan led the pack into the staircase. There was no visible light source but the tunnel was lit with a bluish gleam.

The soldiers who had just climbed out of the chopper fired openly at them but missed as the sliding doors closed quickly. Gombu, Kongsi and Damien went past Dragan and took the lead. Farina and the kids stayed between Dragan's team and the Sygods. Despite all the commotions and deadly attacks the kids remained high-spirited. It was surprising how quickly they had adapted to demanding situation. Farina was very proud.

The bombings continued. With each hit the mountain shook in strong spasms. There was no way to know exactly where the bombs were falling.

"We are safe here." Dragan broke the silence. "This tunnel is deep inside the mountain. It won't crumble that easily."

"Finally you did something sensible." Dylan taunted.

"Watch it!" Johra warned. "He is showing us the way out."

"Yeah, yeah. My bad." Dylan muttered. "He started all this, remember?"

Another blast. More tremors. Some loose smashed rocks rolled down the stairway. They paused for a moment, fearing the worst. The tremor stopped.

"What are they trying to do?" Miller asked.

"They are trying to break the door to this tunnel." Roger replied.

The next blast sounded awfully close, as if to prove Roger right.

"Oh damn! Faster! Faster!" Dragan shouted.

They moved quicker, realizing how bad things would turn out if the soldiers destroyed the door and caught up with them.

Another forty-fifty stairs later they came down to a specious platform that was so poorly lit that one could barely see anything beyond a few feet. Dragan stopped here for a moment.

"Roger, you go south." He pointed at a door on his right. "Once you go past the door you'll be inside another tunnel. It'll take you out of the mountain. I doubt the Colonel would harm any of you. If things end safely we'll meet again.

You are a worthy opponent."

"Dragan, where is Meganano?" Roger sharply asked. "I can't let you escape with that."

Dragan burst into laughter. "Meganano! Are you crazy? You have no time to waste. They are coming. Save the lives of these kids first. Go. We can talk about Meganano later."

Roger knew Dragan was right. The soldiers were on their tail. It was only matter of time before the secret door gave up. However, he'd another choice.

"Take the kids and get out of here." He told Farina. "Sygods will shield you. Go on. I must get that Meganano."

He'd barely finished when the door to the hidden staircase blew up with a loud bang; debris flew all over the place, some reaching far below on the platform where they were standing. The tunnel shook up, like an earthquake; a series of tremors passed through. Smoke and dust had carried down quickly, fogging their views. Seconds later the floor cracked in the middle and continued to drift away rapidly increasing the crevice to several yards.

Chapter 46

Run! Run! Run!

Shahed and Farina led the kids toward the south door with the Sygods staying right behind them. It was obvious the most important thing now was to get the kids safely out of that war zone. If they lived the Sygods could always chase Dragan and his Meganano, another time, another place.

Not exactly what Roger was thinking. He wondered if he allowed Dragan to slip away would he (Roger) ever find him again. Would he be able to stop the Meganano from falling into wrong hands? He wasn't ready to take that chance.

The crack on the floor was now more than ten feet and was still growing. Dragan had gone to the north side with his party. Roger knew he'd to go after him. After all these years he couldn't simply let this man escape. He quickly waved at his team.

"Keep going. I'll see you guys outside."

Before anybody had a chance to react Roger took a short run up and jumped over the crevice to the other side. However, he must have misjudged the distance because instead of clearing it he hit the wall and somehow clang to the edge with his fingers.

Johra, surprised, wasted no time thinking. She jumped over the crack safely, grabbed Roger by the hand

and tried to pull him up.

Farina, not sure whether it was adrenaline or just sisterhood bondage, jumped over the crack quickly and gave Johra a hand in pulling Roger up on the ground.

"Thanks for coming." Johra said, admiringly.

"You bet!" Farina grinned. It felt really good. To her Johra had already become a symbol of adventure.

"Oh dang, the girls are taking all the credit now!" Dylan taunted.

"Jump back!" The kids shouted. "The gap is getting bigger!"

They were right. The distance between the edges was now more than twenty feet. There was no way they could jump back.

Farina looked for Dragan and his company, hoping they might still be in the vicinity. She was wrong. They were long gone.
The debris had stopped falling and the dust was settling down. They heard several dozen footsteps rushing down the stairs, right toward them.

"What should we do?" Farina desperately asked.

Roger and Johra exchanged glances.

"We have no other choice." Roger calmly said. "Rana, you guys keep going. We'll find you soon."

"Farina, be careful!" Shahed cried out.

"Don't worry, Uncle Shahed." Farina tried to appease him. "I'll be okay. You take care of the kids."

"We are doing just fine." Stanley roared.

"We are going to beat the crap out of them." Oliver boastfully added.

"Is that after or before you wet yourself?" Preeti scorned.

"Watch your mouth!" Stanley warned.

"Stop!" Dylan stepped in. "One more word and you kids will become the crazy colonel's snack. Move!"

They rushed through the south end door into the adjacent tunnel.

Roger felt guilty realizing how he'd ended up putting Johra and Farina into a horrible situation. If he'd known the girls would come to rescue him he'd have never done it. But it was too late. They had no other choice but to follow Dragan's footstep. Dragan might get mad, but Farina's presence would definitely calm him down. He ran toward the north end door, closely followed by Johra and Farina.

As the soldiers marched down the stairs they fired several rounds of warning shots, each generated an endless string of echoes as the bullets ricocheted on the rocky walls.

"These idiots are going to cause a rock slide." Roger muttered as they dashed past the door that Dragan had taken and stepped into a long, shadowy passage. They saw some movement hundreds of yards ahead. It had to be Dragan and his bodyguards. Roger ran as fast as he could with Johra and Farina following him closely.

Dragan and his team scurried past through another set of doors at the end of the passage. Before Roger and the girls had a chance to slip out of the passage another big blast shook the mountain once again. This time it felt much closer. The air filled with dust dense as cloud. For a few moments they went completely blind and deaf. Once their vision cleared up a little they noticed a section of the ceiling ahead of them broke down and dropped over the passage, completely blocking the exit.

Yet another blast shook the mountain. More rocks slid into the cave and rolled further down the passage. They knew they had to take shelter. There was no way to know where the bombs were going to fall next. The whole ceiling could come crumbling down right on them.

They walked around in the fuzzy darkness stumbling over boulders and rubbles for a little while before finding a corner that looked untouched from all the destruction.

"Damn! We are stuck here." Johra sounded disappointed.

Roger shrugged. "The Great Magician escapes again. The worst part - he takes the Meganano with him. Who knows what he is going to do with it? This idiot Colonel ruined my plan."

"So much for your plan!" Farina teased.

"Okay, may be it wasn't perfect." Roger defended. "I tried."

"What is this Meganano, anyway?" Farina inquired.

"A phenomenal application of nanotechnology, something that Dragan has been working on for decades."

"Flyball mentioned something called nanorobots. Does Meganano have anything to do with that?"

"Well, nanorobots are the building block of all nanotechnology applications. Consider nanofog. It is an entity built with trillions of nano sized tiny computers grouped together, shortly nanorobots. They can be as small as a molecule. You can make them do all kind of stuff by sending proper signals to them. Of course, it would require several supercomputers to control these trillions of nanorobots.

"Meganano is built with an especial type of biological nanorobots. It has the characteristics of an energy cell and can be used instead of gasoline. Dragan took incredible sum of money from the Americans to build this technology. All first world countries want a good alternative of oil to reduce dependency on Middle East, especially America. They are ready to give an eye for anything that looks promising.

"Dragan used them. He never intended to hand it over to them. He believes in balance of power on earth. He is planning to sell this technology to the third world countries. He wants them to rise."

"Why is that so bad?" Johra said, surprised. "If the poor countries can prosper using this technology, isn't that good for the world?"

Roger shook his head in disagreement. "America, perhaps countries like Russia, China or even India could resort to force to get their hands over this technology. There will be wars. There will be blood bath. Innocent people will die. Communities will be destroyed. Kids will meet horrific ends. The truth is - he is going to invite an uncertain future. And he knows that. Stubborn, stubborn fool!"

He'd barely finished talking when a section of the stony wall ahead of them blasted into pieces. Running back they looked for a safe place to hide behind big boulders. The sound of the blast echoed on the walls, the air filled with the smell of ammunition. They could hear soldiers closing on them.

Roger was panicky. "We can't afford to get caught by the colonel. He knows your real identity. Damn it!"

Farina was surprised. He'd never seen Roger so nervous. "Who is this colonel?"

"He is the right hand of General Derek Bowman, chief of Bureau of Crime Reduction. It's just a bogus title. He heads a secret army of devoted American soldiers and officers who would do anything in the name of their country. Anyway, he was the one who made the agreement with Dragan. When he realized he has been conned he became furious and has been looking for Dragan since."

"How would they know my true identity?"

Roger cleared his throat. "We used to work together. Seems like a long time ago. I'd to shake hands with the devil himself to stop Dragan."

"Did he have anything to do with the attack on my mother?"

"I sure have reason to believe so. It couldn't have been anybody else."

"How can you be so sure?"

"He wasn't trying to hurt her. It was just a show. Remember the kidnapping attempt on you? After Dylan had messaged the guy a little he told him somebody offered him ten thousand dollars to make up a scene."

"He was not a real kidnapper?"

"No. He was a retired postal worker, buried in debt. Anyway, looks like we have bigger and real problems to worry about."

The soldiers had now entered the cave. They were carrying powerful flashlights. It took them no time to find the three runaways.

"Colonel Blake!" One of the men called out.

Chapter 47

The Prisoner

A tall, strong, clean shaved man hurried down the stairs and ran into the rubble. He wore full army dress, with a series of badges pinned on his chest as the proof of his heroic achievements over the years.

"That's Colonel Blake." Roger muttered. "Junk soldier."

Colonel held a gun in his hand and a smirk on his face. He ignored Roger and spoke to Farina. "You are the one I was looking for. This time I got Dragan. He won't escape leaving his daughter at risk, would he, Roger?" Colonel's smirk extended into a big smile.

"Who knows, Colonel?" Roger dryly said. "May be Meganano is dearer to him."

Don Blake walked close to them in long stride. "Let's test it. Come on Farina. We'll be going for a short air trip."

He signaled his men to take her upstairs where one of the choppers had landed earlier. As two men stepped ahead to grab Farina, Johra suddenly moved forward and with two successive kicks into the groins took care of them quickly.

Few others came rushing at her, cautiously. Obviously they were already briefed about the Sygods. Johra somersaulted on the ground once and delivered two strong kicks, crashing couple more on the ground. Next she rolled away from the pack, stood up, pulled out some of her Ninja stars and started throwing them indiscriminately. When several soldiers cried out in pain, the rest kissed the ground, their guns drawn.

"Nobody shoots." The Colonel shouted. "I want Farina alive."

Just about that time two heavily built big men entered the cave.

"Jarvis! Harvis!" Colonel happily called out. "Where had you been? Take care of this crazy girl. No shooting." Colonel ordered.

The two brothers nodded and boldly walked toward Johra, dodging her swishing Ninja stars with ease. Johra stepped back, not knowing what she could possibly do to stop these two fast moving giants. Soon she'd no place to go as her back pressed against the hard surface of the cave.

Harvis displayed a gun. "Just give up. No harm will be done."

Johra wasn't yet ready to surrender. With a sudden movement she jumped forward and swung his legs as forcefully as she could at the two, hoping to meet their lower abdomens. She hit okay but to her amazement there was barely any impact on the two.

Johra tried to move away from their reach quickly but apparently the brothers were just as fast. Harvis grabbed her by the hand and in one jerk pulled her body into the air, slammed her lightly on the hard floor. Johra dipped into darkness for a few long moments. Jarvis came forward, twisted her hands back and handcuffed them.

"Now be a good girl."

Colonel was clearly annoyed. "Nonsense! Take Farina to the chopper. "

Harvis effortlessly picked Farina up on his shoulder

and walked back to the stairs.

"You are doing a mistake." Roger grimly said. "She has no role in his life. It wouldn't work."

Colonel smirked. "We'll see. Meganano is mine. Let the game begin."

He scurried out of the cave with his remaining soldiers.

Once they were gone and all he could hear was their decaying footsteps Roger went to check on Johra. He didn't want to give the psychopath any excuse to kill him. Johra was alert and could stand up on her feet on her own. She twisted her arms over her head and brought them in front of her body. Next moment a small hairpin showed up in her fingers. A few seconds later she took off her handcuffs and slammed them on the floor.

"I am going up." She said.

Roger held her hand. "There's no use following them. They have guns. Not only they can hurt us, they can hurt Farina too. Now her life depends on her father and sister. We are practically powerless. Instead of doing something regretful, we should try to get out of this mountain."

Johra didn't try to hide her frustration. "If anything happens to her I'll never forgive me. She is like the sister that I never had."

"I know that." Roger tried to comfort her. "Don't worry. Dragan is not going to take off leaving Farina in danger."

"I hope not." Johra didn't sound very convinced. "Let's follow them to the upper level."

"That's not a bad idea." Roger thoughtfully said. "There's no other way to get out of this rubble anyway."

Johra had already hopped onto the stairs and was

climbing up fast. Roger caught up with her quickly. He needed to make sure Johra didn't rush into something risky. Sometimes she could be a little irrational.

Johra and Roger had just climbed up the stairs to the upper level when Colonel Don Blake and his men flew away in the chopper with Farina. It was out of their sight in mere seconds. Johra ran toward the open mouth. The star lit sky peeked through the rubble. Johra stood by the edge and looked out. To her amazement she saw hundreds of military helicopters hovering around the castle. The strong flashlights from the flying choppers had the whole mountain lit up. Roger ran to her side.

"The castle is defenseless. The blasts must have damaged Dragan's computing facilities." He said. "The pterodactyls were obviously applications of Nanorobots. It would have taken very high computing power to control them. Looks like the Magician's Castle of Illusion have fallen."

Johra wasn't listening to him.

"Where did that devil take Farina?" She muttered looking through the swarming choppers.

"Don't worry." Roger calmly said. "He won't take her too far. He needs Dragan. He doesn't care about Farina. All he wants is the Meganano. Every nut wants more power."

Chapter 48

The Battle in the Cave

After getting separated from Roger, Johra, and Farina, the rest of the team quickly went through the south end door to the narrow tunnel and stood there foolishly for a few moments. The whole thing happened so quickly that none of them had time to think it out.

Dylan, clearly baffled, said, "What's now? Do we go to rescue them or just get the hell out of here?"

Miller shrugged quietly. This was an unexpected situation. Even the Hong brothers hesitated to attempt to jump over the twenty something feet crack.

"We can't leave Sister Farina behind." Zaki said. "We must save her."

"Aren't you guys the Sygods?" Preeti sharply said. "Why don't you do some of your heroic stuff? Don't just stand there doing nothing."

Dylan frowned. "Little girl, why are you being so mean to us?"

"Oh, now you want to pick on us?" Ivana lashed out. "How heroic!"

Rana raised his arms in the air, offering peace. "Farina is with Roger and Johra. She'll be safe. There's nothing we can do for them. You saw the crack. There's no way we can go past that. Right now, we need to get out of here."

"And which way would be out?" Stanley roared.

Rana pointed the tunnel. "There's only one way we can go. Let's hope this tunnel would take us out of here."

They heard a group of soldiers climbing down the stairs.

"Shhh..." Dylan cautioned. "If they hear us they might shoot through the door."

"Walk guys. Quick." Rana whispered.

He took out a small flashlight. "I'll go first. All of you stay right behind me."

They all walked through the dark corridor as Rana occasionally flashed his light to see ahead.

They heard the soldiers running toward the north side. That's the way Roger and the girls had gone. This was not good. They felt the ground shaking several times. Another bomb blasted nearby. There was a major rockslide somewhere.

"What is happening there?" Shahed asked fearfully.

Rana shook his head. "We can't worry about that. We have to keep moving."

"You guys are good for nothing." Preeti muttered.

"Little girl, you are pissing me off now." Dylan whispered. "One more word and you are getting inside a ring with me."

"I was just kidding! Take it easy." Preeti retreated.

Rest of the kids giggled.

"Tit for tat." Stanley murmured.

"Shut up!" Preeti snubbed.

"These kids are crazy." Miller said. "We are in a big trouble and they are squabbling."

"Tell me about it." Dylan agreed.

They moved ahead for almost twenty minutes. The tunnel had slowly gotten wider and steeper. As their eyes adjusted gradually to the darkness they could see a few feet ahead of them even without the flashlight.

Both Millar and Dylan were now holding two smaller flashlights, which they switched on alternatively every few seconds, saving the batteries. They had felt the tremor from more bombings but nothing blew up in their direction.

Just when they were starting to feel lucky and hoped to get out of the mess without any more trouble, they found themselves stranded inside a large cave that had been completely blocked out by rubbles at least forty-fifty feet high.

"When did this happen?" Miller said in frustration.

"They have been bombing everywhere." Rana said. "This was probably done during the first phase of attack."

Dylan was mad. "I wish I could have them for dinner. Jerks! What are we going to do now?"

"Find a way out." Millar said.

"Through this rubble?" Dylan was doubtful.

"There may be a passage through these rocks." Miller insisted.

They used the flashlights to search the rubble; found several pockets large enough to crawl in but soon discovered none went all the way to the other side.

The kids were pretty quiet. By now they were tired, hungry and exhausted. Rana felt bad about them and was about to say something encouraging when his attention drifted toward the sound of several approaching boots. He signaled everybody to remain quiet. The boots were closing on them, slowly but surely.

"They are looking for us." Oliver whispered.

"How did they come over the crack?" Musa said in

disbelief.

"They must have found another way." Zaki said.

"Are we gonna die?" Ivana was clearly shaken.

Rana and Dylan turned their flashlights off. Instantly the cave filled with pitch-black darkness.

"Are they going to shoot us?" Shahed whispered. "I'd have never brought these kids here."

"I am not going to go without a fight." Miller boldly said.

"What choice do we have?" Dylan bitterly said. "What do the brothers say?"

"We fight." Hong Lee sounded sure and confident. "We kill them. Kids hide."

Rana was primarily concerned about the safety of the kids. He passed one of the flashlights to Shahed. "Take them as far back as you can and stay behind the big boulders. Even if the soldiers start to shoot you guys should be safe."

The Hong brothers helped them moving back to a safer part of the cave, behind a small enclave that was created when the roof crumbled down. The brothers quickly returned to their teammates.

The soldiers were now just tens of feet away, still advancing, slowly and carefully as they approached the large cave, their powerful flashlights lit up the narrow mouth.

The Sygods stood silently in the dark hugging the cold cave walls. All they could do was to wait. Two things could happen. The soldiers could start shooting as soon as they saw them or the Sygods could baffle them with a preemptive attack and do some damage before they snapped out of it and attacked back.

The soldiers slowly came around a sharp turn and walked right into the cave. The bright flashlights flooded part of the cave momentarily.

Before the soldiers had any opportunity to realize what they were looking at, the Sygods sprung out of their positions and attacked with full vigor. Outnumbered and cornered, they knew their best weapon against the powerful enemy was to use the element of surprise.

The Hong brothers were first to strike, as usual, with the rest supporting them. With their lightning fast movement and smashing revolving kicks they grounded a few soldiers in a blink.

Millar quickly approached an injured soldier, snatched his gun away and grabbed as much ammunition he quickly could before the shooting started. With the gun in hand his level of confidence went sky high. Now he was ready for the fight.

Dylan knocked down two soldiers with dynamite blows. But he realized this wasn't a fight he could win with bare hands. He also picked up a gun from another wounded soldier.

Rana, staying flat against the wall, used his blowpipe selectively. Several painful screams in the crowd told him he wasn't missing.

The first wave of attack went for about ten-fifteen seconds. That was long enough for the soldiers to snap out of the initial shock. Naturally the next thing they did was to shoot, just about in every possible direction, clearly panicking.

The Hong brothers used the close proximity to the enemy in their favor. They swiftly moved through the soldiers, often rolling, occasionally vaulting, using their hands and legs as pistons to smash anything that came on their way. The bullets that were hurled at them had no chance to meet the constantly moving targets. They ended up ricocheting inside the cave, harmlessly.

Millar struggled to keep his nerves calm and mind clear. He positioned himself low to the ground and took his shots carefully. He wasn't missing, though he wasn't shooting to kill. These soldiers were just following orders; he didn't think killing them was fair when he could just put them out of action temporarily.

Shahed and the kids were equally terrified when the shootings started. By now they had seen some fights but this was the first time they experienced deadly shootings in such close vicinity.

As the sprayed bullets hit the cave walls and ricocheted with bright sparks they knew it simply wasn't safe for any of them to stay there. Who knew how long the battle would continue. There could be more soldiers following. They wish they could help the Sygods but clearly the best way to help in this situation was to stay away from the battleground or if possible get out of the area completely. That would take one headache out of the fighting five's head.

"Musa, can you climb up the rocks?" Zaki said. "There may be some holes up there large enough for us to pass through."

"How is he going to climb up in this dark?" Ivana quickly pointed out.

"I doubt he'll find anything there anyway." Preeti dryly said.

"What's the use of just sitting here like a shooting duck?" Stanley whispered.

"We must try to get out of here. Musa, I'll come with you." Oliver said.

"Dad has a flashlight. Take that." Zaki said.

Shahed knew they had to do something. If the kids

could brave the danger to go up the rubble he saw no reason to stop them. They were lighter and better climber than he was, much better.

Shahed handed over his flashlight to Oliver.

"I guess this is the only choice we have. Oliver, you stay right behind Musa and cover the flashlight before using it. We don't want the soldiers to see you. They might shoot."

"Uncle Shahed, I think we should all move away from here." Ivana said. "If the Sygods lose, the soldiers will come looking for us. If we climb up we have a better chance to hide among the rocks above there."

She was right. Shahed acknowledged. He peeked into the cave to get a general picture of the battle. It was darker now, fewer movements, less gunshots. Obviously many soldiers had either perished or were wounded. He couldn't clearly figure out the condition of the Sygods. But even if they were winning that could change quickly. More soldiers were definitely on their way, he assumed. Colonel seemed to be a determined foe.

He signaled everybody to climb up the rubble, carefully. Musa and Oliver worked their way up slowly and watchfully as Oliver occasionally flashed the light through his fingers. The rest quietly followed their trail. To his relief Shahed found out it wasn't as bad as he thought. The rubble was primarily made of large chunk of rocks overlaying on each other and they easily withstood their combined weight.

A few minutes later, Musa and Oliver reached the top of the rubble. After searching for a short while they found something they liked. Oliver flashed his light a few times to make sure the mid size cavity actually went across the rubble. He showed his thumb and grinned. This was good news.

Everybody was pumped up and climbed faster. When

they reached the top Musa had already disappeared on the other side. Rest of the kids made their way through to the other side one by one. Shahed decided to wait for the Sygods.

Down below, in the cave the shots had totally stopped. He could hear the fleeing boots. Finally the battle ended – he thought. Where were the Sygods? He'd to control his urge to call out for them.

"Shahed!" He heard Rana calling, just seconds later.

"We got to get out of here." Miller said. "They will come back."

"Where did the gang go?" Dylan sounded surprised.

Shahed whistled to get their attention. "Come up here, quick. There is a way out."

They quickly climbed up to him and crawled to the other side of the rubble. Dylan pushed a few large rocks to cover the mouth of the hole.

Once they had safely climbed down and were on their way out of the cave they heard dozens of soldiers pouring into the other side of the cave. A series of gunshots rattled the heap of the rubble.

"There they come." Rana said.

"The Colonel really wants to see the end of us, doesn't he?" Miller said.

"Why?" Shahed asked.

"He is the dog of General Derek Bowman." Miller said distastefully. "There's not a single evil thing they haven't done in the name of country. Naturally, we crossed ways. We caused some serious embarrassment for the rogue general. I guess he didn't like that very much."

"What a baby!" Dylan said. "Can't even take a little animosity."

As they all walked quickly along the tunnel suddenly a

303

cool breeze swept in. This was great news. It confirmed that there definitely was a way out of this tunnel. Hopefully it was still undamaged by the bombings. They moved faster.

Chapter 49

Meganano

Sitting at the back seat of a large combat chopper flanked by soldiers, Farina felt a chill flowing down her spines. She doubted if Sygods could rescue her from this situation. Her father, the scientist, had undoubtedly left the area with his Meganano - whatever it was. He must have had a well-prepared escape plan. Anyway, now that he was gone, what was this stupid Colonel doing flying her around in a chopper? The Magician wasn't going to come back, was he?

The chopper flew around the mountain with the ruins of the glorious castle that ornamented its peak less than an hour ago. A number of strong beams of light scavenged through the ruins. After two full circles they couldn't see a single movement anywhere inside or outside the castle.

The Colonel was visibly mad and ordered the pilot to fly the chopper over the valley, staying near the ruins of the castle. Then, he spoke in a powerful microphone, his voice echoing on the surrounding mountains.

"Dragan Valcovich! Dragan! Dragan!..." He growled with anger and vigor, over his own echoes. "Wherever you are, know one thing... I've something very dear to you. You got ten minutes. You don't show up, you never see her again."

Colonel repeated the same message one more time as his chopper hovered steadily in one spot with several others surrounding it. The deafening noise of their rotating blades started to settle deep inside Farina. She could barely think of anything. It all looked, sounded and felt so bleak and worthless.

There was no sign of Dragan. She didn't think there would be. Not the Colonel though. He acted as if it was only a question of when. He impatiently signaled the pilot to land the chopper on the valley. The chopper quickly dived down and in seconds touched the ground softly.

Colonel pulled Farina out of the chopper and shoved her to an open space nearby. Several strong light beams moved on them, lit the spot up brightly.

Colonel took out a gun and held it high making it clearly visible. His voice echoed again on the microphone. "Time is running out, Dragan. I know you are here. You won't escape leaving your own daughter behind. I can bet my life on that. Now show up. Don't try my patience."

Seconds later a very strange thing happened. A group of large Stingrays appeared through the dark. Their long fins moved fluidly as if they were swimming in water.

They swam in coherence and reduced their speed as they came close to the Colonel and Farina, finally stopping just above a few feet off the ground.

Dozens of flashlights from the choppers followed them closely. A few moments later, once the eyes adjusted to the bright light Farina could see people sitting on the floating Stingrays, which inevitably were some kind of flying objects made to give a magical appearance.

It didn't take her too long to recognize the people who sat on them. Aretha and Diego shared the same

Stingray with Dragan, who looked somber but still confident. It was the face of a man who knew what he was about to lose but yet had no doubt in his mind what he must do. Aretha, sitting in her slightly raised sit looked insipid, distant; as if she'd no idea what was it all about.

Colonel smirked. "Always a showman, huh! You are good at it Dragan, I admit. But I guess I am too cursed to appreciate such art."

"What do you want, Don Blake?" Dragan spoke grimly but strongly. His heavy voice was measured and controlled. "Why are you trying to hurt this young girl? Let her go. Be a man. Let's talk man to man. Such childish act doesn't suit a soldier."

Don laughed. "Don't try to shame me. I've none. My country is my love. That's all I understand. Now, let's talk business. This young girl here, we both know, is your daughter."

"Don't talk nonsense." Dragan objected fruitlessly.

Farina flooded in emotion. She'd thought so much about her real father, all her life. There he was! Was she proud? Was she even ready to accept this infamous man as her father? She'd doubts. But she also knew there was something so lively and decent about this man that it was difficult not to love him.

His futile attempt to deny the inevitable was pitiful. Undoubtedly Don Blake knew everything there was to know. She saw no reason to restrain her emotions and broke into tears.

"Dad! I know. Roger told me."

Her words roared into Don's microphone, echoing into the shadowy valley in ripples after ripples. After a few long moments of silence Dragan flew even closer. He tried hard but couldn't control the surge of emotion that pressed hard to burst out.

"My dear, this is why I stayed away from you all these years. I knew I'd nothing good to offer you but trouble. But a father's heart can only take so much. I don't know why I'd to reach to you. Forgive me for all the trouble I caused."

He turned toward the Colonel.

"Okay Don, what do you want?"

"You know what I want." Don barked. "Give me your nano energy prototype – the Meganano. You took lot of money from us. Now give us what you promised."

Dragan pointed at the ruined castle. "Look what you did. My lab was located in that mountain. Everything has been destroyed, the supercomputer, prototype, data - everything."

Colonel laughed maniacally. "Do you take me for a fool? You think you can play with my mind every time? I don't believe for a moment that you would keep that prototype in the lab. You were definitely prepared to escape. Give it to me."

Dragan shrugged. "How can I if I don't have it?"

Colonel pressed the nozzle of his gun on the temple of Farina's forehead. "Thirty seconds."

Dragan looked helpless. "Don, don't be so headstrong. You know if anything happens to her you are not leaving alive. None of you are."

Colonel cackled uncontrollably. "Who are you trying to scare Mr. Dragan? I've sacrificed my life for my country. I am not afraid of death. Look at her. She is just a kid. You want her to die? Here? Today? Twenty seconds. You give me the prototype or we all die. Twenty…nineteen…"

After walking through a maze of tunnels and caves, uncertain about their destination, when finally they got a glimpse of the open dark sky it was a big relief.

Rana had this miserable thought that they were going deeper into the mountain. Thanks god, he was wrong.

Dylan held everybody inside the tunnel when Miller went ahead to steal a good look outside, just in case the soldiers were around. Looking ahead what he saw was not pleasing. He signaled the rest to walk forward but silently.

Carefully they poured out of the tunnel to a small field at the top of a hill, no more than fifty-sixty feet higher than the core of the valley. Just ahead of them, quarter of a kilometer or so away, inside a bright circle of light stood Farina with the Colonel holding a gun on her head while Dragan floated nearby on an outlandish stingray.

This was not something they expected. When Farina followed Dragan along with Roger and Johra, nobody had any doubt that Dragan would take care of her. Looked like something went horribly wrong. What might have happened to Roger and Johra? Would they allow the mad Colonel to get his hands on Farina if they were alive? None of them knew what to think.

"What are we going to do now?" Zaki almost cried out.

"Nothing." Rana said. "Obviously Don is trying to make a deal with Dragan. I am sure it'll work out. Farina will be safe."

"I hope so. Oh God! I really hope so." Shahed could not hide the trembling in his voice.

"All the stuff that I heard about the Great Magician was bogus." Miller declared bitterly. "How come he can't even deal with this cow dung?"

"May be he lost his touch." Dylan added. "The guy is too busy inventing weird stuff like those swimming stingrays. Looks pretty real, eh?"

"Who cares?" Preeti snapped. "Are we just going to talk about the worthless Magician and not do anything to help Farina?"

"What do you wanna do sis?" It was Dylan, being patient.

"How about we shoot his brain out?" Stanley proposed.

Ivana jumped up. "Yes! Don't you have a gun killer Miller? Shoot that evil guy."

"Shoot!" That was a whispering chorus from the kids.

"Hurry up." Preeti rushed.

Miller shrugged helplessly. "It's not safe. He is standing too close to Farina. I might end up hitting her. In the worst case scenario Don's gun could fire too."

"Just shooting him isn't going to be enough." Rana added. "The soldiers may start shooting at everybody, killing Farina."

"What do we do then?" Shahed tried to be calm and clearheaded.

"Well, our best course of action would be to climb down this hill and try to go close to them." Rana said. "Who knows what opportunity may come. But all of you have to be very quiet. We don't want any attention."

"Isn't Dragan going to save her?" Shahed asked doubtfully.

"Of course he'll!" Zaki and Musa echoed each other as they noticed the strange man stepping down from his stingray.

"He is going to beat the crap out of that dummy." Stanley confidently added.

"I knew that! I knew that!" Oliver exclaimed. "That's it for the clown Colonel."

"That's right!" Preeti backed him up to his

astonishment. "The clown Colonel is about to get what he deserves!"

Johra, standing in the middle of the wreckage, felt restless. Farina was in grave danger and she couldn't do a thing to help her. This was not something she was ready to accept.

"Don't worry" Roger said. "Dragan will save her. I just know it." He tried to sound convincing but the doubt was unmistakable.

"Unless he gets the prototype, the colonel won't stop." Johra muttered. "I don't think Dragan would hand it over to him, no matter what. He has gone a long way to build that."

"He cares for his daughters." Roger reasoned. "Don't forget what he did for Aretha. Calm down. Farina will be fine."

"I must be able to do something." She said, pacing up and down.

"We can't do much from here." Roger shrugged. "We are stuck thousands of feet above the ground."

Suddenly Johra briskly walked closer to the edge and examined the vertical drop of the mountain, all the way to the valley.

"Don't do anything stupid." Roger warned.

Johra quickly got into her jumpies. "If we could climb up with this, we should also be able to climb down."

She didn't wait for Roger's approval. She slowly suspended herself from the edge and started to gently climb down using her fingers to balance.

Roger, after a brief hesitation, followed her down carefully. The jumpies held his weight. "These old bones can't take this anymore," he mumbled.

Dragan walked to the Colonel in small strides, stopped just a few feet away from him, face to face.

"Let her go. We'll negotiate something. You want the prototype, you'll get it." He sounded calm.

"I'll release Farina only after I get the prototype in my hand." Colonel replied coldly.

Farina and Dragan exchanged glances for one long moment. Was there a touch of wetness in her eyes? Dragan couldn't have missed it. He'd sharp mind and sharper eyes. He gave away a deep sigh.

"Okay."

He inserted his right hand inside a hidden pocket of his long, multi-layered coverall, took out a small battery size object. He held it above his head.

"Let Farina go first or I'll throw it away. You may or may not find it. It's a tiny thing."

"No!" Blake shouted stubbornly. "I want that first in my hand." In one quick jerk he threw Farina on the ground and pointed his gun right at her chest. "No tricks. Give that to me right now or she dies."

Dragan realized this was a possessed man. He shrugged helplessly. "Okay, okay. You win. It's yours. Just take it easy. Don't harm her."

"Give me the P-R-O-T-O-T-Y-P-E!"

"Here…"

Dragan had just extended his hand toward the direction of Colonel Don Blake, the small battery sized prototype - the Meganano, was held between his pointer and thumb, when something of enormous proportion happened, something that was totally unexpected, unthinkable, unimaginable.

Chapter 50

Mad, Mad, Thrasher

It all started with a sudden gust of breeze, chilly but nothing unusual for a mountainside. But the very next moment as all the flashlights went dead almost simultaneously, there was clear sign of something disastrous.

With no electric lights the valley dipped into the darkness that bore slight hint of light from distant stars. Completely baffled and wordless everybody waited, not knowing what to expect.

Another gust of chilly breeze, this time much stronger, almost shook even the strongest men off their feet, with it flew in the darkest and heaviest series of cloud over the mountain range in startling speed, covering the starlit sky in a dense sheet of pure diabolic darkness.

And then came the lightening, the gigantic blazing serpentine figures of thundering charges hit the ground in fearsome speed, series after series, the cold blue glow turned the surroundings into a scary zone. The deafening thunders reverberated through the hills and mountains and shook the earth with every roar.

Then, accompanied by a series of loud thunder and branching, blinding lightning appeared a monstrous twister, with hundreds of spinning arms that moved around it like an uncontrollable flames of fire.

It spun ahead to the colonel, blasting everything that it came in contact with, the helicopters, the soldiers, trees. The rage was absolutely unparallel to anything that anybody has ever seen. The volcanic twister sent a spinning arm toward the colonel. The arm grabbed him by the waist, picked him up high in the air and then smashed him right on the ground so violently that the colonel's body tore off in hundreds of pieces.

The twisting monster then went on its carnage, destroying any chopper it could put its hand on, tearing off any soldier it came upon. In just a mere minute the valley became the field of the deaths. The unbelievable destruction that had happened was beyond imagination.

Farina lied on the ground hiding her head inside her folded arms. Only occasionally she could gather up courage to look up and experience the unimaginable. Though, interestingly, no harm came near her, not even a strong gust. Everything happened around her, the deaths, the destructions, the cruelty. She noticed Dragan still standing in his place, as if frozen to the ground.

"Dad!" She called out in panic.

Dragan scurried to her and lifted her up into her strong arms, sheltering her from the ravenous twister.

"That's the Thrasher! Don't worry sweetheart. She won't do any harm to you."

The fury went on. The Thrasher ravaged through the hills and mountains like a mad superpower, uprooted trees effortlessly, squeezed armed men out of their last breath. No choppers flew over the valley anymore, no soldiers were seen. But the rage just won't subside. It wanted more. More death, more destruction. It swiftly moved around the valley looking for preys, roaring so loudly that the valley shook in vibration and the air filled with echoes louder than a thunderstorm.

In all the chaos nobody really noticed when Aretha had flown her stingray to the Tower that still stood proudly over the ruins, and landed on it. With her face slightly up on the sky, she looked focused, distant, unmoved by any worldly events.

Farina saw her first. Dragan followed her eyes and was the next to see.

"Is she doing it?" Farina whispered in disbelief.

"Her power has no match." Dragan murmured. "With her mind she can control trillions of nanorobots! Way more powerful than any super computer! Simply incredible!"

"Is the Thrasher built of nanorobots too?"

"Yes, billions of trillions of nanorobots. Only a series of interconnected very powerful supercomputers can drive them with such extreme accuracy and vigor."

Farina was visibly shaken. "How can it be possible? How can her brain be so powerful?"

Dragan didn't have a chance to reply because something strange and unexpected drew his attention. The kids were hiding behind boulders during the destruction. As soon as the situation turned around they had gathered back their courage and were running at Farina when Thrasher intercepted them and picked them up with its thousands of wiggly smoky limbs. Terrified the kids screamed at the top of their voices as the Thrasher raised them up forty-fifty feet above the ground.

"What's going on? What is she doing?" Farina could not believe her eyes.

"I am not sure." Dragan looked confused. This wasn't expected.

"Aretha!" A desperate Farina called out.

Aretha was too far from her to hear still she'd to try.

"Aretha! Please let them go. They are my friends. Don't harm them. I urge you. They are just kids." .

That didn't work. The Thrasher paid no attention to her pleadings. It neither released the kids nor did anything harmful. The kids remained suspended inside its foggy grips.

"What should we do dad?" Farina was hysteric. "Isn't there any way to stop her?"

"The only way to stop her is to attack the thrasher back but with most of my supercomputers out of order I can't do much. With the little power that I've left I can control a few robots like the Flyball but not billions of nanorobots.

"Boss!" it was Flyball.

"Flyball!" Farina exclaimed. "You are here?"

"I was with the boss, all along." Flyball replied, positioning itself between Farina and Dragan. "If I'd some help I could probably create some chaos into the Thrasher."

"How do you plan to do that?" Farina was doubtful.

"Virus!" Flyball replied. "If I can implant a few self-propagating virus into the memory of some of the nanorobots then the virus would multiply and hopefully make the other nanorobots dysfunctional."

This made sense to Farina. Would it really work? There was no way to know for sure. It all depended on the level of security embedded into the nanorobots. If they were equipped to detect malicious viruses early then there would be no propagation. The plan would fail.

"It's worth trying." She tried to sound confident.

Chapter 51

The Blue Dragon

In the mean time Johra had climbed down the mountain and joined the rest. Her relief to see Farina safe quickly disappeared when she noticed the six young kids dangling in the air at least four storied high. This was bad news.

"Is Aretha doing all this?" She looked perplexed. "I don't even want to ask how. But we need to act quickly. Who knows what that thing is planning next?"

"How are we going to fight against such powerful thing?" Rana sounded hopeless.

"Sometimes strategy works better than just strength." Dragan said. "Do you still have that Blue Dragon with you?" He asked Farina. "That is a special crystal. As I told you earlier, no nanorobot can stay in the close vicinity of it. It has strong electromagnetic fields with a certain pattern. Use that crystal. In this circumstance that's the only thing we have to battle against the Thrasher."

Farina quickly checked into her pocket. Thanks God, the crystal was still there. She didn't pay much attention to it since Dragan had given it to her. The Blue Dragon glistered brightly inside her fist.

"Whatever we do we must do it right now." Roger said with urgency. "I think the Thrasher is getting madder."

That was quite apparent. The mighty Thrasher had

just discovered another chopper that tried to escape its wrath by hiding behind a nearby mountain.

What happened next was very ugly. The diabolic twister rushed to it with uncanny speed and slammed it against the rocky surface of the mountain with brutal force. So brutal was the force that the thing burst into a fireball and instantly turned into pieces of metals. Half a dozen or so soldiers perished with it.

Farina knew Roger was right. They had to act quickly. She looked at the crystal. All they had was this small crystal. Would it really work? Was Dragan speculating about its power or did he really know that it would work? She looked at him inquiringly. Even in this absurd situation he looked proud and confident. Their eyes met.

"Are you sure about this?" Farina almost urged for the truth.

"I am." Dragan was calm, confident. "I personally tested it – in small scale of course. I wish I'd more time to enhance its power. But I guess for now that's all we got."

"But how can we use this tiny thing to beat that incredible whirling, crazy giant?" Dylan gasped. "Any bright ideas anyone?"

"If the nanorobots can't stay near that thing we can essentially use it as a sword." Rana said.

"Right." Farina added. "We can use its power to disintegrate the mighty twister. However, we have to go close to it, very close. We can then throw the crystal through its body. Every time the thing makes a pass inside its trunk there will be a cut."

"If we can do it quickly and long enough then there will be chaos." Roger finished her words. "Excellent idea! The only problem is - how to go near it?"

Johra pointed at the Stingrays. They were now sitting

silently on the ground. "What are they?"

"They are regular machines." Dragan replied. "A special type of hydraulic engine is used to create the smooth motion. Yes, you can use them to fly to the Thrasher."

"How fast can they move?" Farina asked.

"More than hundred miles per hour."

Farina exchanged glances with Roger. He nodded in approval.

"I need as many people as I can get." Farina said. "Who wants to come?"

"We do." Gombu said. He, Kongsi and Damien were standing by Dragan. All three stepped ahead. "Let's move. We have very little time. That thing is going to get meaner."

After a quick discussion it was decided that Roger and Shahed would stay on the ground while the others would fly to the Thrasher. Dragan would go to talk to Aretha in an attempt to calm her down.

"What about me?" Flyball yelled. "I could help."

"We can use all the help we can get." Farina agreed.

"Boss, what do you say?" Flyball asked Dragan.

"There may not be enough power left." Dragan thoughtfully said. "But go on. Whatever you can do will definitely help."

"Y-a-h-o-o!" Flyball cheered joyously. "I am going to call my brothers and be there in twenty seconds."

He became silent. It was obvious he was busy communicating with other Flyballs.

"Are we going?" Johra could hardly wait.

"Go on guys," Roger said. "Good luck."

"You'll need it." Dragan muttered.

"Be careful, Farina." Shahed didn't try to hide his fear.

Farina, Johra, Hong brothers, Rana, and Miller divided into three groups and hopped onto three stingrays with Dragan's associates on the driving seats.

The fish like flying objects ascended smoothly, turned on its axis and sped suddenly toward the raging Twister that howled and growled and spun with its innumerable rotating arms branched almost like a monstrously big tree. The team's target was Twister's main trunk, the thickest part of its body, the center around which the rest of the body revolved in immense speed and power.

They were detected half way down and the counter attack was severe though not deadly, not like anything that they had viewed just minutes ago. The Thrasher sent its thousands of rotating arms that wiggled like snakes to trap them into its misty claws.

Gombu, Kongsi and Damien displayed their great skills in maneuvering the Stingrays, making way through the maze of twisting branches, often avoiding collusions by inches. They randomly changed direction and height of flight, spread out over the valley and kept on closing down on the main trunk from three different directions.

Once they were able to penetrate through the maze of tentacle like smaller twisters, the Thrasher seemed to lose track of their exact location. That became clear when they noticed its attacks were not directed precisely toward them anymore. Instead they were taking place in the approximate vicinity, often as far as ten yards away.

The thunderous howling subsided considerably as the teams rode their Stingrays closer to the Thrashers column like thick, branching, spinning body.

A few moments later they found that the density of the smaller arms had decreased dramatically and they were now in a zone that was free of any nuisance branches. The fifty plus feet wide main trunk of Thrasher was fully exposed before them as it revolved with a ferocious speed, its hundreds of feet tall flexible column like entity wobbled with a rhythmic movement. It was a splendid view to watch. Such mixture of strength, speed and grace was rare. The thunderous noise had lessened considerably and they could clearly hear each other as they shouted.

They knew this was the right place to attack. Each team quickly took position on one of the three points of an imaginary triangle drawn around the width of the trunk hundreds of feet above the ground.

Farina and Johra were riding with Gombu. Rana and Dylan were with Damien and Miller and the Hong brothers were with Kongsi. Farina handed over the crystal to Johra to start the process.

Johra held the crystal briefly. It was heavier than she thought. That was good. She threw it hard across main trunk of the twister, in the general direction of Rana and Dylan. It all seemed kind of strange to her. Trying to destroy such a monstrous thing with a tiny crystal just didn't feel plausible.

To her complete amazement what happened next was simply incredible. As the crystal tore through the trunk millions of small particles zoomed away in random direction, as if some mysterious power forcefully pulled them away.

As the crystal came out at the other side of the twisting trunk Damien quickly moved his Stingray into its course and Dylan caught the small rock like a magnet.

He knew he'd literally no time to waste. Every second counted. The Thrasher was working fast to recover from the cut.

He quickly threw the crystal toward the Hong brothers.

The Blue Dragon shot through the trunk once again,

cutting it like a thick edged knife.

Hong Lee picked it up from the air and threw it with precision to Farina and Johra.

Farina grabbed it, passed it to Johra who threw it again to Dylan.

After just two passes the impact on Thrasher was so dramatic that Farina became truly optimistic. The cuts inside Thrasher's trunk only partially healed in some areas, where in others things looked very bleak. The building elements of the Thrasher were quickly collapsing, failing to synchronize the healing process and in turn creating more chaos and confused array of movement.

"Got to be the work of Flyball and his brothers!" Farina mumbled. "They must have succeeded in planting some self propagating virus into the Thrasher's body."

"Great!" Johra was pumped up. "We'll stop this monster and free the kids."

They continued their effort with the crystal, damaging the main stem a bit more with every throw.

Interestingly the Thrasher had very little guard to secure it from invaders in close proximity to its core. The branches that spread out in the exterior had no access in the inner space. Farina knew it was necessary for Thrasher to ensure its own revolving hands didn't cut through its main body. In this specific case it just worked out in their favor.

The Thrasher bellowed louder and louder, its thunderous revolution over the valley seemed to gather more energy for a brief moment, but then as the main trunk started to become disintegrated slowly but surely the strength started to decrease. The howling was less startling, the spinning slowing down. There was clear sign of disorder and weakness in the Thrasher's existence.

Aretha was losing her control over it, Farina thought.

She was now forced to spend more of her brain power to heal the disorder that continued to spread across the main trunk, leaving less and less for the rest. This was encouraging.

Soon Farina found out that the frequency and speed at which the injuries were being fixed started to slip and at times became almost nonexistent. Chaos was about to take over the main part of the Thrasher's body. The result was obvious. Soon the rest of the body would give up and would probably completely disintegrate.

Sensing that the whole entity could crumble down at any moment Farina and the rest rightly decided to get out of the inner body and quickly flew outside.

The breaking had already started. Many smaller arms disappeared and the higher surfaces way above the ground lost their solid look and was quickly turning into a smoky appearance. As the howling subsided considerably they could now hear the kids screaming. The smoky claws that imprisoned them were quickly losing their shape putting them into the risk of falling down on the ground to their deaths.

The three teams rushed to the kids and picked them up into the Stingrays in no time.

Chapter 52

The Final Destruction

The Thrasher was turning weak. There was no doubt about it. Its movements had slowed down and the countless arms swung aimlessly. Aretha was quickly losing control over the gazillions of tiny nanorobots that made the fearsome monster.

Farina hoped it would all end without any further violence. Too many people had already lost their lives; too many things had been destroyed. No more.

Right at that moment, perhaps only to disappoint her, suddenly the top of the mountain range that surrounded the valley lit up — more choppers with more soldiers. One of the escaped soldiers must have had send a message to headquarter. Reinforcement had been sent without fully realizing the risk.

Farina was terrified. They had just seen Colonel Don Blake and his men got literally obliterated. That wasn't a view that Farina would ever forget. Was it going to repeat? Was the Thrasher still strong enough to be able to incur similar devastation?

She noticed Dragan and Diego were standing on the Tower with Aretha. Obviously they were trying to convince Aretha to stop the carnage. However, she looked straight ahead, still composed, quiet.

Farina could now hear the whirring choppers blasting up the tranquility of the night for a second time. Thrasher noticed them as well. The rage that was slowly evaporating quickly returned. In the span of just few seconds the Thrasher shook up its sagginess and stood straight, its arms still struggling into their spins.

The Thrasher was rising, possibly for the last time before it completely collapsed.

"The Thrasher is mad again. Run!" Stanley shouted and ran away as fast as he could from the freaky monster.

Nobody questioned his judgment. They ran like crazy, looking to reach for large enough boulders to hide.

"Can't we contact the choppers and ask them to stop?" Farina asked Roger, as she ran.

Roger took out a walky-talky from his pocket. "No harm in trying."

He dived on the ground and tried to contact the choppers. The Thrasher was back on its feet and was fuming in rage. The spinning velocity, the deafening howling and the display of immense energy had returned, somehow. It was ready to kill, once again.

Roger had connected to somebody on the wireless. He was pleading. "Please, listen to me. Go back. I am retired colonel Roger Kogut. I beg you to turn around. If you come here, there will be carnage. I can't explain everything now. I can only say your firearms have no impact on this monstrous power. Go back. Now!"

The Choppers continued their advancement. Apparently Roger's request fell into deaf ears.

"This is not going to be good," he muttered in sheer frustration. "Prepare for another hell."

The Thrasher, still frantically trying to heal itself,

watched the advancing army calmly. This wasn't exactly what everybody had expected. Was it too weak to attack? Or did it have some other plan? Was the thirst for blood gone?

Perhaps Dragan and Diego were successful in pacifying Aretha, at least to some extent. But still it was difficult for them to believe that the monstrous power would just quietly disappear. Everybody waited as the seconds ticked away, many silently prayed.

Another few seconds had passed by without any event. And then the Thrasher did what nobody had even thought of. It picked up velocity and with one sudden thrust roared toward the mountain that hosted the magical castle and obviously Dragan's hidden laboratories.

Before the very eyes of Dragan, who had just carried Aretha to his Stingray and was flying away from the Castle, the Thrasher struck the mountain with maximum strength, forcing a large part of it to almost erupt into the air, bursting into a mixture of rocks, soil and dust.

The valley sunk into an opaque layer of dust that momentarily became ubiquitous. As they breathed the dirty air they coughed to get the sand out of their throats. Slowly, after a few long minutes when the dust started to settle down and the view became clearer, the first thing everybody noticed was the fact that the Thrasher was gone.

There was no sign of its huge revolving body and the uncountable branch like hands. It had disintegrated into the dust and became undetectable.

The next thing that they noticed was Dragan and his team had disappeared as well. There was no sign of the stingrays, Aretha, Diego or his three remarkable bodyguards. And finally they noticed the inevitable. The magical and mysterious castle was no more. It was destroyed beyond the slightest sign of recognition. The tall and majestic peak where the castle once stood was half gone; the remaining of it bore the sign of the carnage that the Thrasher had caused.

The caravan of the choppers reached the valley without any opposition. They had seen the huge tornado like entity and the destruction of the castle but as the tornado disappeared in thin air they continued on to find survivors, if any.

Zaki, who stood flanked with Farina through the carnage, whispered in Farina's ears, "Do you think the Magician and Aretha were able to escape?"

"I am sure they did." Farina confidently said. She really believed it. "Aretha was angry but not suicidal."

"Do you think we'll meet them again?"

"For sure." Farina knew it, somehow.

Shahed, recovering from the nasty cough that the dust gave him, walked to their side. He embraced both of them dearly.

"Thanks God, it's over! Farina, I just want you to know that I'd no clue about your relationship with Dragan. I swear."

Farina hugged him quietly. She didn't even try to say anything as she struggled to stop her tears. Knowing an infamous but charming scientist like Dragan was her father was interesting indeed but that wasn't why she was sad. She just couldn't let Aretha get off her mind. In a regular family life two of them definitely would have been great sisters.

The rest of the kids, safe and sound, looked dazed. They had been subjected to something that they hadn't even dreamt of.

Roger and the Sygods walked up to Farina and the kids.

"So, I guess here is the end of the mysterious

Magician for now." Roger sarcastically said. "Now, presumably, that his Meganano has been destroyed he'd definitely have to find another place to put it all back together. In the meantime, we have to continue to look for him. Farina, I just want you to know if he ever tries to contact you don't mistake him to be something that he is not. He is not a regular nice guy, a father that you may want. Guard yourself against his charm."

"Don't tell me you are going to abandon us now." Farina grimly said.

"Not a chance." Roger smiled. "I was afraid of that you wouldn't want to have anything to do with us anymore."

"Let's ask the silly bunch." Farina faced the kids. "So, what do you guys say? We continue to be SciAngels?"

The approval was overwhelming as the kids roared, "Yes! We are the SCIANGELS!"

Chapter 53

Aretha`s Gift

The following year Farina came back to Vienna to play in the Open chess tournament. Shahed had accompanied her, of course.

In addition, this time Roger and Orenda had come with her as well. They both had strong belief that Farina would make the Grand Master norm and they wanted to be there to celebrate it firsthand.

The tournament went very well for her. She'd no difficulty getting the third norm toward the title of grand master. Out of nine games she won seven and drew the other two to become the champion.

This year there was no promise of the privilege to play Aretha. The organizers had mostly kept mum about it. Farina didn't hope to get the opportunity to play against Aretha. Who knew where she was anyway? About six months had passed and no words came from either Dragan or Aretha.

Farina tried to think positive though she knew anything was possible. Even if they had escaped the carnage safely that day they could have become the victim of something else. Too many people wanted Dragan out of their way. All she could do was to hope that they were well.

After the tournament concluded and the prize

ceremony took place the organizers suddenly announced that they had unexpectedly heard from Aretha and offered Farina an opportunity to play one game against her via the Internet.

Farina was ecstatic. Just knowing that Aretha was safe was overwhelming. She wondered why Aretha waited until the end of the tournament to contact the organizers. Was she following the game and only decided to play when Farina became the champion? That was possible.

The game took place in a huge hall room before thousands of spectators. After just ten moves Farina realized her force development had slight disadvantage. While it took extraordinary brilliance to exploit such weakness into winning combinations Farina knew without a shred of doubt in her mind that Aretha had many times more the foresight that was required to win. The super girl who could control trillions of nanorobots with her mind would see through such weaknesses without even trying.

Another eight moves established the weakness even more though still on a level that many grandmasters couldn't see. A defeat was obvious, Farina knew. Was she unhappy to lose to Aretha? She didn't know for sure. She didn't have the unimaginable brainpower that the unfortunate girl had, but yet she believed deep inside that she could beat the super girl in chess, using her own unparallel strategic approach.

She was wrong. The revelation did give her a slight distaste in her mouth. She'd have loved to beat Aretha. A few more moves and the whole audience would see how Farina's position would crumble under Aretha's attack. Farina seriously considered resigning. That would save her the embarrassment. That's when something strange happened. On the large display screen showed up

"Don't forget me, Farina."

Aretha resigned the game and logged out instantly. Why would she accept defeat while she couldn't have lost the game even if she tried? While the audience congratulated her with loud applaud Farina sat on her seat completely clueless. She didn't even get an opportunity to write anything back. Why did Aretha let her win?

A month later Farina received a letter without a return address. Inside she found a short note. No names.

> *Never knew how good it feels to lose*
> *to somebody so dear. One day, we two*
> *sisters will rule this world. There's*
> *none who can stop us.*

Farina hid the letter. Clearly she was going to have a lot of problem with Aretha in future. But she didn't let herself get worried about that yet. In the war between good and evil, the good must always win. The innocence of Aretha would stop the incredible rage and hatred of the Thrasher.

That's how the world has always been.

The End

www.ingramcontent.com/pod-product-compliance
Lightning Source LLC
Chambersburg PA
CBHW062022170626
46813CB00001B/265